DEGREES OF DISTORTION

The Distortion Series, Book 1

By Aimee McNeil

DEGREES OF DISTORTION

Limitless Publishing, LLC
Kailua, HI 96734
www.limitlesspublishing.com

Formatting: Limitless Publishing

ISBN-13: 978-1-68058-732-6
ISBN-10: 1-68058-732-3

DEDICATION

To my fans,
This book is for those who love to get lost in a story
and enjoy the adventure.
I wrote this for you.

And for those who will pick it apart and say nasty
things…I know you're out there.
This is not for you.

PROLOGUE

The room was dark, and the air felt as if it had taken shape and slithered over her skin—cold and damp. Her jaw hurt from the constant chattering of her teeth. The dull ache stretched down her throat, making it feel swollen and tight. Her thoughts jumped from one to the next as her mind refused to focus on anything.

She raised a shaky hand and brushed her hair from her face, noticing her cheeks were damp. She pressed numb fingers to her skin and wiped away tears that were dripping from her chin. She hadn't even realized she was crying. She licked her dry lips and blinked her eyes. The haunting quiet was enough to make her question what was real.

A strange numbness engulfed her as she looked through the rough metal bars that caged her in. A lone lightbulb in the far corner of the room flickered occasionally, threatening to leave her in darkness. She had no concept of time due to the solid walls of concrete around her. The only indication of time passing was the constant drip of water she could

1

hear from the leaky faucet across the room.

The bars that made up the small cell had initially been a source of terror when she had awoken inside them, but now she was grateful for the barrier. They were the only thing that separated her from *him*.

The man sat on the other side of the bars with a suit and blood red tie. His chair was so close that his knees were pressed against the bars. He had been sitting impossibly still for so long she was beginning to wonder if she was imagining him.

When he finally moved, her breath caught in her throat. He loosened his tie and leaned back. The chair groaned loudly in protest, but he remained eerily quiet. He didn't look like a man that was capable of great evil with his expensive suit and well-manicured appearance, but there was no denying there was something unnatural about him. He watched her silently like a lion toying with its food, waiting to strike.

She pushed back the lump in the throat and searched for her voice. "Why?" Her lips felt frozen, making it hard to speak.

He refused to break his silence. He ran his hand down the front of his shirt and began to rub his thighs in long, languid strokes. His gaze never left her, and she cowered away from his frightening presence.

She sat on the small cot pushed up against the wall. It offered no comfort as the frame dug through the thin mattress. A chill rushed over her skin as she pulled her knees up to her chest.

"Why…am I…here?" she cried. The rush of emotion was impossible to stop as it began to flow.

She gasped for breath between her sobs. Her body shook as she wrapped her arms around her knees and made the best attempt she could to shield herself from his view.

He leaned forward suddenly in his chair and grabbed hold of the bars. His abrupt movement startled her. She pushed off the bed and stumbled to her feet. She pressed her body against the solid wall of concrete in the back of the cell. Her heart raced so fast she could taste the metallic pulse in her mouth and the deafening rush in her ears.

"Because you are mine," he said in a voice that reached across the distance between them and grabbed hold of her.

She shook her head. "Let me go," she sobbed. "Please."

"Never," he said as he shoved his chair back. It scraped loudly against the floor. He pulled what sounded like keys from his pocket and walked around the cell. He ran his fingers over every bar until he came to the door. Fear strangled her as the sound of a lock released.

"I will never let you go," he said as he pushed the door open.

CHAPTER ONE

"Come down here now, Lexie! You're gonna get yourself killed."

Lexie looked down at her blue-painted toes. It was her favorite polish. The color had long since chipped away and was in dire need of a new coat. She had used the remainder of the bottle last time she painted them and could not find the shade anywhere. It had to be that specific color. Nothing else would do.

Lexie was standing upon a rock overlooking a sheer drop. Water sprayed and frothed over the edge, showering into the pool of turbulent water below. Her stomach felt weightless and dense simultaneously as she peered over the edge. Her heart beat madly in her chest as fear stretched its cold, dark fingers around her, holding tight. She reveled in the feeling that penetrated the numb fog that had long since settled over her. The warm did nothing to soothe her as it cast its afternoon light upon her bare skin, clothed as she was only in her blue bikini. It was a staple in her wardrobe since summer had begun.

Her eyes fell upon her friend below, Stephanie, her arms waving madly. "I know you can hear me, Lexie. Get your cute butt down here. This isn't funny."

Their quiet surroundings were so peaceful in the hidden oasis, untouched by civilization. She had stumbled upon this place a year ago on their first road trip. It had been a much different experience the first time. That was when she still had her heart, her Alex.

Taking a deep breath, she pushed off the rock. The comfort of the solid surface beneath her feet was replaced with the weightless feeling of falling. Stephanie's scream rang out around her, swallowing the peaceful calm of the morning. Air rushed past Lexie's skin; the fleeting feeling of freedom was liberating before the cold sting of water slapped harshly against her, swallowing her down into its cold, dark depths where the warm sun could not penetrate.

Lexie could feel herself sink, pushed and pulled by the current of the restless water. She opened her eyes to dreamlike surroundings, completely immersed in the hazy water.

"Come on and jump already," Alex called from below, treading water with perfect poise. Years of swimming had him primed to make swimming look effortless. The contagious smile on his face made Lexie laugh nervously. He always had that effect on her. All he had to do was give her his signature smile and look at her with those hazel eyes and she

would fall for his charm every time. She was completely enamoured since the first day she met him.

"Just give me a second. We're not all fearless like you. I need to warm myself up to the idea of throwing myself off a cliff," Lexie complained as she tried to take deep calming breaths. She couldn't believe he had actually jumped from the top of the waterfall. She looked up at the steep incline and shivered. This was as high as she could manage, and it was still pushing it.

"It's less than half the distance I jumped and I made it."

"Yeah, but you're insane and lucky."

"It's safe. I promise."

"Fine. You better save me if something bad happens," Lexie threatened as she readied herself.

"I'll always save you."

Lexie pushed off the rocks. A panicked scream left her lips as she soared through the air. She dropped into the cold water below, plunging under. Alex was waiting for her; she felt his strong arms wrap around her when she broke through the surface of the water. "I told you it was safe." He pulled her close.

Lexie could still remember exactly what he smelled like, still feel his skin against hers as she reveled in the memory. Something moving in the water caught her attention. For a moment, her mind led her to believe it was Alex swimming toward her; for that one blissful moment her heart didn't feel like an empty hole filled with sorrow until his image faded away and Stephanie's face came into view. Her momentary escape was gone, and so was Alex.

Stephanie grabbed hold of Lexie's arm and pulled her up toward the surface of the water. Lexie could feel the temperature warm dramatically as they neared the top, her lungs suddenly screaming for air as her numbness melted away. Lexie drew in as much breath as she could as they swam to the edge. Her adrenaline high crashed quickly, and she was left feeling drained as she dragged herself out of the water.

"What the hell, Lexie? You scared the shit out of me…" Stephanie paused for breath. "Don't take stupid risks like that. You could've been seriously hurt." Stephanie twisted the water from her dark hair before letting her curls spring back to life.

"I just wanted to feel close to him." Lexie sighed deeply.

Stephanie's scowl fell from her face to be replaced with sympathy. "You don't have to throw yourself off cliffs and take the same crazy risks he did. Just take in the scenery and remember him."

"Sometimes it doesn't feel like enough. It's not till I really push myself that I remember him with perfect clarity. It feels like he's with me." Lexie fell back onto her towel, letting the sun warm her chilled skin.

"He'd want you to be safe, Lexie. You know that more than anyone." Stephanie sat down beside her, taking Lexie's hand in hers for a comforting squeeze.

"I know." Lexie breathed sadly before closing

her eyes.

***

"Maybe Alex didn't get it on the trip. Maybe he had picked it up before." Stephanie placed her menu down and looked across the table. Lexie was trying to read the choices, but her mind was too full to comprehend the words in front of her. It might as well have been in a different language.

"No, he said it was a memento from our trip. He gave it to me on the ride home. I remember thinking how ridiculous it was that he bought me nail polish when I never wore it." Lexie gave up trying to read the food choices and ran her fingers through her hair. A laugh bubbled up from her chest. "Who would have thought I would be retracing our steps a year later on a mad hunt to find the elusive color?"

"I think we need a drink." Stephanie leaned back in her chair and waved to the waiter.

"Make that drinks." Lexie sighed. The tavern had an old world feel, with a stage for live performances. The bar was beautifully carved from a richly grained wood, running the entire length of the interior. A small wood floor stood before the stage, worn from years of dancing. A lone woman sat on a stool upon the stage. A spotlight set her sullen features aglow as she sang a sad song. It seemed appropriate for Lexie's mood as she listened to the words. The woman sang about loss and a harsh world. It was sad how very fitting those words fit with her life.

Lexie and Stephanie had come to the final stop

on their road trip. Tomorrow, Lexie would return to the life waiting for her and the inescapable sadness she bore upon her shoulders. Lexie looked at her best friend sitting across the table, the reason she had come this far. Stephanie had stood by her side since the day her world was torn apart; she was her crutch and the reason she found the strength to get out of bed in the morning.

"It's all gone, Stephanie," Lexie sobbed into the phone. The bottle of nail polish clasped so tightly in her hand her knuckles were white. Hot tears ran down her cheeks. "It's gone…"

"What is, Lex? What's gone?" Stephanie's concerned words poured through the phone.

Lexie was tired of being strong. She was tired of trying to convince everyone that she was all right. Tired carrying on with her life like it was natural to move on when her heart was torn from her chest. "The nail polish," Lexie whispered into the phone, collapsing onto the floor. She could see the broken version of herself in her mirror. Anger flared from deep within her like an angry beast breaking free. She threw the polish at the sad, pathetic girl staring back at her. The mirror shattered to the floor, a perfect representation of what was left of her.

"Hold on, Lex. I'm just pulling up to your building. I'll just be a sec." Stephanie hung up. It was only a matter of seconds before Lexie could hear her approaching, hurried steps. Stephanie had her own key. Lexie was grateful because she couldn't pull herself off the floor. She could only stare at the bottle of polish that had rolled across

the floor and stopped in front of her—mocking her.

Stephanie's feet came into view with her favorite sandals that wrapped around her ankles and set off her tanned legs beautifully. "If my feet were the same size, I would definitely steal those shoes," Lexie said in a numb, distant voice. Stephanie grabbed her by the arms and pulled her up to sit on the bed.

"You're scaring me. What happened to your mirror?" Stephanie's warm chocolate eyes lowered to look into hers. "Lexie?" Her hands felt warm upon Lexie's chilled cheeks. She was shivering. The cold felt as if it were originating from deep inside her.

"Why's it so cold in here?" Lexie mumbled.

"It's not. It's hot as shit." Stephanie grabbed the blanket off Lexie's bed and wrapped it around her shoulders when Lexie's teeth started chattering. "Talk to me."

Lexie lifted her hand. The bottle of nail polish lay in her palm.

"Oh, Lex." Stephanie took the bottle from her, looking at the trace amount of the deep blue color left inside. The bottle had become one of Lexie's most treasured belongings.

"I looked everywhere. No one carries this color."

Stephanie wrapped her arm around Lexie's shoulders and pulled her close. "I can take some time off work. Let's retrace the steps you and Alex took, track down the nail polish. Give you a chance to get away and remember the better times."

"Really?" Lexie perked up.

"Yeah, I think we both need this."

CHAPTER TWO

This little town of Sugar Hill was her last hope to find what she was looking for; after stopping at every possible location over the course of the week she was no closer. The small town was on the perimeter of a much bigger city shining bright in the late night hour. It was like watching a fireworks show when you stood outside. The city of Belhaven was a lively bright world in the center of a cluster of small towns. It sat just out of reach with flashing signs, pulsing with life. As much as it called to Lexie to discover its secrets, she knew Alex always avoided the big cities. He wouldn't have found the polish there.

The color, Knockout by Revlon, meant so much more to her than it should, but it was tied to important memories. She was scared they would fade without it, and she needed to see the color on her toes to remember when Alex painted them. She remembered it so clearly; it was the morning before her world fell apart.

"Wake up, sleepy head," Alex's smooth voice brushed against Lexie's shoulder, sensitizing her skin.

"No." Lexie tried to pull the blankets over her head, but Alex refused, slipping his arms around her.

"Come on. I want to see those pretty blue eyes." He rained gentle kisses down her arm.

"My eyes are still asleep. Don't be mean," Lexie complained, opening one to see him leaning over her with a mischievous smile.

"We have places to go and things to see. You need to get your hot butt up and get dressed." Alex climbed out of bed, dressed in only his boxers. His body was lean and cut beautifully from his dedication to swimming. His blond hair was tousled from sleep, and his smile was brighter than the sun peeking through the windows.

"Five more minutes." Lexie yawned, stretching her tired body.

Alex grabbed the bottle of nail polish off her dresser that hadn't been touched since she had gotten back from their trip a few weeks before. Alex sat down on the bottom of the bed and unscrewed the cover.

"What are you up to?" Lexie narrowed her eyes suspiciously.

"Give me your feet." His deep dimples carved into his cheeks.

"Oh god, this won't be pretty." Lexie slipped her feet out from under the sheets and wiggled her toes in front of him. Alex began applying the deep blue color to her nails. It was a shocking contrast to her

normally bare toes. "Why did you pick blue?"

Alex looked up from his careful application. "Because it's called Knockout, and that's how I feel every time I look you—completely knocked out."

A smile broke out on Lexie's face. "Then I will wear it always."

"Good." Alex leaned down and kissed her leg. "Now get up."

"What can I get you, ladies?" The waitress smiled at Lexie and Stephanie with lips as red as rubies. The color was smudged onto her top teeth, and it was all Lexie could concentrate on despite her friendly bright eyes with heavy glitter eyeshadow. Even her lovely locket that hung around her neck didn't hold Lexie's interest. It was only that bright red lipstick smudged across her white teeth. It was a perfect match to the color that haunted her dreams. Red...always so much red.

"Lexie." Stephanie nudged her arm. "Is that okay with you?"

"What?" Lexie watched the waitress's ponytail swing back and forth as she walked away from their table.

Stephanie shook her head with a smile. She was the most patient person in the world, and Lexie was so grateful. "I ordered us a couple of vodka waters with extra limes. Thought we should keep it clean drinking since we have a long drive tomorrow. I don't want to have sugar rot in my guts."

"Yeah, that sounds like a good plan. You and your weak stomach," Lexie teased.

"What was that?" Stephanie looked at her with

wide eyes.

"What was what?" Lexie asked, confused.

"Did you just smile?" Stephanie grabbed Lexie's phone off the table.

"Ha, ha. You're hilarious. What're you doing?" Lexie tried to make a grab for her phone.

"I'm taking a picture so you know what you look like when you smile. You are completely gorgeous."

"Give me my phone back, Steph," Lexie said, completely unamused.

"I will—after you smile for a picture," Stephanie goaded her, waving her phone in the air.

"No."

"Yes," Stephanie demanded as she kicked Lexie's leg under the table.

"Ouch!" Lexie broke out into laughter, and Stephanie snapped a picture. "You're such a jerk."

"And you completely love me," Stephanie said proudly.

"Here you are, ladies." The waitress set their glasses down in front of them.

Lexie and Stephanie lost track of how many drinks they had as they let themselves enjoy the evening. A young man took the stage; his long hair hung in his face as he hid from view. No one expected the voice that projected from him as he had seemed nervous as he prepared his set. His tone was upbeat and lively as he strummed beautifully on his guitar. Stephanie had been right to suggest this getaway even if they hadn't found what they were looking for. She was able to escape the pain for a while. It felt good to smile and remember the wonderful time she and Alex shared when they had taken this same road trip. The memories she could recall left a smile upon her face. Here, away from home, they were not tied to tragedy.

"May I have this dance?" Alex placed his hand over Lexie's menu.

Lexie looked up, a smile completely captivating her face. "Of course, handsome sir." She placed her hand in his. Alex led her out to the small dance floor, completely bare of anyone else. All eyes around the bar were on them, curious why they were on the dance floor while the musicians were between sets. "You do realize there is no music right now, right?"

"There is always music playing when I'm with you." Alex kissed her hand before spinning her around.

"Oh yeah, what does it sound like?" Lexie smiled up at him as he wrapped his arms around her waist. He was a dream she fell in love with years ago. The first time she saw him, he stared at her without saying a word. Little did she know then that the speechless little boy would become the love of her life. Alex told her it took him three years to work up the courage to ask her out. She knew without a doubt she would have always said yes to him.

"Something like this…duunnn dunnn…duunnn dunnn."

"Hey!" Lexie smacked him playfully on the chest.

"I'm kidding. It's more like this…" Music

started to play, a soft beautiful melody spilling out of the speakers.

"Wow, you're good."

"I am, aren't I?" He smiled and kissed her.

They both looked over at the woman singing upon the stage. She smiled at them as she continued with the beautiful song about young love. It was perfect.

"Hey, Lexie, come here. You've got to see this." Stephanie waved her over to dozens of pictures lining the back wall. Lexie finished her drink, discarding the glass on the table before heading over. The pictures were old from the looks of the clothing the people wore.

"Look!" Stephanie's mouth remained open as she gawked at the photograph.

"Where?" Lexie leaned in closer and gasped when she saw the exact likeliness of her mother, twenty or so years younger, sitting in this very bar. "Holy hell, that's my mom."

"Stand next to it and I'll get a picture." Stephanie held up her phone and Lexie leaned in, pointing toward her mother's picture.

"This is unreal. Look at this one, she's mixing drinks. Maybe she worked here." Lexie noticed her mother's face among others. "Mom told me she never left our small town of Freyview in her entire life. In fact, the idea of travelling always made her nervous."

"Guess your mom is full of secrets." Stephanie wiggled her eyebrows excitedly. "Maybe she has a whole secret life."

"Yeah right, my mom is the definition of boring. She's worked the same job for as long I can remember and has always lived in the same place. The next day is exactly like the last, never stepping outside the box. This doesn't make sense."

"Well, based on these pictures, she lived outside the box at one time." Stephanie stood on her toes to see a picture of Lexie's mom pouring a long row of shots before a full crowd of onlookers. "Your mom looks amazing in these pictures. She had to have some excitement—she had you, didn't she?"

"I didn't say she didn't have any secrets, but she's not the same person in these pictures."

"Hello, ladies."

Lexie and Stephanie spun around to see a tall, imposing man. At first glance, fear spiked in Lexie's blood. He was rough around the edges with his unshaven face and striking dark eyebrows that slashed across his face in a permanent scowl.

"Hello." Lexie smiled tentatively.

"Didja want me to take a picture of you two?" he offered kindly. He seemed less threatening with a smile warming his features.

"That would be lovely, thank you." Lexie held out her phone. His eyes looked almost black in the light as his gaze followed her. It was difficult to determine his age because of his hard edge. His skin had seen many days of sun, but his features still held an intensity that spoke of much fire in his blood. Something about him did not sit well with her. "I'm Jason, by the way."

"I'm Stephanie, and this is Lexie." Stephanie spoke up when Lexie hesitated.

Stephanie wrapped her arm around Lexie's shoulder. The flash flared to life, capturing them. "Did I overhear you know Mary Connors?" Jason flipped Lexie's phone around in his hand. A sudden chill flashed over Lexie's skin.

"Mary? No, the woman in the pictures looks like my mother, but her name is Beth."

"Isn't that funny." Jason looked up at her with a sly smile. "I bet you look exactly like your mother."

"So I'm told." Lexie forced a smile. Lexie was struggling to find the pieces of the puzzle dumped on her. As far as she knew, her mother had never been to Sugar Hill, but despite the fact that these men knew the woman in the photographs as Mary Connors, Lexie knew without a doubt it was her mother. Besides the exact likeliness, they both had the exact same tattoo inside their right wrist. It was barely visible in the pictures, but it was there. Lexie knew it well. She pulled her phone from Jason's hold, seemingly reluctant to let it go.

The bartender approached the end of the bar. "You givin' these ladies a hard time, Jason?" The grey-haired man wiped down the counter before he threw his rag over his shoulder.

"Naw, Mac. Apparently this young lady's mother looks just like our Mary." Jason grabbed for the beer Mac dropped in front of him.

Mac's eyes focused calculatedly on Lexie as he scratched his chin. "The resemblance is uncanny." As much as Lexie thirsted for knowledge in regards to a life her mother had sheltered her from, she could detect the undercurrent of danger in these two men. She did not want them to know she suspected

19

the two women be one and the same.

"Does Mary still come here?" Lexie tried to seem unaffected by their attention and to reiterate the fact that this woman was not her mother.

"No, she hasn't been around these parts in over twenty years. She left quite the legacy."

"Yeah, she looks like she left a lasting impression." Stephanie spoke up, waving her hand toward the wall.

"You could say that," Mac agreed offhandedly, slapping two glasses upon the bar top, pouring two glasses of vodka waters, and sliding them over to the girls. "On the house."

"Thanks." Stephanie picked up her glass and sipped it with a nervous smile. Lexie wrapped her fingers around the glass but made no move to drink.

"How old are you, Lexie?" Jason asked. He was prying. Lexie's attempt to brush off the resemblance obviously wasn't fooling this man.

"As much as we would like to stay and talk, we actually need to be going. It was nice to meet you both." Lexie didn't wait for a proper goodbye. She grabbed Stephanie's arm and pulled her past the men and toward the exit.

"I agree the whole thing was a bit odd, but I don't understand why we're suddenly running off? I still need to use the washroom," Stephanie complained.

"I don't like the feeling I get from those men. I think we should leave." They both turned to see the men staring after them. There was nothing pleasant in their demeanours, no fond memories surfacing of the Mary Connors they knew and remembered.

"You're right. I'm suddenly getting an axe murder vibe. Let's get out of here." Stephanie picked up the pace, pushing through the exit door. Lexie had no intention of returning. They stumbled upon a past her mother might have buried for a reason.

CHAPTER THREE

Lexie pulled her suitcase through her apartment door, swinging it closed behind her with her foot and sliding the chain lock in place. It felt good to be home.

Her one bedroom apartment was modified to house her photography equipment. She used her bedroom as a small studio. Her bed was placed into her living space off the kitchen, piled with pillows that spilled over onto the floor. The rest of her furniture was placed where it could fit in the small space. It wasn't ideal, but it was hers.

Lexie's walls were filled with photographs, all taken with her own camera. Years of her life played out around her. Some hung from strings running back and forth on the walls, some were framed, and others merely tacked to the wall with a painted border on the area around them to make them look finished.

Alex looked back at her in so many pictures. His bright beautiful smile used to talk her into anything. She would say yes before he even finished his question. As much as it stung to look at his face, it brought her solace.

Lexie turned on her music, filling her apartment with comforting sound. She hated the quiet and where her mind would take her should she let it wander. Having music on was a much needed distraction.

Lexie lifted her suitcase onto her bed, unzipped it, and tossed all of her clothes into her hamper. She grabbed her cosmetic bag and walked into her bathroom. Turning on the shower, she slipped out of her shirt and pants and looked at her reflection. She was wearing her favorite lingerie; the delicate lace bra and panties were both a pale shade of blue that looked great against her sun-kissed skin.

Lexie ran her fingertips over the lace cup of her bra. Closing her eyes, she tried to recall what it was like to feel pleasure. It seemed a lifetime ago when she craved touch and release. She remembered when it consumed her thoughts, when she would dress to impress, and engaged in flirty behavior. Those days she wore a smile everywhere; life was beautiful then. She couldn't remember that version of herself now. She didn't yearn for pleasure anymore. She didn't even know if she was still capable of feeling it. She felt cheated, angry, sad, and she didn't know how to get past these emotions ruling her life.

Lexie was just about to step into her shower when a noise called her attention from inside her apartment. She froze for a moment, trying to hear over the music. She slipped out of the washroom on hesitant feet, searching for her purse, thinking the sound must have been her phone, but there were no new messages.

Lexie was startled there was movement in her peripheral vision. She gasped, placing her hand against her chest, trying to calm her racing heart. The curtains were swaying gently. Lexie slowly slid open her kitchen drawer and wrapped her fingers around the handle of a knife. Numerous scenarios played in her mind, none of them good. She could taste her heartbeat as it rose in her throat. She walked over to the window, her panic in full bloom. Taking a deep breath, Lexie grabbed the curtain quickly and yanked it open. She knew she hadn't left the window open when she had left for the week, though, looking at the window now slightly ajar, she began to question whether she had missed it. At a quick glance, she might have thought it closed.

Lexie closed it tight and turned the lock, making sure it was secure. Giving one last glance through the window, she noticed her neighbour staring at her from across the street. He was sitting out on his balcony with a newspaper in hand. Lexie looked down and remembered she was only in her underwear. She whisked the curtains closed quickly.

"Well, I just gave beer guy a little show. At least someone is getting some excitement." Lexie sighed, turning to go back to her warm shower. Her eyes fell on her apartment door. The chain lock was unlatched. "I'm going crazy," Lexie complained as she grabbed for the chain and slid it securely in place. "I seriously thought I locked you...and now I am talking to my door," Lexie moaned in disbelief as she stomped off toward the shower sweetly calling her name.

The water melted away her tension as it heated her skin to the point where it turned a bright pink. Leaning against the shower wall, she closed her eyes and concentrated on the sound of the water spraying against her body. As hot as the water was, it could not penetrate the frigid temperatures of sadness burrowed deep inside her. She felt as if she was destined to walk the earth for the rest of her days numb and cold, constantly seeking heat that would never truly warm her. Eventually she talked herself into turning off the water.

Lexie pulled on an off-white sundress covered in tiny flowers of different shades of blue, with the occasional purple thrown in the design. She loved it for its imperfection. She was the purple flower in the sea of perfect blue as far as the eye could see. She dried her hair, powdered her nose, put on a little blush, mascara…and shuffling through a basket of lipsticks, she found a shade called "So Good." She ran the bright pink across her lips, waiting for the so good feeling to overcome her. Lexie turned her lipstick on the mirror and drew a circle around the reflection of her face, then proceeded to turn it into a frowning face. She snapped on the cover and dropped it back in the basket before flipping off the light.

Slipping her feet into her favorite sandals, Lexie pulled her camera bag over her shoulder and set out into the late afternoon. She walked up her street, watching the world around her through the lens of her camera. She loved to capture candid moments, interactions of people, and their real emotion when they didn't know the camera was watching them. A few people waved in greeting; others knew Lexie well enough to know she was on the hunt for her pictures, letting her pass through as they carried on with their routines.

Lexie kept walking until the pavement turned to sand beneath her feet. The beach that drew tourists to their small town of Freyview year after year was one of her favorite places to take pictures. The descending sun was still hot upon her skin as she took in deep salty breaths of ocean air. Children lined up for ice cream, screaming and laughing while they waited. Lexie lifted her camera to see what the camera would capture when it looked at the innocent faces of youth.

Lexie had sold ice cream from this very stand years ago, while she was still young and carefree like the kids behind the counter. Scooping endlessly, she served the line of people yearning for the cold sweet treat while the sun rained down on the sandy stretch of paradise. It felt like forever ago.

Lexie turned her camera on the surfers. She recognized every one of them...especially Evan; his red bathing suit stood out like a target, drawing her eyes. He looked up and noticed her, lifting his hand in a wave. They both were forever haunted by the same truth. Lexie waved when they all turned in her direction before turning on her heels and moving on. Her last encounter with Evan had been surreal. A line had been crossed, and she didn't know how to deal with him now. She didn't know if he expected anything to change.

***

Lexie pushed through the doors of a diner, a place she had come to more times than she could possibly recall. The familiar tinkle of the bell sounded over her head as she stepped onto the worn black and white tiles. The delectable scent of apple pie assaulted her, making her mouth water.

Eats and Treats Diner was famous for its pies, always served with a large scoop of delicious vanilla bean ice cream they made fresh every day. It was a hot spot for tourists as well as the locals, and it was rare to see an empty seat in the room.

The space was newly renovated. A refreshing pale blue paint covered the walls. Framed photos that Lexie herself had taken covered the walls from the last ten years from the moment she fell in love with photography. It had become an addiction, a fascination, a calling. The evidence surrounded her.

Her mother worked at this diner for the last twenty years. She had bought it from the original owners eight years ago when they retired. Lexie herself worked within these walls until her photography became profitable enough to pay her bills. Lexie continued to visit on a daily basis because everyone who worked there had been a part of her life and she considered them family.

"Miss Lexie." Molly's smile lit up the room when she noticed Lexie's arrival. Molly worked at the diner and was her mother's closest friend. Molly had bright red hair and a mischievous personality that tended to get her into trouble, but her heart was pure gold. "How was your big adventure?"

"Hey, Molly. We had a great time. Mom in?"

"No, sweet pea. She was off about an hour ago. Did you try calling her?"

"Yes, but you know how reliable Mom is with answering her phone." Lexie rolled her eyes with a laugh.

"So true! It drives me crazy." Molly set two plates down in front of a couple of regulars sitting at the bar before turning her attention back toward Lexie. "Sit, honey. I'm going to feed you." Molly pointed toward a newly vacated stool against the bar.

"Well, if you insist. I can never turn down good food." Lexie slid into the stool. Lexie pulled out her phone to see her mother still didn't return her call. A plate slid across the counter. Lexie looked up to see a piece of warm apple pie. The ice cream was melting as it nestled beside it.

"*Oh my god*, I love you," Lexie said as she took the fork Molly held out for her.

"It's so nice to see that beautiful smile again," Molly said, reaching across the counter and placing her hand on Lexie's arm before scurrying off to serve another customer.

The bell chimed again, and Lexie turned to see who entered. Lexie knew immediately the two men were not locals. They were dressed casually enough, but the way their eyes took in the entire interior told that this was their first time entering the diner.

Lexie sat up a bit straighter as she studied them. They had a dangerous energy about them, something that made her instincts flare to life. They were not simple tourists, looking to taste the famous pies from Eats and Treats. They had calculated gazes as they scanned the people in the room. They were both tall and intimidating. One had dark black hair, cropped short, with a neck tattoo peeking out from under the collar of his shirt. The other was only an inch or so taller, with lighter brown hair and a scar that ran through his brow. Their gazes fell on her simultaneously with expressionless faces before they walked to a nearby booth and sat down.

Lexie turned her back to them. She felt a chill rush over her skin with the sensation of being watched. She tried to dismiss their attention, knowing she did nothing to warrant any trouble. She glanced back toward their table to notice that the dark-haired one was staring at her. They were not even trying to be discreet.

"Looks like you can add some admirers to your list." Molly startled Lexie. She wasn't expecting her to lean over the counter. Lexie placed her hand against her chest, feeling her racing heart. The men had her on edge. Molly was looking at her with raised brows.

"They give me the creeps," Lexie whispered.

"Oh, I don't know…I think the dark-haired one is cute in a rough cut kind of way."

"No way." Lexie slid her plate across the bar. "I'm gonna swing by Mom's to see if she's home."

"Sure, hon. Come back and see me when it's not so busy. I want to hear about your trip." Molly collected her dish.

"Of course." Lexie tried to slide some money across the counter.

"Don't you dare," Molly warned.

"Love you, Molls." Lexie slid off the stool.

"Not as much as I love you. Now go find your Momma. She's been worried about you." Molly placed her hands upon her hips.

"Yes, ma'am."

Lexie walked out, refusing to glance toward the two mysterious men. Their gaze gave her the sensation of spiders crawling upon her skin, and she wanted nothing more than to leave them behind and wipe her memory of them.

***

Lexie pulled up in front of her mother's small house, which was nestled on a mature property a short drive from town. It was the same house Lexie grew up in. Coming back always brought her comfort; this place held so many wonderful memories. She wished she could go back to her innocent youth before life told her too many secrets and tainted her view.

Lexie took a deep breath when she stepped out of her car. The flowers were in bloom, and they made the property smell lovely. Lexie and her mother had a ritual of planting new flowers every year, and the garden had grown vastly over the years, though Lexie hadn't participated the last two years and the thought suddenly saddened her. That cold dark feeling tightened its claws on her again, a reminder that she was now a stranger to the girl that dug in the dirt, laughing with her mother on hot sunny afternoons.

The broken trellis still sat under her old bedroom window. She knew her mother would never touch it. Alex had used it for years as a ladder to crawl in her bedroom. Many nights he would come to her and crawl into her bed, kissing her gently and falling asleep with his arms around her. A tear slipped free, and Lexie quickly wiped it away.

"I want to keep you forever," Alex whispered in her ear, his arm wrapped around her waist, pulling her close.

"I'm yours," Lexie whispered back. The only light was the moon filtering in through her curtains.

"Forever?"

"Forever."

Lexie's mother knew she could not keep Alex from her. The two of them were inseparable until everything changed and Lexie discovered forever has an end.

Lexie pushed her key into the front door and stepped inside. Her mother's car wasn't outside, so she dialed her mother's number again.

"Hey, baby."

"Hey, Mom. Where are you?" Lexie walked into the kitchen and noticed her mother had picked flowers and placed them in a large vase upon the table, bringing the delectable scent inside the house as well.

"I had a few errands to run after work, just finishing up. How was your trip?"

"It was nice to remember him...go to the places he loved." Lexie tried to make her voice light, but she could not fool her mother.

"I'm glad. You know I would tear the world apart to find your happiness again if I could. I want to put that smile back on your face for always. You deserve it more than anyone."

Lexie took a deep breath. "Thanks, Mom." Lexie ran her fingers over the silky petals of the flowers. "I made a strange discovery on my travels…"

"Oh yeah?"

"I did, *Mary Connors*." Lexie teased lightly. She was met with a silence that scared her. "Mom?"

"What did you just say?" Her mother's voice was now small, retracted with traces of fear.

"Mary Connors. We were at this bar in Sugar Hill…"

"Who did you talk to?" Her mother's voice exploded with a rush of emotion.

"I noticed your pictures on the wall and this man named…James—or no, Jason maybe. The bartender knew you too. I got a strange vibe so I said it wasn't who I thought it was."

"Where are you now?" Her mother's tone was unsettling.

"I'm at your place."

"Were you followed?"

"What? Mom…you're scaring me." Lexie swallowed the fear that climbed up her throat.

"Listen to me, baby. Go upstairs in my bedroom right now. Hurry."

"Okay." Lexie darted up the stairs and into her mother's room with the sensation of fear nipping at her heels. "What's going on, Mom?"

"Move my dresser out from the wall. There

should be a plug cover directly behind it."

Lexie held the phone against her shoulder and pulled the dresser out. "I see it."

"The plug isn't real. It's just a false plate. Kick the wall to the right of the plug."

"What the hell, Mom? You want me to kick a hole in the wall?" Lexie stood in front of the plug; disbelief felt heavy in the pit of her stomach.

"Just do it, Lexie!"

"Fine, but I'm not paying to fix it." Lexie kicked at the wall; it gave slightly, but her flip-flops did little damage. Lexie pulled the plate out of the wall and reached in to pull part of the wall away. "What am I looking for exactly?"

"A bag."

A large piece of wall gave way, and a black bag came into view. "Hold on." Lexie pulled it through the small opening. A small journal fell to the ground that had been wedged under the bag. Lexie picked it up and flipped through the pages. It was filled with her mother's handwriting. The dates indicated it was from before Lexie was born. Lexie decided to keep it, shoving it into her purse. She planned to ask her mother about it later. "Okay, got it." Lexie unzipped the bag. "Oh my god, Mom! It's filled with cash!"

"Listen to me closely, baby. I need you to take the cash and get out of town for a bit. Do not go back to your apartment. There's an envelope in the bag with your name on it. It has an address for a place I want you to go. You'll be safe. I need to stay there until I contact you. Under no circumstances can you use your bank or credit cards. Do you hear me?"

"Can you at least tell me what's going on?" Lexie gasped in disbelief. She felt like she was suddenly dropped in someone else's life. Her mother did not stash bags of cash and make escape plans. The whole situation seemed surreal.

"We don't have time right now. I need to make sure you're safe."

"Safe from what? You're freaking me the hell out."

"The key to the place is with the letter. Did you notice anyone suspicious since you got home?" Her mother's tone was disturbingly calm as she carried on with the ridiculous conversation.

"No…well, yes. At the diner, there were a couple of strange men with tattoos that showed up when I was there."

"Shit!" Lexie's mother swore uncharacteristically.

Movement outside caught Lexie's attention, and she walked toward the window. "Mom? Did you just pull in the driveway?"

"Get out of there, Lexie! Go out the back; leave your car. If you run a few miles through the trees, you will come out near the old gas station. I need you to go to the bus stop and get on the bus."

"Mom…"

"Hang up your phone and leave it at the house. There's a phone in the bag. I'll call you."

"I can't leave my phone. All my pictures…"

"*Goddammit*, Lexie. Do what I say now or none of it will matter! Hang up and go *now*!"

Lexie covered her mouth as a sob escaped her.

She hit end and glanced at her phone for a fleeting moment. It had all her favorite pictures of Alex. The sound of a car door closing snapped her focus back into play. Terror pumped her heart furiously. She dropped her phone on her mother's bed and threw the bag strap over her shoulder. She ran into her old bedroom. It looked strange without her belongings filling the space. It was now only a ghost of her youth. She pulled the window open and slipped a leg outside until she felt the roof ledge beneath her foot. Her eyes widened in panic when she heard noises inside the house—downstairs. She slipped out, sliding the window closed, and climbed over the edge of the roof, using her feet to find the trellis below. When she was close enough to the ground, she let go and jumped down onto the grass. The weight of the bag caused her to stumble slightly, but she quickly regained her footing.

Lexie pressed herself against the house and glanced through the window. She noticed one of the men from the diner walking into the kitchen. Her stomach fell, and panic closed around her throat. Ducking under the window, she took off through the trees at full speed.

The sound of her heavy breathing completely enveloped her hearing, drowning out everything else. She continued to run as adrenaline pumped through her system. She pressed forward when her muscles began to burn and her chest ached. She was familiar with the woods, knew exactly where she was going. She and Alex used to go to the old gas station and stock up on their favorite snacks when they were younger. In fact, the last time she stepped in these woods, she was with Alex. The memory of her hand in his washed over her. Sometimes when she thought about Alex she could almost feel him, like he was still with her. She needed him now. She needed his strength. She needed him to take her hand and pull her the rest of the way because her body was growing tired as she ran over the uneven ground.

The trees began to thin, and finally she broke free of the forest. Lexie leaned on her knees and desperately drew breath into her starving lungs. She needed to collect herself before she headed toward the bus stop; she didn't want to raise any flags. If she ran to the bus like a crazed girl, someone was bound to notice. Her mother was insistent she slip away unnoticed, and until she got answers, she would do just that.

CHAPTER FOUR

Lexie walked to the back of the nearly empty bus, collapsing in a seat. Her legs felt like they could no longer hold her weight. She was exhausted and unsure what had just happened. She was trying to find a reasonable solution to the insanity that just fell into her lap. Ringing sounded from a side pocket of the black shoulder bag. Lexie scrambled to retrieve the phone. The screen indicated a blocked call when she held it up.

"Hello?" Lexie answered hesitantly.

"Are you on the bus?" Her mother's tone was nothing but direct.

"Yes. The men from the diner were at the house, but I don't think they saw me leave."

"Good. I'll call you soon."

"Mom?" Lexie tried to catch her, but the line disconnected. "Dammit!" Lexie cursed. Anger was starting to bubble to the surface. Her mother left her completely confused, unprepared, and running from her entire life.

Lexie threw the phone back into the bag and

leaned back against the seat, closing her eyes. "Wake up…please just wake up," Lexie whispered, running her hands over her face. She pulled out an envelope that was in the same pocket as the phone. It had her name written across it in her mother's handwriting. Ripping the seal, she pulled out a piece of paper and unfolded it.

Lexie,

If you are reading this, things have probably gotten out of control. I'm sorry I had to keep you in the dark. I need you to follow the directions below to a place I set up as a safe house should the situation arise...

Lexie looked at the detailed instructions that followed her brief, unsatisfying explanation and sighed. She tipped the envelope up, and a silver key fell into the palm of her hand.

Despite the fatigue that gripped her, Lexie couldn't rest. Her mind was running rampant with possibilities of what her mother may be involved in. Every idea that came to mind seemed entirely unlikely of the woman she knew as her mother. She could only stare out the window and watch the horizon become more and more unfamiliar.

Lexie remembered the journal she had found. Retrieving it from her purse, she opened it up to take a closer look.

March 2, 1992

Last night was one of the most wonderful nights of my entire life. Karen and I were waiting in line to get into The Compass, our usual dance club of choice because at happy hour drinks are only a dollar. It is, of course, the most logical choice for students.

We were approached by a well-dressed gentleman named John Stodden. He was beautiful and made my head spin. He was the kind of beautiful that made music play from nowhere and your heart race. He had a wonderful charm about him and a face that I could not stop staring at. He offered to take us to Obelisk. We had heard about it but never imagined actually going. It was a club that tailored to the rich and famous. We couldn't imagine our luck.

It was everything we envisioned and more. The music sounded better, the drinks tasted better, and the people... wow!

John introduced us to many new faces throughout the evening and always made sure we had a drink in hand. We felt *like celebrities.*

We danced our asses off and met some of the most beautiful people I had ever seen. John kept me by his side, his hand constantly touching me. I loved it. He never let me out of his sight. I felt beautiful.

I am practically jumping out of my skin.

Before he dropped us home, he asked for my number. He wants to see me again. I keep pinching myself. This definitely calls for a new outfit!

The entry sounded innocent enough. Lexie closed it up when guilt began to claw at her. Maybe she shouldn't be reading her mother's personal journal. Tucking it back into her purse, she decided to leave it alone for now.

***

Hours passed, and after one stop to switch buses, Lexie finally came to her stop. Grabbing her things, she headed for the unknown. Stepping off the bus, her stomach tightened. She wanted to stomp her feet and scream out in frustration, but it would solve nothing. It would only draw attention and possibly the police if someone thought she was crazy enough. She wondered why her mother didn't call the police to deal with what was happening. The only thing she could come up with as a solution was that her mother wasn't innocent.

Night had already settled; everything seemed eerie. At first glance the stop looked like it was in the middle of nowhere. The long street was heavily lined with thick trees. She knew she was in the right place based on her mother's description. A lone bench next to the bus sign was painted to look like it was covered in tiger stripes under a bright street lamp. A narrow road a few yards from where she stood was marked with multiple signs for various house numbers. The number of her destination was not indicated, but she knew it wasn't far. She began the walk down the long, dimly lit road.

Her mind was so full of conflicting thoughts, and she found herself in a daze as she listened to the crunch of the gravel under her feet and the gentle wind in the trees. She tried to retrieve her phone only to remember that she no longer had it. The pictures she had stored on it were a source of comfort when things became too much. Now she didn't know what to turn to. She needed something to ground her.

Lexie used her mother's cell phone for a flashlight; the streetlamps were spaced far enough apart that it left black voids along the road. Lexie was nervous walking along such a long dark street late at night with a bag full of cash. Nothing about her situation was safe. She spun around when she heard a noise behind her. Her heart raced in her chest as she waved her flashlight around the treeline. "Where the hell did you send me, Mom?" Lexie shook her head as she spoke to herself.

A car approached and passed her by, the lights blinding in the darkness. She gave a gentle wave and continued on her way. She quickened her steps until the silhouette of the cottage came into sight. It was nestled in a row of others that all lined the water, separated by only a thin line of trees. The number forty-eight was nailed to the tree at the top of the driveway. It was completely dark and looked like it had been years since anyone stepped foot on the property based on the overgrown grass that no longer resembled a lawn.

Lexie pulled the key from her pocket and slid it into the front door. There was a little resistance, but the key turned. Holding up the phone, she shone the light into the dark interior. She swallowed the lump in her throat, convincing herself to step over the threshold.

Lexie flicked on the switch and flooded the small space with light. Her nerves uncoiled a bit now that she could see the inside. Locking the door behind her, she looked around. A laundry room and bathroom were on her left and a bedroom on the right side. The hall opened into a small kitchen and living space. It was all furnished with the basics, but it looked unused. Everything was too new to be convincing as a cottage, despite the layer of dust that coated the room. It was as if someone filled the entire place with the necessities and then walked out the door and never came back. Maybe that was precisely what her mother did.

Lexie walked up the narrow staircase that led to

a small loft with a bed sitting in the center of the space. She dropped her purse and bag on the bed and sat down on the edge. Tears started falling, and she couldn't stop the flood that followed. She curled up into a ball. The emotions of the day could no longer be contained.

***

Lexie woke with a start the next morning. Exhaustion had finally claimed her when her tears dried up. The night had been so quiet, no sounds of cars or commotion that usually took place outside her bedroom window. It felt like she'd lain awake for hours waiting for sleep to come, staring at the shadows that crawled across the walls from the trees dancing in the breeze.

Lexie walked into the washroom and opened the cabinets. A couple of new toothbrushes and toothpaste were in the drawer. She ripped open the package and slathered it with paste.

Running her fingers through her hair, she made it as presentable as possible. She rummaged through her collection of lip glosses in her purse to find one that was suitable for the occasion. "Optimism...that will work." Lexie pulled the cover off and painted it over her lips. "I am in serious need of optimism and caffeine right now."

Lexie needed to find a store. She wasn't sure how long she would be staying, but she knew she needed to eat and also more than just the clothes on her back. Lexie slipped her camera strap over her head and collected her phone from the charger, tossing it into her purse. She would not miss a call from her mother. She had too many questions floating around in her head that needed answers.

Lexie walked out into the warm morning sun. The air tasted fresh and smelled woodsy from the thick forest winding tightly around all the cottages. She wished circumstances were different and she could enjoy the scenery. She took a deep breath and lifted her camera up to view the peaceful wilderness through her lens. The ability to capture a moment forever with one click of her camera always fascinated her. She loved the power to stop time, hold on to it, and revisit it whenever she wished.

The sound of a car door closing pulled her attention away from a couple of birds chirping in a nearby tree. Lexie looked next door at the sleek black car that she hadn't noticed the night before. Her knowledge of cars was slim to none, but it looked like it was built for speed and nothing practical.

The front steps groaned loudly in protest as she stepped down, alerting the owner of the car. His attention drew to her as he swung a black duffle bag over his shoulder. She froze like a deer in the headlights. He was tall and shaped like a man that did nothing but physical activity. His intense eyes were staring back at her, and her heart throbbed so loudly she could feel it in her fingertips.

She imagined it was like crossing a lion in the wild. He was captivatingly beautiful and terrifying at the same time. He gave her a friendly wave and, unlike her, seemed completely at ease.

Her flee response screamed at her because she

knew if she tried to engage she wouldn't be able to form a coherent thought. She was too drained from the night before to muster up a proper conversation. She gave a small pathetic wave in response and quickly walked up the driveway toward the main dirt road. She could feel the heat of his eyes on her back, and she forced herself not to look back no matter how much she wanted to.

Once the cottage faded from view, Lexie let go of the breath she was holding. She was definitely awake now that a hefty dose of adrenaline was pumping through her system. She wasn't sure how she felt about discovering her next door neighbour was the embodiment of a fantasy. The memory of his eyes on her was not easy to shake, nor was anything else about him.

Lexie knew a store was nearby; the bus had passed it before her stop last night. As she walked, she noticed a few signs pointing her in the right direction. Some of the areas she passed were campgrounds with trailers parked and people cooking on portable BBQs. Lexie could smell bacon and pancakes as she walked by, one site in particular causing her mouth to water. If it weren't for her circumstances, this place would be the perfect relaxation retreat. A few children raced past her on their bikes, and she turned to watch them drive off into the distance. She was jealous of their carefree laughter.

The path opened up into the back of the parking lot after walking a good thirty minutes. It was scattered with vehicles. A couple of older gentlemen were chatting next to a pickup truck. A woman unloaded her groceries while trying to calm her fussy baby. She took a deep breath and headed toward the entrance of the store. A bit of tension eased from her shoulders, and the tight coil of discomfort was beginning to unfurl in her stomach. The danger she felt the night before felt a lot less potent with the light of the new day. As long as she didn't dwell on the previous night's events, she could almost see herself enjoying this place. The only thing she needed was for her mother to call and explain what was going on. She reached into her purse and wrapped her fingers around the phone. The urge to call Stephanie was suffocating, but she had no idea what to tell her. She knew Stephanie would demand answers. She decided to wait for her mother to call first and then ease Stephanie into the situation once Lexie had a handle on it herself.

When Lexie entered, a young man greeting customers smiled so big she thought it would crack his features. She gave him a polite nod and grabbed a cart. Her list was formulating in her head as she walked through the store. After a quick pass of the women's section, grabbing anything that looked wearable, she moved onto the cosmetics department.

Standing in front of a huge display of nail polishes, she searched for the one particular shade she needed. Running her fingers over the smooth bottles, she held that hope tight in her stomach...please be here. An empty spot on the shelf with the name of the ever-evasive color mocked her. "Knockout" was sold out.

Lexie looked down at her toes, the color almost

completely chipped away and non-existent on her baby toes. Lexie pulled in a deep breath until her lungs screamed in protest. If she let her emotion show, she wasn't sure if she could stop the tidal wave that would hit her. She needed to be strong now.

Lexie collected a few other items, including a blush called "Happy" and a soft mauve eyeshadow called "Lucky Girl." She desperately wanted luck and happiness. Wearing them might be the closest she could get.

Her cart filled with all the necessities and food she gathered to hold her over for a few days. Her mother said nothing about being frugal with the money. She tried to spend wisely, but even just the necessities seemed to add up considerably. Luckily, she always kept her camera in her purse; otherwise she would've had to invest in another one. A camera was one thing Lexie could not live without.

On the way to the checkout, Lexie decided to pick up something sweet. She was in the need for some sugar after a stressful few days—not to mention she was hungry and she was never one to make wise decisions in the grocery store on an empty stomach.

With her mind completely captivated by the entire aisle of sweets, Lexie didn't notice that someone was in the path of her cart until she collided with them. "Oh my god! I didn't see you," Lexie gasped.

She looked up into eyes that pulled all the breath from her lungs and sent a scorching heat flashing across her skin. Her mouth dropped open as she watched the contents of his cup absorb into his t-shirt. The dark wet stain crawled across his chest, sticking to lines that made her legs shake. It took a moment for Lexie to realize her impossibly beautiful neighbour was standing in front of her. He stared back at her with dark, dangerous eyes she knew she could get lost in.

"Oh god!" Lexie looked for anything to help him wipe up the mess she made. "I'm so sorry." Lexie grabbed the scarf tied to her purse—the only thing that looked useable. She untied it with trembling hands and quickly pressed it to his chest. "Here. I'm so sorry." Lexie kept her focus on her hands pressing the material to his wet shirt, not daring to look up into his eyes again. It made a strange feeling bubble up through the chaos in her stomach. She could feel his gaze on her. It heated her and made her aware of every inch of her body. His hands remained at his sides while she held the fabric to his chest. The subtle hint of vanilla from his drink mixed with whatever godly scent was coming from him made her head feel light. His skin felt hard and unyielding beneath the thin material. The realization of what she was doing hit her hard in the chest. Heat seared her face as she stepped back. "I'm pretty sure I just molested you. Oh god, can this get any worse?" Lexie placed her hands over her face and took a deep breath. "I should leave now before I make this situation worse. Keep the scarf, and here…let me give you money for dry cleaning…" Lexie grabbed for her purse.

"I don't want your money." He chuckled lightly.

Dear lord, his voice sounded like a bass

instrument, vibrating deep and low.

"I feel like I should give you money after what I just did. Please, just take it." Lexie held out a fifty dollar bill. She knew her face was a prefect representation of the color red.

He looked at the bill and raised his brow, passing her the scarf back.

"Think of it as compensation for the emotional trauma I just caused you." Lexie waved it at him.

"My emotions are just fine."

"Good to know." Lexie tucked the bill in his hand quickly and grabbed her cart. "Sorry again." She walked as fast as she could in the opposite direction, leaving him and her scarf behind. She continued around the outer edge of the store until she made her way to the checkouts. Luckily he was nowhere in sight. Her embarrassment eased up as the cashier rang through her items. There had never been someone she wanted to see so bad and yet never again. The overdose of intense emotions made an uncomfortable knot form in her stomach.

The cashier probably thought her rude because she could only bring herself to nod at her friendly questions.

Loaded with bags that got heavier with every step, she walked through the doors and came to a sudden stop. *He* was standing directly in her line of sight leaning against his car—staring directly at her.

Lexie felt like she was hit in the stomach. She couldn't breathe. Adjusting the bags in her hands, she forced her feet to move forward.

"Are you going to yell at me or something?" Lexie asked hesitantly when she approached. "I am really sorry about your shirt."

"No." The edges of his lips curled up. "I was going to offer you a ride."

"Oh…no thank you." As soon as Lexie finished speaking, the bottom of one of her bags gave out and the contents scattered on the pavement. Lexie dropped her shoulders. "I'm not usually this much of an idiot." Lexie sighed.

"I think it's cute," he said with an amused tone.

One of her lip glosses rolled over and stopped against his foot. Luckily her bottle of wine that was in the same bag didn't smash when it hit the ground. Lexie took that as a sign she was meant to have a few drinks tonight, and she was delighted the universe agreed. Lexie quickly grabbed all the items and stashed them in her other bags. When she looked up, he was holding out a few of her things, luckily none of them embarrassing.

"Thank you." Lexie took them from his hand. Touching his skin was like lighting up every nerve in her entire body. She imagined it was similar to taking a hit off a drug that gives you an amazing high. Retracting quickly, she tucked the things away, trying to ignore the sensation lingering on her skin.

"I'm heading back. Let me drive you so you don't lose anything else along the way."

"I don't trust you," Lexie blurted. She could feel her eyes widen in panic when she realized how ridiculous she must seem. "Listen, I had a really bad day yesterday…well, actually I have had many bad days lately, but yesterday's events leave me unable to feel comfortable around strangers right now. I hope you understand."

"Fair enough." He took Lexie's bags from her hands. He smelled of the woods mixed with spice and heat. It was delicious and enough to make her swoon. Lexie didn't know what was getting into her. She shook her head to clear her thoughts.

"What are you doing?" Lexie's focus snapped back into play.

"Being neighbourly and helping you back to your place."

"I don't want to get into your car. This is the perfect set up for some murder mystery. Girl ruins guy's shirt. Guy pretends to forgive her. Girl stupidly gets into his car. Guy chops her up into a million pieces and scatters her body in the ditch and no one ever knows what happens to her." Lexie's voice cracked, showing her nervousness.

"That is completely unrealistic. First, do you know how long it would take to chop a body into a million pieces? And then there is the fact that I wouldn't throw you in a ditch where it would draw attention to the crime. I would have to be more discreet unless I wanted to get caught," he said in a completely serious tone. Lexie unconsciously took a step backward.

"Relax. I was joking." He chuckled. "Listen, I will help you carry your bags back to your place and come back to get my car. Better?"

"You don't have to walk me."

"I insist." He raised his hand for her to lead the way. "I'm not a stranger, after all. I am your neighbour, and I'll admit I am exceptionally good at scaring off strangers. So this works in your favour."

Lexie sighed in defeat, letting her features soften enough to manage a smile. "My name is Lexie."

"Jackson."

"Thank you, Jackson, for being a gentleman despite the fact that I assaulted you with my cart and spilled your drink all over you." Lexie felt the need to properly apologize, especially now that he was helping her home.

"Don't forget the part where you molested me." Jackson laughed.

Lexie covered her face with her hands in mortification.

"Oh my god," Lexie complained. "It's not too late to change your mind. You don't need to walk me."

"I never back out of anything," Jackson said. His lips curved up deviously, and his grey-blue eyes seemed to reach deep inside her and wreak havoc on her insides.

There was something about Jackson that screamed danger—she couldn't decide if it was his unwavering confidence, his strong brow that shadowed his stormy eyes, his high defined cheekbones, or his scruffy, unshaven face. He looked like a beautiful predator stalking his prey— her. She couldn't bring herself to walk away from him, though. Despite her reservations, she was more terrified of being alone.

Even though her instincts were unsettled by his presence, she couldn't stop the pull toward him. A heat grew inside her, feelings stirring where they had been absent for so long. Guilt clung to everything she felt, but she held on regardless. She felt alive.

"Are you staying here long?" Lexie attempted easy conversation.

"No. Just passing through." Jackson looked ahead thoughtfully, and Lexie took the opportunity to appreciate the view. He had a strong jaw that was cut perfectly. The thought of what his scruffy face would feel like against her skin grabbed her attention, and she could feel the flush creep along her neck. She tried to find a flaw that would make her realize he was just as human as everyone else. She couldn't help thinking that Jackson was as hard as Alex's features had been inviting. She didn't know what possessed her to make the comparison.

"Are you on a road trip adventure, or looking for something or someone?" Lexie forced her voice to seem casual.

"Something like that."

"Well, you're an open book, aren't you?"

"No, but you are." His penetrating eyes held hers, challenging.

"Oh yeah, how so?" Lexie desperately tried to keep her eyes locked with his.

"You're scared of me. Your eyes give it away. You swallow a lot, which indicates you are uncomfortable. The color of your skin and the way you keep licking your lips tell me you are also attracted to me."

Lexie's breaths became deeper and more frequent. "I'm not scared of you," Lexie said defensively.

A satisfied look brightened his features. "You are also a horrible liar. Since you bought all these

53

necessities," Jackson held up her bags to verify his point, "I know you ran off unexpectedly. Now, you're all alone in a cottage in the middle of the woods next to someone you don't know if you want to run to or from. See, Lexie, you are an open book."

Despite the unease that he was able to read her so well, she couldn't help the thought of how good her name sounded coming from his lips.

"Obviously I need to work on my game face. It was just a fun last-minute getaway. I have people meeting me here. They should be arriving anytime."

"Mmm hmm," Jackson responded in a tone that indicated he was not convinced at all. "Like I said, terrible liar."

CHAPTER FIVE

When Lexie opened her front door, Jackson insisted on bringing the bags inside. He looked so much bigger inside the cottage as he walked in. She wondered what it would be like to roam the world with confidence like his, never seeming out of place. He set the bags on the small round table. Picking up a pen, he scribbled on the notepad sitting next to the bags before he turned toward Lexie. When his gaze fell on her, she tried to hide the fact she was trying to see what he was writing.

"Um…thanks again for helping me home and sorry about your shirt." Lexie's nervousness skyrocketed now they were alone. This seemed riskier now that they did not have the background of happy campers to diffuse her nerves.

Jackson looked down at his shirt, the stain barely visible on the grey color now that it had dried. He reached over his head and pulled his shirt off. Lexie backed up until the refrigerator pressed into her back. She knew her mouth was hanging open. She couldn't pry her gaze away from his beautifully tanned skin. His body was carved into the most delectable male form she had ever seen. Coiled muscle after muscle molded his flesh into a body made for sin. He tossed it into the garbage can next to her.

Jackson looked at her, his eyes carving through the distance between them like a hot knife through butter. He ran his fingers through his thick hair, and Lexie felt like melting. His gaze was enough to stop time, and she found herself completely lost in his captivating eyes. She doubted she had the will to stop whatever his intentions were.

He moved closer. Lexie swallowed her nerves. They were wound so tight in her stomach it ached. When he came toe to toe with her, Lexie's breath broke as it escaped her. Her mouth watered from his nearness and enticing scent. She grasped the handle of the fridge like it would save her from falling.

He placed his hand on the top of the refrigerator, and Lexie felt the strength in her legs seep to the floor. Her whole body shook as he grazed her cheek with his. Lexie closed her eyes and tipped her head back. All logical thoughts were a distant memory as she held her breath in anticipation. She was completely under his spell.

His heat was suddenly replaced by the cool air of the room. Lexie's eyes flashed open to see him standing a few feet away from her. "Your faucet is dripping."

"What?" Lexie gasped. Her eyes flew open, and she looked over at the sink. Sure enough, there was a slow drip she hadn't even noticed until now. She was breathless from the build-up of sexual tension that had her squeezing her thighs together. He walked out of her kitchen and down the hall without another word. Lexie was left speechless, staring after his retreating form as he opened the door. He looked back at her, his large frame filling the doorframe.

Lexie lifted the camera that still hung around her neck and snapped a picture before he left. She needed a picture to convince herself this really happened because as soon as she came down from this strange high she was bound to question her sanity.

"Dear God…what the hell was that?" Lexie ran her hand over her sensitized chest, her nipples straining through the material of her dress. She couldn't understand why her body decided to fire up now. Her life was crumbling around her, but a moment ago she would have agreed to anything to have Jackson's lips against hers. All thoughts of her mother and the men that had been after her and even Alex had completely faded away. The realization scared her. She had been a slave to what Jackson waved in front of her. Now that he was gone, she was relieved things didn't proceed further. She needed to stay away from him. Jackson was the last thing she needed in her life right now.

Lexie walked back to the garbage can and pulled his shirt out. The material felt so soft against her skin. There was no way she was leaving it in the garbage. It just needed to be washed—eventually. Lexie held it to her nose. It smelled of vanilla and Jackson—delicious.

On the refrigerator Lexie noticed the fifty-dollar

bill she had given Jackson under a small magnet of a horseshoe. He placed it there when she thought he was going to kiss her. Her lips still tingled with anticipation. She didn't understand the feelings that swirled within her. It was as if a part of her she forgot about was suddenly waking up and demanding attention. Thoughts of Alex made guilt twist violently in her chest. She shouldn't want to kiss someone else.

Lexie grabbed a grocery bag off the table and began placing a few items in the fridge, taking long slow breaths to slow her still frenzied heart. She placed the milk, butter, and eggs in the fridge and closed the door.

"Holy crap." Lexie's hands flew to her chest when she noticed Jackson walk back into her kitchen. He was wearing a new shirt and carrying a toolbox. "You're back?" Lexie looked up at him questioningly.

"I want to fix your drip." He lifted his tools with a raised brow. He set the box on the counter and opened it.

"You have already done enough. You don't need to fix my sink too." Lexie made sure to keep her distance this time. She grabbed the material of her dress and twisted the fabric between her fingers. He made her incredibly nervous.

"I already whipped out my tool, Lexie. No going back now. When I see something that needs doing, I do it." Jackson held up a wrench and threw a seductive smile her way. "I can't leave a beautiful woman in distress."

"Oh." Heat flashed across Lexie's face as she

tried to keep her mouth from falling open at his suggestive tone. She wasn't sure she could survive the physical affects Jackson had on her body. "Thank you."

Jackson opened up the cabinet doors and leaned in under the sink. Lexie took the opportunity to move over to the table. She pulled out a chair and sat down before the rush of hormones knocked her off her feet. She tried not to watch Jackson as he climbed under the sink and made a few adjustments. She quickly found out how impossible it was to ignore him, especially the way his body flexed and his shirt rode up to reveal abs that she could easily imagine running her tongue over. She could feel her body temperature rise. It was as if she hadn't eaten in days and he was a big plate of things she knew would taste divine. She avoided his gaze when he turned around. She had to work on discretion or he was going to think her an awkward mess. He dropped his tools back in the box. "All done."

"That's it?"

"Yep." Jackson wiped off his hands and grabbed a small box off the windowsill that Lexie hadn't even noticed before now. "Do you want to play?" He held it up, and Lexie realized it was a pack of cards.

"Play what?" Lexie asked hesitantly. She was mentally trying to get her body under control. She was beginning to think all of these crazy emotions were the start of a mental break.

"Black Jack." Jackson pulled out a chair beside Lexie and sat down. Taking the cards out of the box, he began shuffling.

"What are we playing for?"

"Answers. I know you're dying to ask me questions." He raised his brow knowingly.

"And you'd actually answer them?" Lexie narrowed her eyes suspiciously.

"One answer per hand you win."

"Okay, deal."

Lexie watched Jackson deal out the cards as she swallowed the emotions working their way up her throat. Jackson dealt the cards, and Lexie looked down at her card facing up—an ace. Lexie picked up her other card to peek underneath. A victorious smile spread across her face. "Twenty-one," she said.

"Ask your question then." He leaned back in his chair, resting his arm over the back.

"You didn't even look at your hand." Lexie waved to his untouched cards.

Jackson picked up a card and placed it next to his eight. "I'm bust."

"Who are you?" The question tumbled from her lips.

"That's a pretty broad question. How about you narrow it down a bit?" Jackson said with a raised brow.

"Okay." Lexie tapped her fingers on the table. "What do you do for a living?"

"I'm a cop," Jackson answered casually.

"A cop?" Lexie asked in disbelief. "You're joking, right?"

Jackson reached into his pocket and pulled out his wallet. Opening it up, he laid it down, sliding it across the table. A shiny metal badge stared up at

Lexie.

She ran her finger over the intricate design. It was cool to the touch. "I think a cop would have been my last choice. You look more like a break-the-rules type." Lexie looked up to see him studying her. She desperately wanted to know what he saw when he looked at her. She wondered if he saw that she was just broken pieces barely clinging to each other.

"Cops can be the worst kind of rule breakers," he replied with a frown.

"And do you break many rules?"

"You already asked your question," Jackson said as he began dealing another hand.

She looked down to see an ace on her face card. She threw him a glance before she peeked underneath to see the same card as before. "Are you allowing me to win?"

"I want you to know about me."

"Why don't you just tell me then?"

"It's not as fun." His lips turned up in a crooked grin.

"Why are you here?" Lexie asked curiously.

"Because of you."

"Me? Why me?" Lexie leaned back in her seat. His answer made her nervous.

"Since I saw you hop down your front steps, that camera wrapped around your neck, and that white dress showing off your sinful legs I haven't been able to think about anything else." His dark eyes cut deep into her, causing goosebumps to flash across her skin.

Lexie was not expecting him to say the words

that just flowed so casually from his lips. She wasn't even sure if she heard him correctly and couldn't bring herself to formulate a response. Jackson stood up and pushed his chair into the table.

"Where are you going?" Lexie asked.

"I don't want to play anymore."

"Why?"

"Because I said all I wanted to say and if I stay, all I'll be thinking about is bending you over this table and fucking you until you can no longer walk."

Lexie swallowed the enormous lump in her throat. "Is that a bad thing?" Her heart was furiously thumping in her chest to the point she feared it would overheat.

"Yes, because you're the type good guys keep, not the kind the bad guys fuck."

"Does that mean you're a bad guy?"

"I don't know what I am." It was the first time she saw his confidence stripped away and she glimpsed something else in his gaze. Something she recognized because it felt familiar to her.

"I feel the same about myself." Lexie stood up, holding onto the back of her chair in case her legs didn't cooperate.

"You are not what I expected, Lexie," Jackson said thoughtfully.

"I can say the same about you."

"It's been a pleasure." Jackson grabbed her hand and brought it up to place a kiss. She immediately turned her hand to cup his cheek. This suddenly felt like a goodbye, and it surprised her how much this terrified her.

"You make me want things I shouldn't," Lexie confessed in a rush, completely letting go of her filter.

"I can say the same about you." Jackson gave her a sad smile as he used her words. He gave her hand a squeeze before he turned and walked out the door again, leaving her completely dumbfounded. This time he didn't return.

***

Lexie paced back and forth in the small interior of the cabin. The walls felt like they were closing in on her. Every second that passed she swore the room felt smaller. She struggled with conflicting emotions. Her loyalty to Alex was being tested by a man she barely knew. She placed her hand against her chest; her heart belonged to Alex. It would always belong to Alex, but her body had other plans. It now thrummed with energy that was hard to contain because Jackson looked at her with eyes that could pull all the breath from her lungs. She was so tired of feeling stuck. Maybe allowing herself a guilty pleasure with a stranger would give her enough of a nudge to feel alive again. She was tired of feeling so empty, alone, and trapped.

The guilt of thinking of another was easier than dwelling on the unknown when it came to her mother and the men that chased her from her mother's house. It was difficult to grasp the situation when she felt like she was blindfolded and walking through a minefield. She was so tired of staring at the phone, waiting for the screen to light up.

Lexie looked over at the two bottles of wine she had set on the counter. She was in need of a drink and fresh air or she would combust at the seams. She grabbed the bottles and her phone before heading outside.

CHAPTER SIX

Lexie sat on one of two wooden chairs positioned perfectly to look out over the calm water. A beautiful pink cast stretched across the horizon. The evening sun felt like a warm blanket on her skin as she sipped the rich red wine straight from the bottle. She had searched every cabinet for wine glasses to no avail. Apparently her mother didn't anticipate her need to drink should she be thrown into these turns of events. She stared at the phone, willing it to ring. The longer she stewed with her unanswered questions, the angrier she became.

She had spent the afternoon taking pictures among the trees that surrounded the handful of cottages. Most of the land was untouched, left to its own accord with a raw, natural beauty that Lexie loved to capture. Normally she would have pulled her pictures up on her computer and worked her magic but she didn't have access to her computer, or anything in her life.

Lexie tipped the bottle up to her lips, taking a long swallow. The spicy plum flavor warmed her stomach. Lexie picked up her mother's diary, running her fingers over the leather-bound book. In her current state of mind, she didn't care if she was intruding upon her mother's privacy. She was in the middle of nowhere with nothing but her thoughts to occupy her. This terrified her more than the men that had followed her to her mother's house.

March 5, 1992

John took me out on an official date tonight. It was a beautiful restaurant, and the food was like tasting heaven. The chef even came out to speak with us personally to see if we were enjoying our meal. I've never experienced service like that before.

I feel like any moment he is going to realize I'm just a small town girl with only a few dollars to my name. This is definitely not the lifestyle I am used to. I don't know why he's insistent on spending time with me when he is constantly surrounded by beautiful woman, dressed in clothing that probably costs more than my car.

He is incredibly handsome, and he treats me like a princess.

I think I am falling in love.

I cannot think about anything else but

his amazing blue eyes that I want to dive into and stay forever.

And our kiss...a moment I will never forget.

I never want to wake up from this dream.

March 7, 1992

In the middle of my physiology class a letter was delivered to my desk by another student. All eyes were on me as I opened it. It was from John, and it simply said, "I miss you."

I wore a stupid smile for the rest of the day...

The phone ringing pulled Lexie's attention abruptly from her mother's words. She practically knocked over the bottle of wine in her frantic effort to grab the phone. "Mom?"

"Lexie, are you at the cottage?" It was her mother's voice, but something was off. It was too cold and direct.

"Yes. Where are you?"

"Stay there. I will come to you. I will explain everything when I get there."

"Are you all right? Where are you? Shouldn't we call the police?" Lexie had to cut herself off before the flood of questions followed.

"We can't call the police, Lexie. Not now. I will be there as soon as I can. I will explain when I get there. I love you, Lex."

"When are you going to be here?"

"As soon as it's safe. I have to go."

"You better explain this insanity when you get here," Lexie demanded, but her mother was already gone. She listened to the silence on the other end of the line. She wanted to throw the phone into the lake in frustration, but she knew she would immediately regret it.

Lexie instead held her phone out and stared at it. She was not good with sitting and waiting. She was about to crawl out of her skin. She needed to talk to someone and dialed the first number that came to mind. The one person who always made her feel better.

"Hello?" Stephanie said hesitantly.

"Steph, it is so good to hear your voice." Lexie leaned back into her chair.

"Where are you? I've been calling you all day! Holy shit, Lexie. I've been going out of my mind."

"I don't even know where to start, but I'm fine."

"You just disappeared without any word. Never do that again."

Stephanie listened quietly as Lexie tried to explain the last two days after they returned from their trip. The men at the diner, how her mother reacted to the name Mary Connors, being followed, the cash, and the fact that her mother made her run out of town without an explanation.

"Holy hell, Lex! What did your mom get herself into?" Stephanie finally exploded. "What are you going to do?"

"Wait, I guess. What else can I do? She didn't tell me anything."

"Wow! I still can't believe your mother was involved in something...dangerous," Stephanie said in disbelief.

"You and me both. Let's talk about something else. I need to get my mind off this craziness." Lexie sighed, rubbing her forehead.

"How can we talk about something else? It's like a huge bomb went off."

"Yeah, well, it's not the first time it's felt like this," Lexie said sadly. Stephanie immediately quieted on the other end of the line. "I really need a distraction before I go crazy."

"Okay...How about the fact that Evan has been calling me nonstop, looking for you? What happened between the two of you? He seems a little panicked like you're upset with him," Stephanie asked cautiously. The night Lexie was trying to pretend didn't happen settled in the forefront of her mind and refused to be ignored.

"Hold on a sec!" Lexie called out from the shower. The insistent knocking became impossible to ignore. Fear of something wrong caused her to jump out of the shower and hastily wrap a towel around herself. "I'm coming!" Lexie called out as she made her way toward her door.

When she looked through the peephole, she could see Evan leaning against the doorframe. She unlatched the lock and pulled the door open. "Evan? Is everything all right?" Lexie questioned.

As soon as she noticed his unruly hair that looked as if he raked his hands through it too many times and his bleary eyes, she knew he was drunk.

Whenever she looked at Evan, she couldn't help but think of Alex. They both had the same mouth, dimples, and green eyes. Evan's hair was darker, but there were many similarities that made it painfully obvious they were brothers. A dull ache throbbed in her chest at the sight of him.

"Hey, Lex." Evan drew the words out slowly. A lazy smile curled his lips.

Lexie sighed. "Come in." She opened the door wider and waved him in. "Just let me finish up in the shower and we can talk." Lexie had known Evan since Alex came into her life. He was barely a year older than Alex. They had not only been brothers but the best of friends. Lexie had dated Alex for years, and Evan had always been part of the package. They had leaned on each other more than anyone when Alex had died.

Lexie started toward her bathroom when Evan called her name. When she turned around, she wasn't expecting him to be so close. "I need you, Lex." He reached for her, wrapping his strong arms around her tiny frame. Lexie immediately wrapped her arms around him and squeezed tight. She knew the turmoil in his heart. He was the only person who understood the depth of her own pain. He held her tightly. His fingers caressed her still damp shoulders. "I need you," he whispered against her ear.

"I'm here, Evan. I'm always here for you." His touch slowly became more than merely seeking a

comforting embrace. "Evan?" He kissed her neck, and then his hands dipped under the material of the towel. "Evan? What are you doing?" Lexie pushed his shoulders back, searching his expression.

"I miss him. I miss him more than anything, Lex." Evan searched her eyes.

"Me too, Evan." Lexie reached for his hand.

"But...sometimes I think that maybe since he's gone, you won't see me as just Alex's brother anymore."

A lead weight dropped in Lexie's stomach. "Evan..."

"Don't say anything. Just let me finish...I loved my brother, and I loved that you made him happy but...I want you. I have always wanted you. I'm in love with you, Lexie. I have always been in love with you." Evan placed his hands on the sides of her face. His eyes were full of emotion. "I don't want to pretend that I just want to be your friend anymore. I need you." The desperation in his eyes terrified her.

Tears threatened to surface as she watched him confess something she wasn't prepared for. His eyes dropped to her mouth, but before she could say anything, his lips were against hers. Shock clouded her senses as she tried to register what was happening. Lexie pulled away from his hold, looking at Evan for answers.

"Lexie, I need you. Please." Evan stepped closer, backing her against the wall. His fingers wrapped around the towel, pulling it free. Lexie felt numb; she couldn't register his touch as he ran his fingers along the skin of her side. It felt like she was

immersed in water as the world seemed to blur. Evan's hands explored every curve as his breathing became heavy.

This was the same person that had consoled her for hours, a constant by her side as they both tried to work through the grief of their loss. Her heart loved him, but as a friend.

She closed her eyes. She had told Evan countless times that she would do anything for him, but she never imagined he would ask this of her. Tears fell. She could feel them running down her cheeks. It was the only thing that felt real as Evan's lips found her breasts.

"I can't do this," Lexie sobbed. Evan wiped her face and kissed her lips.

"Just tonight, no expectations, no promises." Evan placed gentle fingers under her chin and tilted her eyes up to meet his. "I just need to feel something good." He was still the same person, and she trusted him. Those soulful green eyes that he had shared with Alex stared back at her.

"Just tonight," Lexie whispered.

Evan pulled his shirt over his head and took her hand, leading her to the bed.

"He showed up at my place a few days before we went away, drunk and a little emotional...he probably just wants to make sure things are good," Lexie said in the most casual voice she could manage.

Lexie knew Stephanie was trying to read between the lines. She never usually held anything back where Stephanie was concerned, but Lexie couldn't bring herself to talk about what happened yet.

"Is that what brought it on? The nail polish incident?" Stephanie asked cautiously. She was referring to the night she found Lexie an emotional mess, the very episode that brought on their last-minute road trip.

"Maybe…" Lexie grew quiet.

"I'll let it go for now, but will you promise to talk to me about it later?" Stephanie always knew what Lexie needed. She was a better friend than she deserved.

"I will. I promise."

"Tell me something good about this whole scary situation. There has to be some light in this shitstorm," Stephanie said hopefully.

"I'm still trying to come up with something. Will you have a drink with me? I need the company," Lexie asked, leaning back in her chair. Just hearing Stephanie's voice was enough to allow her to feel a bit more grounded.

"I'm already with you. On my second glass."

"Do you think my life will ever be able to go back to some kind of normal?" Lexie asked thoughtfully as she stared up at the stars.

"I fucking hope so." Stephanie sighed.

"Me too."

"Can I come to you, so you're not alone?"

"No, definitely not. As much as I would love to have you here, until I know what's going on, I need to listen to my mother and wait for her. I couldn't risk bringing you into the middle of this. I probably shouldn't have called you…"

"What? No way. Stop talking like that. I was ready to call the police in a complete panic until you called."

"Don't call the police. That was one thing my mother did say."

"I can't help the scenarios going through my head. She actually said not to involve the police?"

"Yep."

Lexie tipped the bottle of wine up to her lips and drained the rest of the contents before she grabbed bottle number two. "Well, I am certainly glad I bought two bottles of wine, because one was not enough to make me numb."

"Slow down, Lexie. I'm not there to help if you pass out on your face." Stephanie laughed.

"That's okay. I have an incredibly hot neighbour that apparently likes to be helpful," Lexie joked.

"Say what now? Hot neighbor?" Stephanie asked with excitement. Lexie couldn't help but smile when she heard Stephanie hiccup. It was a sign she was nearing the end of her bottle of wine. "I think we might have just found a light in this fucked-up situation. Let's pretend nothing else happened and you just tell me about this hot neighbor. We can pretend to be normal for a little while at least."

"I ran into him earlier. He walked me home and carried my groceries, even after I spilled his coffee all over him when I literally ran my cart into him. He is seriously like fell-out-of-the-heavens hot."

"And?"

"He fixed my sink."

"And?"

"We played cards."

"And?"

"He's a cop."

"What? How weird is that? So I'm guessing you didn't tell him why you're there."

"Definitely not."

"What else happened?"

"Nothing. When he left, it felt like goodbye. I can see his driveway from here. Hasn't been back all day. For all I know, he's long gone." Lexie drew out her words slowly.

"Did he mention leaving?" Stephanie asked.

"No, he's not much of a talker when it comes to himself. Maybe I should call him…"

"You have his number?" Stephanie's voice squeaked and was followed by a hiccup.

"Yes…I found it scribbled across a notepad in the kitchen."

"You're so drunk, Lex." Stephanie giggled.

"So are you!" Lexie took another drink. The flavor was no longer distinguishable on her tongue.

"That seems like a strange coincidence—him being a cop." Stephanie trailed off thoughtfully.

"You think he could possibly have something to do with this?"

"I don't know. It might be worth doing some investigations."

"I'm drunk. What could I possibly investigate right now? Besides, if he's doing some undercover stuff like they do in the movies, he wouldn't have told me he's a cop," Lexie argued.

"Go into his place. Have a quick little look around to see if anything looks suspicious."

"What the hell? That seems like a sure way to

get myself into trouble when I'm trying to lay low."

"You said he's gone and you're in the middle of nowhere. What could happen? At least then you would know if he's on to you."

"On to me? Oh god, Stephanie. You watch too many bad movies," Lexie complained.

"If you get in there and the place is clean…"

"*What*?"

"Yes," Stephanie said like she'd just concocted a fool proof plan. "How else would you know if he's undercover and he's looking into your mother who is involved in this big conspiracy?"

"You are suggesting I commit a felony," Lexie complained.

"It's quite the coincidence that a cop shows up next door when all this happened. Don't you want to make sure? You should have told me this before I was drunk, but since you didn't, this is the best I got."

Lexie took a deep breath. "Hold on." Lexie tipped the bottle up to her lips and let the wine flow down her throat. "Okay, screw it. Just so you know, if I get arrested, I'm naming you as an accomplice. I'll prove he has nothing to do with this."

"Keep me on the phone. If I'm going to be named as an accomplice, I want in on the details."

"Heading over…whoa, I think the ground is spinning…I think I overdid the wine," Lexie complained, squeezing her eyes tight to focus her vision.

"Whatever you do, don't pass out in his house."

"I'm good. I'm good. Don't worry. I can hold my liquor."

"Yeah right. You forget who you're talking to." Stephanie laughed.

Lexie walked up to the thin line of trees that separated the two cottages, hesitating for a moment. Jackson was intimidating, dangerous, and ignited something deep within her she didn't know existed. She wanted to embrace it even for a fleeting moment because it overshadowed everything else. It felt like a blissful escape when her thoughts were with Jackson.

The entire cottage was dark, consumed by the late night hour, still no sign Jackson had returned.

"Okay…here goes," Lexie said before she pushed off a tree and quickly walked toward Jackson's place.

"Oh my god! I need to pour myself another drink," Stephanie squealed. "What do you see?"

"Nothing at all. It's completely dark," Lexie whispered. Lexie pressed herself against the outside of the cottage and moved closer to a window. "There are definitely no lights on." Lexie couldn't see anything inside, not even shadows. She grabbed the doorknob of the back door and slowly twisted it. "Holy crap, it's open," Lexie said in a rush.

"At least you don't have to break in! That will definitely lessen your sentence," Stephanie joked.

"You're not helping," Lexie whispered. She walked in, closing the door behind her. "I can't see anything. It's too dark. I have to use my phone as a flashlight." Lexie held the phone up to shine around the room. The layout was identical to hers, though there was no sign that anyone was staying there. It looked recently cleaned with no personal items lying around. "I think he's gone. It looks too clean," Lexie whispered. "Ouch!" Lexie bumped into the table. A few items scattered across the surface of the table and dropped to the floor. She slapped her hand over her mouth to stop the gasp that erupted. "I just ran into the table. I can't believe I'm doing this." Lexie dropped down and picked up a small round salt shaker and placed it back on the table. "I can't find the pepper."

"What?"

"I knocked the salt and pepper shakers off the table, and I don't know where the pepper went."

"Forget about the pepper. Just be careful! Check the bedroom," Stephanie whispered. Lexie took a quick look around with the same conclusion. The bedroom was bare and the bed made.

"Nothing…" Lexie sat on the bed and leaned down close to the pillow. "No pictures pinned up on the wall or cop stuff lying around. This is ridiculous. What should I be looking for? Our pictures with targets painted on them?" She knew she was way too drunk to think clearly. Wandering around his place was a stupid idea. "He must be gone," Lexie stated disappointedly.

"In the movies they always find the clues."

"Because it's a movie." Lexie shook her head.

"I guess him being a cop is just coincidence then," Stephanie said quietly.

"I'll call you back."

"What? Why? Did you find something?"

"No. I just want to look around a bit more."

"You better call me back," Stephanie pleaded.

"I will. I promise," Lexie assured her before

ending the call.

Jackson's delectable scent hit her in a rush. She didn't think a man could smell so delicious. Her nervousness had faded away, and excitement had taken its place. She couldn't resist pulling back the covers and lying down for a moment. Lexie bit her lip as her drunk thoughts swirled in her head. She decided to throw caution to the wind. She began thinking about his lips and how they felt on her hand. She wanted to know what they would feel like on hers. She wanted to know what would have happened if he had stayed. His words from earlier began to heat her blood. Lexie flipped on the bedside lamp and looked around the room to confirm she hadn't missed anything. She was surprised by the strange feeling that held her insides. The idea of never seeing Jackson again was hard to accept.

She found she wanted to reach out to him in a way that would get his attention. She didn't want him to forget about her—she would always remember him and wonder what would have happened had circumstances been different. She could only think of submitting to these feelings and desires. Taking a deep breath, she pulled her shirt over her head. Unclipping her bra, she dropped it on the floor. Her shorts followed before lying back on the bed. Once she positioned herself, she slipped her fingers under the waist of her panties. The thrill of doing something completely out of character had her reeling with heightened emotions. Holding out her phone, she snapped a picture.

Looking at the picture, she liked the girl who

was looking back at her, a seductive smile upon her lips. She wished she was that girl. The girl in the picture didn't look like she had a history that threatened to tear her apart. She wanted Jackson to have a picture of who she wished she was when she was with him.

Lexie pulled up Jackson's number on the phone.

You didn't say goodbye.

Lexie attached the picture and hit send. She leaned back against his pillow. She could seriously fall asleep surrounded by Jackson. Closing her eyes, she let herself relish in the moment. She wasn't sure how much time had passed, but the sound of the front door opening snapped her into motion. Lexie jumped off the bed. She didn't have time to grab her shirt before Jackson filled the doorframe.

Lexie stared at him through the haze of alcohol that currently clouded her senses. She wore only a lacy pair of panties. Her bare chest was covered by her hands as she stood in the bedroom of a man that both terrified and excited her. She wondered how she ever thought this was a good idea.

"Hi," Lexie said nervously.

Jackson held onto the doorframe, his knuckles turning white. His eyes looked dark and perilous.

"Hi," he said tightly.

"You didn't leave?" Lexie asked, ignoring the fact that the answer was staring back at her.

"I didn't leave," Jackson confirmed. He clenched his jaw, his gaze never leaving her.

"I had a few drinks...maybe a lot. This seemed

like a good idea a few minutes ago," Lexie said in a rush of words. "Are you going to arrest me?"

"No." A grin pulled at his full lips. He was so beautiful, it was impossible to look away.

"So...can we pretend I didn't just get naked in your bed? Because I'm not sure why exactly I thought this was a good plan." Lexie smiled nervously.

"Definitely not, Lexie." The way he said her name made heat pool in her stomach.

Jackson picked her shorts up off the floor and knelt down in front of her. He held them up for her to step into. He pulled them slowly up her legs, his fingers grazing her skin the entire length. The contact was intoxicating; her head swam and her body felt too hot. Excitement twisted through her core, and her body wanted to be closer to his. She wanted to touch him, wanted to know what he felt like.

He grabbed her shirt and stood up. Holding it up, he closed his eyes, waiting for her to take it from his hand. Instead of taking her shirt, she ran her hand over his chest. He squeezed his eyes shut as his breathing became more pronounced.

"Can I touch you?" Lexie whispered as she leaned in closer. He nodded slightly, keeping his eyes closed. He remained perfectly still.

Lexie stood up on her toes and ran her fingers over his neck, watching goosebumps flash across his skin with the contact. She twisted her fingers up into his thick hair as she leaned in and skimmed her lips along his jaw. His rough skin tickled her tender skin. He held his breath as Lexie neared his lips.

She gently touched hers to his, waiting for him to respond, pulling his bottom lip into her mouth.

"You should go," Jackson whispered.

Lexie pulled back; his eyes were still closed tightly as if in pain. "Oh…I'm sorry. I thought with what you said earlier…I thought you wanted this…" The word was almost a sob with his rejection. Her embarrassment burned through her lust. Lexie grabbed for the shirt he still held out for her. Holding it to her chest, she ran as fast as she could. As soon as she closed the door to her cottage, she released her breath. She climbed the stairs and threw herself on the bed and buried her head under her pillow. She never wanted to face Jackson again.

CHAPTER SEVEN

Lexie opened her eyes and looked up at the pine ceiling. The details of the night before came crashing down. She raked her hands down over her face and whimpered in disbelief. She was not ready to face the day that awaited her. "You are such an idiot," Lexie scolded herself.

Dragging herself from bed, she climbed in the shower and let the hot water burn away the throbbing pain in her head. Normally she loved the smell of the coconut shampoo, but it smelled too potent, causing her stomach to churn. She tried to convince herself the memories from last night were merely a dream. How the hell did she ever think that was a good idea? First she was going to call Stephanie and yell at her.

After dressing, Lexie went to grab her phone only to discover she didn't have it. Realization hit her like a brick wall. She'd left her phone at Jackson's place. Lexie tried to convince herself for a moment that she didn't need her phone, but she knew that was ridiculous. She had to hang her head in shame and drag herself next door.

Lexie felt sick to her stomach as she knocked on his door. It swung open before she could prepare herself—there he was. He was quite possibly a contender for the eighth wonder of the world. He was only wearing a pair of pants, riding low on his hips. Lexie tried not to notice all the delectable dips and lines of muscle that were staring back at her, and those eyes could arguably see into people's souls.

"Now you knock?" An amused expression graced his features.

Lexie snapped her eyes closed and held out her hand. "May I please have my phone back?"

"Why are you closing your eyes?"

"You closed your eyes last night when I didn't have a shirt on. I'm just returning the favor. Can I have my phone?" Lexie gave her hand an impatient shake. The truth of the matter was staring at all his perfection made her legs shake and her embarrassment fire hot.

Lexie heard Jackson chuckle as she nervously shuffled her feet. She could feel him lean in closer. He placed something in her hand as he whispered in her ear. "I peeked."

"What?" Lexie snapped her eyes open. Lexie looked down to see her bra hanging from her hand. Her face exploded with heat.

"I'm only human." Jackson pushed off the door frame and walked toward his kitchen.

"Well...I still need my phone," Lexie demanded, following him inside.

"Your friend Stephanie seems nice."

Lexie wasn't expecting his comment. "How do you know about Steph?"

"She called your phone after you left. We had quite the conversation about you." Jackson sat down on his sofa, stretching out his long legs in front of him.

"Oh yeah, well, I'm going to have words with Stephanie later. Can I have my phone now?" Lexie stood at the entrance of the kitchen, refusing to come in any further.

"Why the big rush?" he asked, throwing his arm on the back of the sofa, his devious eyes watching her. Lexie noticed his phone sitting on the table. She grabbed for it.

"I'll give yours back when you give me mine." The screen lit up when she picked it up. It was the picture she had sent him—as his lock screen. Lexie gasped when she saw it. She wasn't even smart enough to leave her face out of the picture when she took it. There she was almost completely naked, sprawled out on his bed. "Holy hell! Take this off," Lexie panicked.

"Why? You sent it to me." Jackson was trying to keep a straight face, but she could tell he was holding back his laughter.

"This isn't funny. You need to erase this picture. I was drunk. I didn't know what I was doing."

"I know. That's why I couldn't kiss you back," Jackson confessed. His playful tone faded away.

"What?" Lexie was surprised by his confession.

He stood up and walked into his bedroom to return a few minutes later with her phone in hand. "Here."

Lexie took the phone from his hand. "You wanted to kiss me back?"

"Yes."

"I wanted you to," Lexie whispered.

"What about now, Lexie?" His gaze was so intense she had a hard time not melting under the heat. "Do you want me to kiss you now?"

Lexie drew in a shaky breath. "No…yes."

"You should have said no." Jackson grazed his fingers along her cheek.

"Why?"

"Because now that you've told me yes, I won't be able to stop myself." Jackson grabbed hold of Lexie's waist and lifted her onto the counter. She gasped in surprise, grabbing hold of his arms for support. The feel of his hard, unyielding flesh under her fingers was exhilarating.

The cool counter was a stark contrast to the heat of her skin. Her skirt rode dangerously high on her thighs as his eyes greedily drank her in. He nudged her knees apart, moving his body between, placing his hands on either side of her face.

"Don't stop," Lexie whispered. Her gaze was on his lips as he moved closer. She was desperate to taste him, to feel him against her. She was high on whatever drug his presence pumped into her blood. She felt like she was in a dream.

His lips were soft and tentative at first, the hunger growing until they both unleashed their desire. He devoured her lips like she was the sweetest of desserts, and her head swam with lust. Lexie's body demanded more as she pressed herself against him. She moved her hips, rubbing her desire against his. The friction caused an intense pleasure to build. Her body was already primed from being in his presence. His hands grazed her legs until his touch found her center. He stroked her with the pad of his thumb, and the heat he stirred sent her reeling.

Wrapping her legs around his waist, she pulled him closer; the thin barrier of her underwear did nothing to lesson her pleasure as she became a victim to her desires. Lexie pulled at his flesh hard enough to leave marks upon his skin. Running her fingers through his hair, she deepened their kiss until she gasped against his mouth when she came undone. Pleasure exploded through her so intense she lost touch with reality and melted.

Small rays of clarity began to dissipate the fog of her mind, and she realized that she just had the most intense orgasm of her entire life and she was still clothed. Jackson leaned against the counter with his head down. She would have given anything to know what he was thinking. Embarrassment and lust seemed to be the most prevalent emotions she was plagued with where Jackson was concerned. His muscles were coiled so tight she thought he might snap.

Lexie concentrated on regulating her breathing as she watched him silently. "Holy shit, Lexie." Pushing off the counter, he raked his hands down his face and walked out of the kitchen. Lexie heard the bathroom door shut and the shower turn on seconds later. Lexie took a deep shaky breath. She slid off the counter and righted her clothes. Grabbing her phone, she walked quietly past the bathroom door and slipped out the front door.

***

"Lexie, I was wondering when I'd hear from you." Stephanie's voice caused emotion to stir in her stomach. "Lex? What's wrong?"

Lexie released a long, slow breath. "When I kissed Jackson, I didn't even think about Alex. It was like he didn't even exist for that moment in time. I forgot...I forgot to miss him." Hot tears started to fall. Lexie couldn't hold onto them.

"Okay, just hold on a second. You kissed Jackson?" Stephanie asked in disbelief.

"Yes."

"How did it happen?"

"Jackson said he was talking to you, so I guess you already know he caught me last night."

"He wasn't mad at all. He actually seemed very comfortable with the idea of you checking him out. What happened, anyway?"

"It was a disaster, and I planned never to see him again, but when I woke up this morning and realized I forgot my phone, I went back...I tried to make a stand but I can't stop wanting him. It's like I'm a whole new person with him. I don't recognize myself. I didn't want it to stop."

"Is that a bad thing?"

"Not when it was happening—but after. I feel like I let Alex down. I shouldn't have these feelings. Not to mention the timing actually couldn't be any worse." Lexie rubbed her temple. She could feel a headache coming on from all the emotional stress.

"I feel like there's a war going on inside of me, and I have no idea what side I'm on."

"I know you don't want to forget him, Lex. I know it terrifies you to move on, but you need this. Alex would want you to enjoy your life. You can't spend your whole life stuck because you're afraid that someone else will claim a piece of your heart that you're keeping for Alex. You have a big heart. There's room to let someone else in," Stephanie said. "I wish you weren't so far away."

"I want to come home," Lexie sighed, wiping the tears from her eyes.

"Oh I just remembered...I ran into Marley from your building. She said there was a strange guy hanging around your apartment. She said he looked a little scary. Do you think it's one of the guys that followed you from the diner?"

"I don't know...you didn't tell anyone where I was, did you?"

"No, of course not. Not even Evan, who is constantly harassing me."

"Thanks. I need to lie low until I get some answers from Mom. Don't go near my apartment just in case."

"It sounds like you're out of breath. Where are you?"

"I'm heading to the store. They had a label for the nail polish, but it was sold out. It was the closest I've ever come to finding it. I'm going to check and see if they got any in." Lexie picked up her pace.

She could hear Stephanie sigh on the other end of the line. "Okay, but can you promise me something?"

"What?"

"If they don't have it, can you buy a different color? Just whatever grabs your attention and paint your nails. I promise that you'll find out that you'll still remember everything about him."

"I have to go. I'll call you later."

The trees fell away, and the parking lot was sitting in front of her. Lexie didn't even attempt to smile at the greeter when she walked into the store. She headed straight for the aisle that displayed rows and rows of polish with the hope that they restocked the shelves. The empty hole on the shelf made her stomach drop.

"Excuse me?" Lexie called to a young girl with short cropped hair and artsy glasses, straightening the next shelf. "Do you know if you will get any more of this color?" Lexie pointed to the empty spot in the rainbow of nail polish.

She pushed her glasses up her nose before frowning. "We haven't had the color in about a year. I think they discontinued it."

"Oh…thanks," Lexie said despondently.

"Can I help you find another color? We just got in this really pretty pink with sparkles," she said excitedly, picking up a polish that was sitting in its own display.

"Thanks. It's very nice." Lexie took the bottle.

"Let me know if you need anything else," she said politely before she went back to fixing the shelf.

Lexie stared down at the bottle of polish in her hand before squeezing tight and walking toward the cash register. She was going to take Stephanie's advice and buy the polish. Her heart raced with fear; she was terrified of buying it. On a logical level, she knew it was just polish, but her emotions were irrational and right now they had a tight hold on her physically.

She walked up to the same cashier she had been to the day before. This time she made the effort to force a smile on her face, despite her inner turmoil.

When the front doors opened, Lexie instinctively turned to see who entered. A man walked in with a black shirt and dark jeans. His arms were covered in sleeves of tattoos and firm set to his jaw. He was followed by another man that was similarly dressed. They looked out of place and immediately reminded her of the men that followed her to her mother's house. Lexie turned her back to them, ducking behind a rack of chips displayed next to the register. She didn't want to take any chances. She was listening to her instincts. "See the men that just walked in?"

"Yes," the cashier said slowly; her eyebrows rose in question.

"Can you tell me when they're not looking this way? We had an awkward run in earlier, and I would really like to avoid them," Lexie lied, hoping the cashier would be sympathetic.

"Oh." Her eyes immediately sought out the men in question. "One is heading down the aisle and the other...you should be good if you head out...now."

"Thank you so much." Lexie smiled before quickly heading toward the entrance, making sure not to look back. She scanned the parking lot to make sure nothing was amiss as she walked away from the building. Once she was at the mouth of the path, she took off as fast as she could.

Adrenaline pumped through her body as she ran with the occasional glance behind her to make sure she wasn't being followed. She pushed until her legs began to feel numb and the cottage came into view. She ran into the backyard and collapsed in the wooden chair, drawing air desperately into her lungs as she tried to calm her racing heart.

Lexie closed her eyes and took deep satisfying breaths. Her mind started to settle from the panic, and she realized she was being ridiculous. She was scared of everything because she didn't know what the danger was. Lexie opened her hand and looked at the bottle of polish that she had gripped so tightly it left an imprint on her palm.

She wasn't sure how long she was staring at it, but when a pair of well-worn leather shoes stepped into view, she looked up to see Jackson staring down at her hand.

"Painting your nails?" he asked with a raised brow.

"I couldn't find the right color. It's discontinued," Lexie said sadly, looking down at what now remained of the blue color. She looked up and found him looking at her toes.

"The pink suits you more," he stated with a thoughtful frown.

"You think so?" Lexie tilted her head and sighed. "I have always hated nail polish."

Jackson took the bottle from her hand, looked at it for a moment. "Flirt? What a stupid name." He threw the bottle as hard as he could out over the water, and they both watched the splash as it broke through the surface. "Problem solved."

"Hey! Why the hell did you just do that?" Lexie scowled at him.

"You said you didn't like nail polish. You have been staring at it like you were waiting for it to grow wings and fly away. It made sense to eliminate the problem."

"You are such a guy." Lexie shook her head. She didn't really care that her new bottle of polish was now at the bottom of the lake. She only watched as the ripples dissipated to the original calm of the surface. "What am I going to do now? The color is almost gone on my toes."

"I like your toes better naked," Jackson said as he sat down on the chair beside hers, stretching his long legs out in front of him.

"How old are you, Jackson?" Lexie looked at his dark, seductive eyes that spoke of pleasure and danger. His body was primed and always ready for action. He never seemed to relax or let a smile easily grace his lips. She wondered if she looked hard enough if she could find the answers in his enchanting eyes.

"Older than you."

"Will you at least tell me if you like to swim?" Lexie stood up and pulled her shirt off.

She watched him watching her, his eyes drinking in her flesh as she stood before him in her bra. She slid her shorts down her legs slowly, watching his reaction. Tossing her shorts on her chair, she walked to the edge of the water. Dipping her toes in, the water only had a slight chill against her warmed skin. She walked in until the water reached her thigh. She glanced back at Jackson, who was holding his phone up taking a picture. She laughed before diving into the water. The cool enveloped her, and she found it refreshing and soothing to release herself to the weightlessness of the water.

When Lexie broke the surface, she turned around to see Jackson pulling off his clothes. He dove in, and the water instantly felt warmer. She couldn't see him as he remained immersed. It made her nervous.

Lexie felt a gentle brush against her back. She spun around and saw him behind her. He was so quiet she didn't hear him surface. She had so many questions but no desire to ask any of them. She would let him keep his secrets. She just wanted to exist here and now with him. She lay back in the water, floating as she looked up at the pale blue sky surrounding the bright hot sun. It was peaceful, and she wanted to freeze the moment to keep forever.

When her fingers grazed his, she grabbed hold of him, taking his hand in hers. She felt him squeeze her hand in return as they floated side by side. Time escaped them as they remained in blissful silence. She didn't understand how she could find comfort with a man she barely knew, but she wanted to hold onto this moment for as long as she could.

Lexie's phone began to ring, and regretfully she released Jackson's hand to swim as fast as she could toward the shore. Trying to catch it before the caller hung up, she did not want to miss her mother's call.

"Hello?"

"Lexie! The police just questioned me. Your

mom's house was completely ransacked. They are conducting an investigation. Everyone is in a panic because both you and your mother are missing!" Stephanie spoke so fast Lexie had a hard time understanding her.

"Did you say anything?" Lexie asked nervously.

"No, but please tell me you heard from your mom," Stephanie asked hopefully.

"Yesterday. She said she would meet me here. I just have to sit tight."

"I'm going out of my mind. Can I come to you?" Stephanie sounded very nervous.

"No, I don't want you involved in this. I don't even want to be involved. Give me a few more days. I'll let you know when I have some answers."

"I'm scared, Lex."

"I know…so am I. I will hopefully be home before long and we can put this craziness behind us." Lexie tried to sound strong, but she wasn't fooling anyone.

"This is seriously scary shit. I hope your mom knows what she's doing."

"You and me both." Lexie watched Jackson step out of the water. He looked like a dessert with his skin glistening in the sun, making her mouth water. Her stomach exploded into butterflies as he neared her to gather his clothes. He gave her a look that could stop traffic and then headed back toward his place.

"So about Jackson…" Stephanie began.

"Yeah about that…what did you talk about?"

"Nothing much, trying to get information out of him was like pulling teeth. He's not much of a talker when it comes to himself, but he was curious about you. He sounds hot though…"

"Yeah, that's pretty much him in a nutshell. What did he want to know about me?"

"Um…he guessed you're a photographer. He asked about your family. He also wanted to know if you had a boyfriend…"

"He asked that?"

"Yeah, he asked me exactly that. I said no boyfriends but lots of admirers. That's about it."

"Okay, I'm going to go hop in the shower. I'll call you later," Lexie said.

"You better," Stephanie ordered. "And your most persistent admirer is knocking on my door right now. God, Lex, you may have to call him and tell him you're still alive."

"Tell him I'm fine and will call him when I get back. Make sure he doesn't tell anyone."

"Will do."

CHAPTER EIGHT

The rain started with gentle tapping upon the roof until it began to thunder down. It was still early evening, but the skies had darkened considerably. Lexie pulled a bag of popcorn out of the microwave. Sitting down on the sofa, she wrapped a blanket around her and opened her mother's diary.

"Give me something, Mom," Lexie whispered as she looked for the last entry she'd read. She still hadn't heard from her mother, and uneasiness was settling deep in her stomach. She glanced over a few other entries of flowers, dates, kisses, and late nights. Nothing seemed unusual as she read words of a young woman falling in love. Then something began to change; longer stretches of time would pass between dates. The excitement began to fade, and there began to be reservations in her words.

John had asked her mother to move in with him after six months of dating; she did so and that was the beginning of a different person behind the pen. Instead of the excitable girl that was alive and well in the beginning of the diary, she was now reading the words of a suspicious, cautious woman who feared John may not be the man she believed him to be.

Sept. 9

At first when John told me he ran the nightclub, the idea of it seemed so grand and exciting. The glamorous lifestyle was addicting. My new spacious closet in our condo became a boutique of beautiful clothes fit for royalty. Every time I opened the doors to get dressed, I would have to pinch myself. Months before I was a girl who practically lived in her favorite jeans. I had two dresses to choose from, and then suddenly my options were endless. I was spoiled. John called me his girl and loved to show me off. I didn't know it then, but I was another of his possessions. He adored me as long as I played my part.

A week ago he came home late. I waited up for him. He was my everything until I finally opened my eyes and began to see flaws in the beautiful picture he had painted me.

He walked into the bathroom and

loosened his tie. I followed him, wanting to cheer him up. I remember asking him if he hurt himself when I noticed blood on his shirt. The look he gave me made my blood freeze. He ordered me to go to bed.

That night when he came to bed, he no longer touched me like a man in love. He tore my favorite night dress off and ignored my cries. He was a man possessed. I was terrified. I remember how scared I was when he closed his hand around my neck and squeezed tight. I thought I was going to die. My sight began to fade and my chest screamed for breath until he finally released me. My body felt broken, and I couldn't stop the tears.

After, he wrapped his arms around me and told me I was a good girl. He refused to let me go. The only thing I could think of was he was evil. He was not my beautiful John. I was not a girl in love. I was just...his.

Lexie blinked tears away and rubbed her hands over her face. She set the book down on the coffee table and leaned back on the sofa, letting her mother's words sink in. Suddenly it didn't feel so unlikely that answers were written in this book somewhere. The rain still poured from the sky, reminding her how alone she was in the strange cottage. The book kept calling to her until she finally gave in. She told herself she would only read a little more. It was the closest she could be to her mother right now, and she needed her.

Oct. 12

Tonight, one of John's important business associates arrived for a meeting with him at the club. He was preoccupied and paid no attention to me...no one did. I knew this meeting was important because he was wound tighter than usual. I didn't mind...it meant that I had some freedom.

I took the opportunity to explore. I snuck into the back rooms at the club that were normally off limits. Luckily one of the guards was busy flirting with one of the waitresses and didn't see me slip by.

Most of the doors were locked. One handle turned. I slowly opened it to peek inside. A man was involved in a very compromising position with two women. I didn't stick around to find out who they were. I felt sick to my stomach. I quickly passed a slightly open door. A few men in suits were doing lines. From what I could see, these rooms were for sex and drugs...nothing out of the ordinary for a nightclub.

I ducked into an empty room when one of the doors swung open. I hid just out of view, but I saw a man in an expensive suit walk by. He met someone in the hallway, and then they proceeded toward the back of the building. I knew that John must have another exit in the building because there was no way these men in suits would blend into the club. These were business men, not the type that were here to dance and drink the night away. This man in particular seemed out of place. Once the men were out of sight, I ducked back into the hall and tried the door he had exited. It was open. I listened to make sure no one was inside. I pushed the door open and slipped in.

A woman was on the floor next to the

bed. I locked the door and quickly ran to her side. She was naked and curled up in the fetal position. Her lip was bleeding, and a bruise was forming under her left eye. I couldn't get a coherent response from her, but I recognized her instantly.

I remembered a few days ago when an officer had come to the club asking people if they had seen this girl. She was a tiny thing with thick dark wavy hair. I knew it was her because she had the same tattoo of a rose on her neck.

I wasn't thinking. I ran out in the hallway. I should have called the police...

John no longer leaves me unattended. As for the girl...She is still missing. John said I would find out what happened to her firsthand if I didn't leave things alone.

I have to be smarter...

But I will not leave things alone, and I will never forget about the girl with the rose tattoo.

Nov. 14
I couldn't stop thinking about that poor

girl. No one would give me any answers. I secretly contacted the officer that had been searching for her. He met me in the park, sitting on the other side of the bench. I was terrified that one of John's men would see us. Officer Finley arrived dressed in jogging clothes as to not appear out of place. He sat down behind me and raised his phone to his ear. I did the same as we spoke only loud enough to hear each other. This is what my life has become. I am terrified. I no longer see the side of John I fell in love with. He holds me prisoner in this life, and I am forbidden to step out of line.

I had to tell him I saw the girl he was looking for. I told him exactly what I saw, including seeing the man leave the room where I found her in a drug-induced stupor. Apparently none of this surprised him; they have had their suspicions about John and the business he conducts in the nightclub, but they have been unable to collect enough evidence.

He wants me to be an informant, to collect the info they need. I'm scared.

These are dangerous men. I know better than anyone.

Nov. 28

I have played nothing but the loyal girlfriend for the past few weeks. I am not as closely watched anymore. I think I convinced him that I would never betray him again. I record any conversations I can overhear, but they are careful around me.

I believe they are smuggling drugs into the club in the food trucks. They come twice a week, but some of the boxes are moved to a different location.

Only the high-paying customers and VIPs have access to the back rooms. They have to be granted access by John himself. The number of guards has tripled in the last few weeks. I don't think I can get back there anymore.

One of the waitresses told me that John brings in women and pays them under the table to entertain certain guests and stay discreet about what happens behind closed doors. Her cousin ended up attending one of their private functions. She was offered a drink beforehand and then the events of the evening became skewed. They drugged her with something. She remembered enough to know that what took place was not what she agreed to. Her cousin is still struggling with the aftermath. She was threatened not to speak of anything that happened or there would be consequences.

The more I look, the more I find...which only leaves me with more questions.

Jan.25

John bought me a bar in Sugar Hill. I think he prefers I not stay at his club. He knew it was a dream of mine to own a bar with live music. I had told him this when I was on the high of what I thought was love. I don't tell him much anymore.

I feel guilty that I love the bar.

I have been in touch with Officer Finley a few more times...telling him what information I have gathered. John is good at covering his tracks, and nothing I come up with seems solid enough for the police to take action. The only thing I could find about the girl with the rose tattoo is that she was taken to "the lake house." I don't know what this means, and neither does Finley.

He asked me to wear a wire, but I can't. John would find it. He rarely lets me wear clothes when we are alone.

I know that I'm not the only woman John is sleeping with. I feel no jealousy, only relief that it is one less time that he will turn to me.

Jan. 27

I managed to track down a girl that was rumored to entertain the some of the men in private quarters. I have a contact number. I want to give her the description of the man I had seen to see if she knows who he is. I'm planning to call her tomorrow when I am out for a run. It seems to be the only time I feel alone, although I know John has men watching me.

I was told that the girl will not talk to

the police so I must do this alone.

I hate John. It is so hard to keep pretending, but if I stop, I don't know what he'll do to me. People in John's world have a habit of disappearing.

If I disappear, there will be no one to look for me. My parents are gone, and John made sure my friends wanted nothing to do with me.

I am the loneliest girl who is never alone.

Lexie's phone ringing scared her enough to make her jump from her seat. "Hello," Lexie said cautiously.

"Lex...this may be nothing, but I am having a complete panic attack."

"Slow down. What happened?" Lexie rubbed her forehead, setting her mother's diary on the table.

"I wrote the address you gave me on a post-it note. You know how I am with remembering stuff like that. It was in case of emergency. I wanted to know how to find you..."

"Okay...?" Lexie said with a sigh, knowing she was not going to like what Stephanie was telling her.

"It's gone. The note is just gone," Stephanie said with building panic.

"Maybe it fell down behind your desk or something?"

"My apartment door was open when I got home," Stephanie said in a rush. "The lock was broken."

"What? Did you call the police?"

"Nothing looks like its missing that I can see...I've been gone all day. I don't know when it went missing. It could have been this morning, for all I know. What if the people after you and your mom found it? What if I gave away your location? *Oh God, Lexie!*"

A knock sounded on Lexie's front door. "I'll call you back, Steph."

"Are you mad at me?"

"No, of course not. Just give me a few minutes," Lexie reassured her.

Lexie pulled up Jackson's number on her phone.

Lexie: *Are you at my door?*

Lexie stared at her phone waiting for his reply, but nothing came. She was desperate to believe it was her mother, but she hadn't heard from her. Fear had her on the edge of her seat, unsure if she should answer it. Lexie stood up slowly and approached the door. Taking a deep breath, she reached for the handle. When her fingers barely touched the cool metal, a loud thud sounded on the other side of the door. Lexie covered her mouth before she released a scream and scrambled away from the door. She ran back into the main living area, hand over her heart, desperately trying to think through the explosion of fear. A shadow passed across one of the windows, and Lexie gasped. She looked around the room for anything that could be used as a weapon. She darted into the kitchen and opened the drawers, looking for the largest knife she could find.

Something hit the back door, the window rattled, and Lexie dropped behind the small island in the center of the kitchen. She could hear a struggle on the back porch and could make out dark figures through the window. She held the knife tight in her grasp, trying to stay calm as she peeked around the cabinets.

Lexie screamed when the window shattered. Glass and rain sprayed into the room as two figures barrelled through and crashed onto the floor. They continued their struggle as they threw themselves around the room. The lamp was knocked off the table, and the shade twisted free of the light, causing the unfiltered light to cast strange shadows within the room. Lexie crawled over toward the living room and noticed one of the men was Jackson. Lexie recognized the other as the one from the store earlier that day. Her instincts had been correct when she had fled.

Something dark and heavy slid across the floor toward her. Lexie scrambled to her feet and looked down at a handgun. She picked it up with shaking hands.

Both men smashed into the island. Lexie stumbled backward, trying to steer clear of the danger as both men fought with scary savagery. This was clearly a language they were both familiar with, though Jackson had a clear advantage with his precision and size. He was not a stranger to violence; he knew the language well. This was not like a typical bar fight that she had witnessed before. They were trying to kill each other, and her insides twisted tightly with realization.

When Jackson wrapped his hands around the man's neck, squeezing the life from him, Lexie screamed out for him to stop. "I want to know why he's here," Lexie said nervously when Jackson's dark gaze found hers. He had a cut on his brow that was dripping blood down his cheek, and his lip looked swollen. He looked vicious, and if she was honest with herself, incredibly sexy as he looked at her like he was peeling all of her layers away to stare deep inside her.

"He doesn't have any answers, Lexie." The version of Jackson staring at her now did not look like a cop. This was a man that fit into the embrace of violence far too well to play by the rules, but what surprised her most was the fact that she didn't fear this side of him. She was drawn to the power reflected in his dark eyes.

"Please." Lexie tried to force strength into her voice as she circled around the island and stood before the man Jackson hauled to his feet. She held the gun up toward him. It visibly shook, but she was determined to gain some control over the situation.

The man glanced at Jackson before they both spurred into action. Lexie didn't realize she lowered the gun until Jackson grabbed her hand, pulling the trigger as the man lunged toward Jackson with the knife she left on the counter.

Lexie screamed as blood splattered on her clothes and the man dropped to his knees. Blood bubbled from his mouth until he collapsed to the floor. Lexie looked down at the dark puddle forming beside his unmoving body. She couldn't pull her eyes away as she looked at him.

Images of the night that had been haunting her came crashing down on her. She was frozen. Her chest felt stiff, and it was hard to draw in breath. She could barely feel Jackson peel her fingers off the gun. He had pulled the trigger, but she had been the one holding the gun. Lexie stared at the man's lifeless body, his blood slowly spreading across the floor.

Jackson stepped between her and her view of the dead man, leaning down, his dark eyes looking into hers. His lips were moving, but she couldn't understand a word he was saying. She couldn't hear that soothing, deep voice that usually made heat pool in her stomach.

His arms wrapped around her and lifted her from the ground. Lexie curled into his chest as he carried her. She didn't know where he was taking her. She didn't care. She buried her face into his wet shirt, trying to surround herself with his scent, blocking out everything else that was assaulting her. She retreated deep inside herself, trying to escape the pain that dug deep in her chest.

When Jackson set her down, she was in his cottage. He knelt in front of her, pushing her hair from her face. She could hear her name like it was being called in the distance, and then suddenly her hearing snapped back into focus. "Lexie, look at me."

Her surroundings slowly came into view. They were in his room.

"He wasn't alone. I saw him earlier at the store. He was with someone else…there is someone else," Lexie gasped.

"There is no one else. I took care of it. Listen, Lexie…I need you to wait here. I'll be right back."

"You're leaving me?" Lexie grabbed hold of his shirt and held tight. She was terrified.

"I'll be back as soon as I can. Here." He passed Lexie a glass of water, releasing her firm grip on his shirt.

"Do you think he was trying to kill me?" Lexie asked as she looked down at her shaking hands.

"No." Jackson tipped the glass up to her lips and made her drink, but her throat felt too tight. She could only manage a small sip. "Put this on." He placed a shirt into her hand. "Don't go anywhere. Do you hear me? Do not leave this room," Jackson ordered before he was gone.

Lexie reached out where he had been standing, but her fingers found nothing. Her reality still felt distorted, as if her brain could not register what had just happened.

Lexie collapsed backward on the bed, looking at the boards that constructed the ceiling. She tried to count how many there were, but she couldn't even get her brain to cooperate. The simple act of counting seemed impossible. She needed to distract her mind, but the only thing she could concentrate on were the dark, painful thoughts that were pulling at her consciousness.

"That was absolutely amazing," Lexie said excitedly as she pressed herself into Alex's side.

"Yeah, now I totally want to take up guitar lessons. Did you see how many girls were practically throwing themselves at the stage?" Alex laughed when Lexie gave him a playful slap on the chest. "I'd still only have eyes for you, baby," Alex said, pulling her close and kissing her on the head. "Let's grab a slice of pizza before we head home."

"Are you ever not hungry?" Lexie shook her head with a smile.

"I need my energy for all the dirty things you're going to make me do tonight." Alex wiggled his eyebrows.

"Pizza actually sounds really good, now that you mention it," Lexie said, grabbing Alex's hand and heading across the street. The line was already forming from hungry concert goers.

The concert was an annual event for their small town, and it drew a crowd from all over. The live music played for three days straight, and one day blurred into the next to create the best summer high imaginable.

Lexie sat down in a booth as Alex waited in line to grab their pizza. She turned on her camera and looked through the lens, capturing Alex making a goofy face. He was so used to seeing Lexie with a camera in front of her face, she was glad he was always a wonderful sport about it. Pulling up her pictures on the digital screen, she flipped through some of her shots of the concert. She was excited to get them up on her computer.

"Hey there."

Lexie turned around to see a group of guys at the table behind her. She could tell they were here for

113

the festivities. They looked a little bleary-eyed as they started at her.

"Nice camera," the one closest to her said. They all looked a little rough around the edges but seemed friendly enough.

"Thanks. Did you come from the concert?" Lexie asked politely.

"Sure did."

"Hey there," Alex said tightly to the guys before he dismissed them. He sat down across from Lexie, sliding her pizza over to her. It smelled delicious, making Lexie's mouth water. Lexie barely got through her food before she started to yawn.

"Ready to go?" Alex stood up, grabbing their plates to toss in the garbage. She could tell the group of guys behind them were making him nervous.

"Yes." Lexie hopped out of her seat and took his hand as he led her out the door. They walked a few blocks before someone approached them from behind.

"Hey, camera girl." Alex swung around.

"Fuck off, man," Alex bit off, when he turned to see the same three following.

"Don't be like that, man." The one who had spoken to Lexie before continued to approach. Chills raked across Lexie's skin. These guys were trouble, and seeing Alex's posture stiffen, she knew he was fully aware of the danger of the situation.

Lexie grabbed Alex's hand. "Let's go."

Lexie wasn't even sure what happened next. The turn of events shifted so suddenly she lost track. Two of the guys threw themselves at Alex, and the other came after her. She tried to scream when he grabbed her, but his hand clamped around her mouth. She was no match for his strength in this position as she tried to pry it from her mouth. She could barely breathe because of his relentless hold as he hauled her toward an alleyway.

Lexie was shoved against the harsh brick wall. She struggled, but her attacker pressed his body against hers and pinned her. Lexie tried to scream and fight, but a cold sharp object was pressed against her throat. The only thing she could manage was a whimper. The man grabbed her skirt and lifted it up, grabbing for her underwear. She could hardly breathe as his hands pulled at her flesh, searching and imploring.

"Don't fucking touch her," Alex wailed, throwing himself at the other men.

"Just give us your fucking wallet and we'll let her go."

"Take it," Alex said, pulling his wallet out of his pocket and throwing it at the men.

"Alex…" Lexie's words were cut off as the guy pressed the blade harder on her throat. The sting made her eyes water.

"Don't fucking make a sound!" he barked against her cheek. She knew he had broken skin; she could feel the blood drip down her neck. He ran his hand up under her skirt and began pulling her underwear down.

"Lexie!" Alex screamed, throwing himself at the men standing between him and her. He fought desperately to get to her. It was too dark to see what was happening as she watched them struggle. She

was absolutely terrified what these men were capable of.

"*Let's get the fuck out of here,*" one of the other attackers shouted as he stumbled away from the fight.

When the man grabbed her camera, Lexie drove her knee into his crotch. The man groaned, and the knife slipped enough for her to wiggle out of his grasp.

"*Alex!*" Lexie called frantically.

"*Shit! We have to go now!*" one of the others shouted. The one who had been holding Lexie pushed off the wall and took off after the others. Lexie gasped in relief. She stumbled over to Alex.

"*Lexie?*" Alex said as she approached him. He dropped to his knees in front of her. Lexie threw her arms around him.

"*I was so scared.*" Lexie sobbed into his neck. She held him tight, running her hands over his chest. Her hand hit something hard…"*Alex!*" Lexie gasped. She pulled back and looked down at the hilt of the man's blade protruding from Alex's chest.

"*I'm sorry…*"Alex forced his words in pained breath.

"*No…no, Alex, stay with me!*" Lexie tried to hold him, but his body collapsed to the ground, and the only thing she could hear were her screams, which drowned out the entire world. "*Don't leave me!*"

CHAPTER NINE

Lexie snapped her eyes open when she felt the bed dip. She looked up into dark, entrancing eyes. His hair was wet from the rain. His shirt was soaked through, hugging his perfect lines as he leaned over her. One hand placed on either side of her as she lay on his bed. She could feel the moisture seeping into her shirt where he touched her.

"Who's Alex?" His voice was hesitant, as if unsure where the answer would take him.

"What?" Lexie asked, trying to clear her foggy mind. She felt completely drained as she tried to make sense of where she was.

"You kept saying his name. Is he your boyfriend?" Jackson pushed off the bed but continued watching her. Dirt was smeared across his shirt, but his hands and face were spotless. He followed her eyes to his clothes, noticing the stains. He pulled his shirt over his head and laid it over the back of the chair before walking into the bathroom. He turned the water on in the shower.

Lexie stood up and slowly followed him. Her

eyes found his in the mirror as she entered. She had so many questions; she just couldn't remember what they were. Lexie looked at her own reflection. Tears immediately began to flood her vision.

"It was real," Lexie sobbed. Blood was splattered on her shirt, and a few drops had dried upon her cheek. She frantically wiped her face, trying to remove the evidence of what she had hoped was only a nightmare.

Jackson turned on the faucet and wet a face cloth before passing it to her. She wiped away the blood before looking down at her clothes. She needed them off immediately.

She hastily pulled at her clothing; she slid her pants down her legs before kicking them onto the floor to meet her shirt. She didn't want that man's blood on her. She wrapped her arms around herself, trying to hold herself together.

Jackson lifted his hand for her to take. Lexie wiped her eyes and hesitantly slid her hand into his. He pulled her closer, and she wrapped her arms around his waist, burying her face into his chest. She let her tears fall as she held on to him. He was the only thing that felt real, and she clung to him.

When she finally stepped back, she wasn't sure what was going through his mind. He hadn't said a word as he held her and let her shed her tears. He always looked at her like she was a puzzle that needed to be solved. She wished more than anything he could figure out how to put her pieces together.

"You'll feel better after a shower," he whispered.

Lexie nodded before taking a deep breath and

stepping into the water. She didn't pull the curtain closed behind her because she needed to see him. She was scared to be alone again and find herself back in haunting memories. "Will you stay with me?" Lexie asked.

"Yeah." Jackson leaned against the bathroom counter, crossing his arms over his bare chest.

Lexie reached behind her and unclipped her bra, peeling away the wet material. She hung it over the curtain rod. Looking over at Jackson, she saw his intense gaze was consuming every inch of her exposed skin. She could see his muscles tense as he rubbed his hand down his face. He squeezed his eyes closed.

Lexie removed her underwear and let the hot water burn her skin, but it would not stop the chills that made her shiver. She picked up the soap and slowly lathered her entire body, letting the water rinse it away.

"Will you come in with me?" Lexie asked with a small voice.

He clenched his jaw while her question lingered in the air. His dark eyes swirled with a storm. She knew she was in dangerous territory; she didn't know if she should trust him with this vulnerable version of herself.

He slowly pushed off the counter and stopped in front of the tub as Lexie remained under the spray of water. He braced himself on the wall with his hand. He looked so deep in her eyes she felt him inside her, stirring her insides, melting the ice that formed in her stomach.

"Can I touch you?" His voice was rough, almost

pained.

Lexie only nodded as she stepped back for him to join her. She watched Jackson unbutton his pants and disrobe before he stepped into the tub with her. The water sprayed his shoulders and ran down his hard body, coiled tight with honed muscle. This was a powerful man that was capable of great and horrible things. This man did not open doors or offer sweet smiles. He carved his path too close to danger to be safe. She could see it in his eyes as they promised her dark and beautiful secrets.

His hand slipped around her waist and pulled her against his unyielding flesh. His erection throbbed against her as it dug into her stomach. His lips grazed her neck as he held her, seemingly hesitant to push her too far in her fragile state. Lexie grabbed the soap, lathering it between her hands. She then rubbed them on his chest, watching the bubbles cling to him as she delightfully explored his body. He was quiet and unmoving like a statue as she ran her hand down the grooves of his stomach until wrapping her fingers around his steely length. It pulsed in her hand.

Heat pooled under her skin, her legs practically shook with need. Lexie didn't understand this version of herself. She felt alive when she was with Jackson. She could forget everything else and get lost in him. The scared, broken version of herself that she had come to know faded away, and she was left with a swell of feelings so big and hot, they felt like they would break through her skin. He offered her a moment of peace, and she wanted to indulge completely.

She squeezed her grip firm as she slid up and down his length. Jackson braced himself on the wall, and Lexie watched his muscles tense. He was the true embodiment of raw beauty, and she wished she had her camera. She wanted to capture this man. Keep this moment in perfect clarity.

The water suddenly snapped her senses into reality when it became cold. Lexie's scream of surprise erupted into giggles as she scrambled out of the shower.

"*Fuck*, that was cold," Jackson bit off as he turned the water off and grabbed a towel. Lexie couldn't help the laughter that bubbled out. He looked at her then, and that's when she saw it. A truly beautiful sight—his smile. Not just a sly, mischievous grin but a complete, utter reflection of pure happiness. She couldn't help but wonder how rare it truly was for him.

Lexie stood up on her toes, placing her hands on either side of his face, and pressed her lips against his. A moan of appreciation escaped him, flooding her mouth as she drank him in.

He picked her up, holding her body tight against his. The feel of her naked body against his was like a drug. Her head swam with feelings too unreal to understand. Lexie ran her hands over his broad shoulders. She felt safe in this moment in the strong embrace of a man that also terrified her.

Lexie squealed as he let her go, and she fell back onto the bed. He looked at her with a raw savageness that spoke of lust and hunger.

"Jackson?" Lexie whispered.

"Yes." His eyes snapped to hers.

"Make me feel good," she ordered. There was no question in her words. She wanted him to make her forget the world. "And don't be gentle."

He raised his brow as he looked down at her.

"Gentle is for love," she clarified.

"No gentle, got it."

Lexie flipped over onto her hands and knees. Looking back over her shoulder, she watched him caress her with his eyes. He ran his hands down the length of her back and over the curve of her hips, squeezing her skin as he studied her as if she was a piece of art.

The sting of slapping flesh burned across her behind, and she gasped in pleasure. "Again," Lexie moaned. The feeling intensified as she felt the pain so closely tied with pleasure.

Jackson nudged her knees apart. His fingers explored her entrance before he pushed inside. He rubbed the inside of her walls until the entire world collapsed around her and she was floating in the clouds. His teeth pulled at the curve of her behind as he melted her core with his touch. He withdrew his fingers, pressing her shoulders down into the bed.

He entered her again, but this time it was not his fingers. She felt much fuller as she stretched around him. He moved slowly, almost painfully so until he forced the rest of the way, pushing her down into the bed. His thrusts were deep and powerful, pulling forcefully from her pool of desire until she could no longer form a coherent thought. Lexie cried out as the pleasure pulled too tight, almost suffocating as he pushed against her limits.

She felt her body reel as intense heat burned her from the inside out as he caressed her inner walls until she exploded. Her body fell apart underneath him, and she was left gasping for breath.

When she found the strength she flipped over, watching him still leaning over her. His eyes were closed as he took long, deep breaths.

She wrapped her fingers around him, and a sound of appreciation rumbled from deep inside his chest. She stroked him hard and fast until he roared out in release and sprayed his hot liquid over her breasts.

Jackson ran his hand over her breast, rubbing his semen into her skin gently. His strokes were slow and lazy and somehow more intimate than when he had been inside her. He leaned down and gently kissed her lips before he pushed off the bed. He picked up one of the towels they had dropped and came back to wipe her off. It was strange how he could be so wild and untamed as he took her and now gentle as he wiped her off.

"Will you hold me?" Lexie asked, this time there was no confidence in her tone. She felt vulnerable now that he managed to claim a piece of her, even though he was not aware and she did not wish it. It was supposed to be just sex, just a momentary escape. She needed his comfort now. She needed him to hold her together.

Jackson threw the towel into the bathroom, flicked off the light, and then crawled into the bed. He wrapped his arm around her and pulled her against him.

Lexie concentrated on the gentle stroke of his

hand against her stomach, trying to force her mind to quiet. All the things that refused to let her rest but most of all, it was the image of the man's face before he collapsed on the floor haunted her.

"I'm scared," Lexie whispered.

Jackson remained quiet, responding with only a squeeze of his hand.

"Are you scared?" Lexie flipped around so she could see him. The room was dark, but she could make out the lines of his beautiful face and she could feel his eyes on her.

"No," he answered easily.

"What did you do with the man?" Lexie's question felt like poison in her mouth when she spoke. She wasn't sure if she really wanted to know the answer.

"All you need to know is he's gone."

"Just like that?"

"Just like that." Jackson rolled onto his back and looked up at the ceiling with a sigh.

"Why are you really here, Jackson?" Lexie asked. The question burned for an answer.

"Get some sleep, Lex."

Lexie watched him until his breathing became slow and steady. She slid out of bed, grabbing the clean shirt Jackson had given her, and headed into the kitchen. She quietly opened the cabinets looking for glasses for a drink of water.

Leaning against the counter, she let the cool liquid soothe her dry throat. Glancing at the table, she noticed her things sitting in a neat pile. She picked up her purse, opened it, and was relieved to see her mother's diary in the very bottom where she had frantically tucked it away.

She pulled out her camera. Turning it on, she flipped through the pictures she had taken the last few days. She had too many emotions clawing at her insides to sleep. She wanted to find a way to quiet her mind. Lexie walked over to the sofa and sat down, tucking her feet underneath her. She wished she had her computer to load the pictures and view them on a larger screen.

Something drew her attention in the background of a few of the pictures that she hadn't noticed before. It looked like a shadow in the trees. She zoomed in as far as possible and could just make out a figure—Jackson.

Jackson had been watching her that day, before she knew who he was. Lexie's hand flew to her mouth. She slipped her feet from under her, placing them on the floor. Her foot hit something hard under the sofa. Setting down her camera, she knelt down to feel a bag tucked underneath. She recognized it immediately as the bag he had been carrying from his car when she first saw him. Unzipping it, her eyes fell on countless weapons—knives and guns. She didn't know much about hardware, but these did not seem like the kind of weapons a police officer would carry.

Lexie looked up to see Jackson was standing in front of her. She let go of the bag and stumbled to her feet, looking at him for answers.

Lexie raked her fingers through her hair. "Are you really a cop?"

"Yes." Jackson ran his hand over his face; he looked exhausted. "Just not the kind that writes speeding tickets or does traffic stops."

"It's not a coincidence you're here, is it?" Lexie asked, twisting her fingers in the oversized shirt she was wearing.

"No."

"Does you being here have anything to do with John Stodden?" Lexie demanded. She stood up, despite her shaking legs.

"You do know who he is then?"

Lexie ignored his question. "Are you after him?"

Jackson nodded.

Lexie waved her hands between Jackson and her. "What was this for? To get me to fall for you so I would willingly go along with whatever plans you have?"

"I never wanted you to fall for me."

Lexie nodded her head as tears fell from her eyes. "I didn't fall for you."

"Good."

"So you tracked me down because you think you can use me to get to John?"

"That was my original plan, yes."

"And now?"

"I don't know." Jackson raked his hands through his hair. "Things became complicated."

"How did you and the other men find me?"

"I have my ways. As for the others, apparently they tracked down your address."

"Stephanie…" Lexie whispered worriedly.

"It won't be long before someone else comes after you."

"I'll take my chances with them." Lexie squared her shoulders.

"No, you won't."

CHAPTER TEN

Lexie sat in the passenger seat of Jackson's car, watching the dark shadows of trees pass as she leaned her forehead against the window. She refused to look in Jackson's direction. She was so angry that fire stirred deep in her stomach, and she knew if she opened her mouth she would breathe fire. She was trying to get her head together because his deception hurt her much deeper than she realized it could. She refused to give him the satisfaction that he affected her.

After their confrontation, he ordered her to get dressed because they were leaving. Lexie refused to listen to him, refusing to do anything he asked. She did not want to go anywhere with this man. She wanted to wait for her mother.

Lexie stood in the kitchen with her arms crossed and the best defiant face she could manage.

"Get ready. You can't leave wearing that, and besides, I want my shirt back," Jackson ordered.

"I am not getting dressed. I'm not going

128

anywhere with you," Lexie bit off angrily.

"You forget I have guns." He pointed to the bag. *"I can make you."*

"Now you're threatening to shoot me?" Lexie crossed her arms.

"We can't stay here, Lexie. Others are probably already on their way."

Lexie grabbed the hem of the shirt and pulled it over her head. Stomping forward, she thrust it into his chest. She didn't care that she was completely naked. *"Here's your stupid shirt."* She crossed her arms and glared at him.

"Get dressed," he demanded. His eyes were so dark they looked black in the dim evening light.

"No." Lexie narrowed her eyes defiantly. *"Screw you. I want the truth and the whole truth before I go anywhere with you."*

"If you don't get dressed, you're leaving naked." The look in his eyes told her that he wasn't to be challenged. She believed with all certainty he would follow through on his threat.

She grabbed her bag and purse off the table before stomping into the washroom, slamming the door behind her. Once in the washroom, she unzipped her bag, pulling out her clothes to reveal the cash was still there. The only thing she knew for certain was that he was not after her money.

"Where are we going?"

"Somewhere safe until your mother contacts you."

Jackson stopped on a dirt road that looked like it led nowhere. There were no streetlights or signs that anyone lived in the area.

"Why are we stopping?"

"I need to sleep." Jackson locked the doors and pulled the keys from the ignition, tucking them into his pocket.

"Where are we?"

"Nowhere. Get some sleep." Jackson reclined his seat and situated his gun that was tucked in his belt. "Don't think of running off. I'm much faster than you."

"You're an ass is what you are." Lexie rolled her eyes. She leaned back in her seat, closing her eyes with the intent of letting him fall asleep and then she would figure out how to get away from him. It wasn't until she leaned her head back against the seat that she realized how exhausted she was.

***

When Lexie opened her eyes, the car was filled with light. The clock on the dash said it was 7:45 a.m. She silently cursed herself for falling asleep. She looked over at Jackson, still in the same position as when he fell asleep. If he wasn't currently on the top of her hate list, she could appreciate how beautiful he was. His hard brow was relaxed, and his full lips looked so soft. Her mouth watered deceivingly as she looked at him.

She could see the handle of his gun sticking out above his belt. Lexie very slowly reached for it. All she needed to do was get a grip on it then she would be able to turn the tables. Find out exactly what he had planned and who he was. She did not want to be some pawn in his game. She wanted to find her mother and get answers. As soon as her fingers touched the hard surface, Jackson's hand closed over hers.

"You better be reaching for something other than my gun."

"You wish." Lexie wrenched her hand out from under his and growled out in frustration.

He repositioned his seat and ran his hands over his face. He pulled his keys from his pocket and started the car.

"Was that cottage next to mine even yours?" Lexie didn't take her eyes off him as he turned the car around and headed back toward the main drive.

"Nope."

"How did you know whoever owned it wouldn't come looking to have a nice family weekend at their beloved cottage?"

"I didn't."

"You are so frustrating…" Lexie threw herself back into her seat. "Are you planning on handing my mother and me over to John?"

"No."

Lexie rolled her eyes.

"You should be thankful you have me on your side," Jackson said.

"Are you really on my side?" She wasn't sure if she should trust him at all.

"Yes. If I wanted to hurt you, I already had plenty of opportunities."

"Just because you didn't hurt me yet doesn't mean we're on the same side." Lexie grabbed her purse and opened it, looking for her phone. "Just because you have a badge doesn't make you a good guy," she mumbled as she rummaged around, pulling various things out when her search became frantic.

"Missing something?" Jackson asked with an amused expression.

Realization dawned on her. "You took my phone," Lexie accused.

"Of course I took your phone."

Lexie threw her purse down. "I seriously want to punch you in the face." Lexie covered her eyes with her hands and took a deep breath. The last few days had been an absolute mind trip, and it was far from over. "Why are you after John?"

"I didn't exactly say I was after John, but I would find immense satisfaction in ending him."

"At least we have that in common." Lexie huffed. "Are you going to tell me your plan then?"

"Not yet."

Lexie leaned back in her seat; she looked over at Jackson. He looked completely comfortable behind the wheel, as if he was made to drive. Despite the fact that when it came to him every red flag was triggered, he did offer some sense of security. He also seemed irritatingly comfortable with silence. Lexie began tapping her foot. He glanced her way, the crease deepening between his brows.

"Am I distracting you?"

"Nothing distracts me." His eyes remained on the road, and he returned to ignoring her.

"Is that so?" Lexie narrowed her eyes.

She kicked off her flip-flops and placed her feet up on the dash, slowly pulling the material of her dress up her thighs as she ran her fingers seductively along her legs. She noticed the quickest glance in her direction. She planned on pushing him to the edge. She was tired of feeling like she was clinging to her sanity while he sat comfortably without a care.

Lexie lifted herself off the seat and slid her underwear down her legs and tossed them at him. They landed in his lap. He grabbed them and held them in his hand as he continued to drive. She grinned at the thought that he kept them. She slowly sucked on her fingers before she began touching herself. Her dress was pulled up so she was completely exposed as she dipped her fingers into her slick heat, making sure to let him know how good it felt. She pulled the straps of her dress down, releasing her breasts. She was going to make sure he was distracted as she fondled herself.

"What are you doing, Lexie?"

"I'm messing with your head like you did to me."

Initially she had only wanted to tease him, but the act excited her. Her skin began to burn hot as intense sensations began to spread through her, making her rock her hips as she continued pulling pleasure from deep within her. She couldn't stop herself now that her blood pumped hot through her veins. His eyes on her thrilled her to no end, pushing her to the edge. She cried when Jackson slammed on the brakes, jolting her unexpectedly.

"Fuck!" he yelled. A car horn sounded. Jackson pulled off the road and stopped the car. "This isn't a fucking game, Lexie."

"No, it's not!" She unbuckled her seatbelt and lunged at him, hitting him. He wrapped his arms around her and held her still. He was so much stronger than her, but she did not let it deter her fight.

"Stop, Lexie." He pulled her down on his lap, making her straddle him. "Stop," he whispered close to her ear. He placed his hands on either side of her face, looking deep into her tear-filled eyes. When his eyes dropped to her lips, all the fight left her. He crushed his mouth to hers, pulling her bottom lip into his mouth. His hands greedily grabbed her over-sensitized skin. She was practically naked on his lap. She moaned into his mouth as his hands teased her nipples. She wanted more. She wanted to feel his skin against hers. She grabbed his t-shirt and pulled. Jackson broke away and pulled his shirt over his head, and Lexie grabbed for his belt. It was frantic, and they were both desperate.

Jackson reclined his seat, and Lexie pushed his pants down, freeing him. He pulled her body against his, his erection rubbing against her core. Lexie grabbed hold of his hard length and led him to her entrance. The excitement dripped from her, allowing him to plunge deep inside.

Lexie slid up and down, slowly at first until she couldn't hold back anymore. She grabbed hold of the back of Jackson's seat, sliding herself up and down. He grabbed her breasts as they bounced, his thumbs rubbing her aroused nipples.

She lost touch with reality as her head fogged with pleasure; her body felt too hot and light as she moved against him. Everywhere he touched made her ache for more.

"Jackson," Lexie moaned. "Oh…Jackson!" She screamed as she felt all the built-up bliss explode through her body, and she felt like she completely dissolved.

Jackson grabbed her hips and gave a few more forceful thrusts before he growled with pleasure. She collapsed against him, unable to move.

When Lexie regained her senses, she climbed off Jackson's lap. Righting her dress, she sat back in her own seat. They both didn't speak a word as they situated themselves. Jackson started the car and pulled back on the road. She was desperate to crawl inside his head and rummage around, but she was embarrassed by her actions. Sleeping with him only complicated this situation further, but for some reason she couldn't stop herself from wanting to. "I'm not falling for you."

"Good to know. I'm not falling for you either." Jackson looked at her then, the way he did when he reached inside her and stirred things around.

"I don't believe you," Lexie challenged. Something about the way he said it made her doubt him.

"Good. Don't ever believe me."

They both remained quiet as Jackson drove. Lexie watched him clenching his jaw; his eyes trained on the road like his life depended on it. The silence was maddening since he refused to put on the radio. She attempted to turn it on once only to have him turn it off immediately after.

"Can we stop to get something to eat? I really

need to use the washroom." Lexie finally spoke up when she could wait no longer.

She wasn't sure if Jackson was going to entertain her request or not, but she breathed a sigh of relief when he pulled into the parking lot of a gas station. She wasn't going to complain—food was food at this point, and any washroom would do.

When he stopped the car, Lexie opened her door and grabbed her bags out of the backseat. She turned around to find Jackson directly behind her. "Why are you taking everything with you?"

"I need to change after...*you know*. I want to freshen up. Am I not allowed or something?" Lexie forced enough poison into her words to let him know she would not make this easy for him. Looking into his eyes, she felt the embarrassment seep into her. She couldn't believe she gave in to her desires. For some reason, all logic fled her in the heat of the moment.

The self-destructive part of her seemed to be drawn to him like a moth to a flame. He mesmerized her. She needed to clear her head and form a plan. Maybe staying with him was not a good idea. She wasn't sure if she could trust the part of her that wanted him. He stepped back and waved his arm to let her pass, though he remained tight on her heels.

Lexie pushed the doors open to the convenience store; she was met with the smell of stale coffee mixed with lemon-scented cleaner. The young man behind the desk looked up from his phone and perked up with her entrance.

"Where can I find the washroom?" Lexie asked

when he smiled brightly at her. He pointed toward the back corner. Lexie immediately headed in that direction without a backward glance. She could feel the heat of Jackson's stare on her back, and she refused to look back at him. Her attraction for him was clouding her judgment, and she wasn't sure if trusting him was a smart plan. She had no way of knowing the truth.

When Lexie walked into the single washroom, her attention was immediately drawn to the window. She locked the door behind her and dropped the bag. Unzipping the duffle bag, she pulled out a change of clothes; she quickly changed before throwing her dress in the garbage. She didn't want the reminder of what happened in his car. She needed to forget him, not lust after him.

Climbing on top of the counter, she pulled herself up to the high window that ran into the ceiling. She pulled the screen out as quietly as she could, setting it down on the floor before trying to pull the window open. It groaned in protest, but she managed to open it enough for her to climb through. She could see the treeline behind the building and a few cars in the back of the lot. Lexie jumped off the vanity and grabbed her bag and purse. She peered out the window one more time to make sure the coast was clear before she pushed her bags out and pulled herself up on the ledge.

The drop was higher than she realized, and it jolted her ankles. Picking up her bags, she peered around the corner of the building.

Two older men were talking next to their vehicles. One man leaned against a cab, smoking a cigarette. The other sat inside his truck, sipping on a coffee as they both spoke on familiar terms.

"Excuse me?" Lexie called out as she approached. Both men turned to acknowledge her. "Is that your cab?" she asked, pointing toward his car.

"Yes, miss, do you need a lift?" The man, who looked to be in his early fifties, threw his cigarette down and stepped on it.

"Yes, please. I was hoping you could take me to the nearest bus stop."

"Most definitely. I'm heading out anyway." He turned back to the man in his company. "See you later, Frank." Frank waved with a friendly smile before he started his truck and pulled away.

Lexie climbed into the cab when the driver opened the door for her. "It's not too far." He pushed his glassed up his nose and closed her door before circling around the car and climbing in. He was right; it was only a short drive. Lexie was nervous that the bus wouldn't come before Jackson caught on to her.

"Thank you." Lexie tried to hand him some cash, but he refused to take it, telling her he was off duty and it was his good deed for the day.

"Take care of yourself," he said when Lexie climbed out of the car. She gave him a small wave before closing the door.

Lexie took her sweater out of her bag. Wrapping it around her, she pulled the hood up over her head. She slipped inside the bus stop shelter, trying to be as discreet as possible. Her nerves were wound tight in her stomach. She was worried Jackson would come tearing down the street and throw her into his car. She had no idea what he was capable of, and she needed to keep that in mind.

Lexie was on the edge of her seat when the bus pulled up ten minutes later. She jumped to her feet and approached it. Her stomach dropped when she caught sight of Jackson's car in the intersection. The doors of the bus were barely open when she darted in. The bus driver seemed unconcerned with her frenzied entrance. He didn't pay her any mind as she dropped money into the fare box. She watched Jackson's car through the window as she found an empty seat. Quickly ducking down, she dared not look for fear he would see her. She could hear him speed up and tear off on the opposite side of the road.

Lexie released her breath and collapsed back into her seat. Her heart was racing so fast it felt like it was in her throat. When the bus pulled away, she breathed a sigh of relief. She glanced around at the other people sitting on the bus and noticed she was getting curious stares.

Sliding down out of sight, Lexie pulled her mother's diary out of the bottom of her purse. She wished she had her phone. Her mother had no way to get a hold of her. Flipping it open to the last entry, she read. She tried to distract her mind with the search for answers in her mother's words.

Jan. 31

I spoke to the girl on the phone. Her name is Marsha Peterson. She seemed hesitant to speak to me at first, but I explained to her the situation and the missing girl. She finally agreed to meet me and talk. She wanted to meet at a coffee shop just outside of the city.

She didn't show up...I waited for three hours. I tried calling her and no answer. She must have changed her mind.

Feb. 6

Marsha Peterson's body was found in the park a few days ago. I saw the headline in the news: "Woman's Body Found In Park." Even before I read her name, I had a sinking feeling I knew who it would be. A couple of children found her body in the bushes. They are saying that it looks like she overdosed. All I can think about is if I hadn't called her maybe she would still be alive. Some days I wonder if it would just be best not to get up in the morning. I find it harder and harder to face the days knowing the world I am a part of.

Feb. 8

Every time I saw Marsha's face on the news, I got a haunting feeling that I might meet the same fate someday. I went to her funeral, sat in the back, and listened to all the wonderful things people said about her.

Everyone wondered what happened to their bright, fun-loving Marsha that made her fall so far.

I wanted to stand on my seat and shout the truth. I wanted to tell them all that I knew who threw her on the dark path that eventually killed her, but I knew John's men were watching me. I could see Mark, one of his goons, standing at the back of the church. His eyes were on me. I wish I wasn't so scared; I wish I could be brave...I know John won't be happy I went to the funeral. I know I will pay for this, but part of me yearns for the physical pain because it numbs the torment inside me.

Mar. 9

I didn't mean for it to happen, but it

did...his name is Dylan. He showed up in my bar with his dimples and blue eyes. I tried to stop it, I really did, but I fell for him. He plays every weekend and draws a full house. He is so handsome and incredibly talented. He has this amazing voice that pulls me inside out, and I can't help but melt. I thought I was doing well, keeping things strictly friendly, but he confronted me tonight. I was checking inventory in the back room when he found me. I had forgotten what it was like to want to be with someone. For so long I have just survived. Dylan opened my eyes to the life I was missing. The life I want.

As happy as I am, I'm terrified John will find out about him. We have to keep it a secret.

Mar.20

I am walking on eggshells. I know Officer Finley wants me to dig deeper. I can tell he is restless, but he is always a gentleman. I feel bad I can't give him the information he needs.

I think John watches me more than I realize.

I told Dylan we have to be careful, but he says that he can't keep his feelings contained. It is beyond his control. I don't feel like I deserve this piece of beautiful in my dark life, but I don't know if I have the strength to let him go. He is the reason I still smile. I keep telling myself just one more kiss, one more touch, but I am addicted to this man.

May.11

I have been wrong my whole life. I thought I knew what love was, but now I truly know. I hope it's not too late.

Tonight Dylan asked me to leave with him. I said yes. I'm going to run away and never look back!

May.28

I couldn't bring myself to write before now...it hurt too much to pick up a pen.

It still hurts so much. My whole body aches, and every moment is a struggle.

I was ready to leave. I had my phone in

hand, waiting for Dylan's text...

John called me and told me to meet him in his office. I went, knowing I had no choice. I walked in, and my heart shattered. My beautiful high came crashing down around me, and I realized I should never have believed I could escape this prison. Dylan was tied to a chair, his mouth taped. I ran to him, but John stopped me. His voice was ice, fitting for the devil himself, and his eyes were bottomless pools of emptiness.

I couldn't stop him. His men held me back as John slowly tortured Dylan. He started with his eyes for looking at me. I screamed, I fought, and I threw up. I couldn't stop as Dylan's muffled screams filled my head. He slowly cut him as he smiled sadistically, enjoying every moment. I knew what he was capable of, but this—he said it was my fault, and I believe him.

I passed out. I wasn't strong enough to stay with my Dylan as John took his life.

I left him when he needed me. I should have fought harder. I hate myself. I did this to him. He was perfect...I am the reason he no longer brightens this world. I shouldn't have given in to my heart, knowing that John owns me.

Jun. 2

I haven't been able to sleep. I'm haunted...

John had a doctor prescribe me some sleeping pills. At least that's where he told me they came from. I didn't see a doctor. I haven't left my room.

John has been strangely calm. He hasn't brought it up again. I wonder when he's going to punish me or if he feels this is punishment enough.

Last night he made love to me like when we were first together. His eyes full of adoration. I tried to pretend. I don't know if he can see through the façade. I don't have the strength to care. I feel like I am a ghost. I feel like I died with Dylan.

I hate John so much that it has become a dark hole inside me.

June. 11

I'm pregnant. This is supposed to be a moment of pure bliss in my life. I'm supposed to celebrate and shout to the world that I'll be a mother, but it terrifies me. I don't know who the father is...the man I loved or the man I hate.

Lexie closed the diary and held it against her chest. Emotions pulled tightly, like a vice around her heart. It was difficult knowing what her mother had endured. She suffered so much loss at the hands of the man that could very well be her father.

When the bus came to the next stop, Lexie got off. She wasn't concerned her surroundings were unfamiliar. She had no idea where she was. She couldn't stand being on the bus anymore. She needed to breathe in the fresh air and try to clear her head. She noticed a sign on the side of the road that pointed toward a beach. She followed the arrows until she could smell the salty air and hear the water calling to her.

The sound of the ocean always brought her comfort, and she needed relief from the crushing weight upon her shoulders.

Lexie kicked off her shoes when her feet touched the sand. Feeling the sand between her toes, she took a deep breath into her stale lungs and sat down.

CHAPTER ELEVEN

Jackson

Jackson knew Lexie was going to run. She was easy to read; her eyes told what her words did not. He didn't try to stop her; he needed time to think. She was a constant distraction, one he was not used to. He followed the bus, giving her enough berth that she couldn't detect his presence.

Those blue eyes pulled him in, and those lips. He remembered all too clearly how they felt against his. Her skin was so soft; the memory of it was still so vivid in his mind of how it felt like silk against his. Jackson squeezed his eyes closed, trying to change the direction of his thoughts. The more he touched her, the more he wanted. The more he thought of her, the more he found his control and clarity slipping. For some reason she got under his skin and shook him up. For the last ten years, he had been on a path toward this goal. Nothing had ever swayed him until now. He couldn't afford to lose his focus. He was not the type to lose his head over a beautiful girl, but there was something in her eyes that made him want to gaze into them forever and it scared him.

He needed a clear head and to remember why he was here. He had been so close to finding answers when John swooped in and took it from him. He wanted Mary Connors to confirm the events that his father's partner had given all those years ago. He needed to make sure all the pieces fit, because something about that night never sat well with him, no matter how many times he read the files. This needed to remain his priority. This opportunity was what he had been waiting for.

Jackson pulled to a stop when he noticed Lexie climb off the bus. Parking his car, he tailed her on foot. He knew it was important to keep eyes on her. John's men were hot to bring her in; it was only a matter of time before they found her. John had eyes everywhere. Jackson knew Lexie needed time to think. She was walking too close to the edge. He could see it in her eyes; he needed her to be strong for what was ahead.

Jackson held back as long as he could, watching Lexie sitting on the beach, staring out into the horizon. He was used to depending on himself; he didn't share or talk to anyone, ever. His silence was what kept him alive this long.

He was not prepared for Lexie crashing into his carefully planned life. He had been so close to his goal he could have reached out and grazed it with his fingers.

He never expected Lexie to have so much sway over him. Especially with his deep-rooted hatred that had propelled him into this life. She was part of the dark hole that consumed him, but when he looked at her he saw a light that had always been missing. He was drawn to her in ways that terrified him because she made him want more.

"Lexie," Jackson called as he approached. He sat down next to her, looking out at the water that had her so mesmerized.

She looked so raw and beautiful with her tear-stained cheeks and her hair dancing in the breeze. Her eyes were the color of the ocean, and when he gazed upon them, they pulled all the air from his lungs. Her fair skin was a stark contrast to her rose-colored lips, and he could think of nothing more than to taste her again. Jackson brushed her hair back over her shoulder, letting his touch trail down the back of her arm.

Jackson wrapped his arms around her shoulders and pulled her against his side. He wasn't sure if was more for his benefit than hers, but he wanted to hold her, and he was grateful she didn't pull away.

"I need to call Stephanie and make sure she's okay. If those men found me because they were in her place...I need to know she's all right," Lexie whispered.

Jackson pulled out her phone and passed it to her. The tension fell from her shoulders as a relieved smile graced her lips. "Thank you," she said as she stared down at the phone thoughtfully for a moment before she looked back at him. "Do you think that John will ever stop trying to find my mother?"

"No."

"I need to know if that is the only reason why you're here with me now, because I'm a means to get to John Stodden?"

"No." Jackson shook his head and ran his fingers along her cheek. "I can't seem to stop wanting you." The confession surprised him, but it was the truth. Something about Lexie called to him on a level that he couldn't begin to understand.

Color seeped into Lexie's cheeks. She suddenly seemed nervous. "What do you plan on doing?"

"I don't really know. I saw an opportunity, and I took it. I don't have a plan."

"That's comforting."

He hoped this detour would eventually lead him back to the goal he had set out to achieve.

Jackson watched as Lexie listened to the phone ring over and over with no answer, a crease forming between her brows.

"She's not answering. She always answers her phone. What if something happened?"

***

"Get down," Jackson told Lexie as they neared her apartment.

She slid down in her seat, looking at him questioningly. "What's wrong?"

"Stodden will most likely have some men watching your apartment. Just stay down." He had fully expected there to be eyes present. He knew John Stodden well enough to know that he covered all his bases. Two men were sitting in the café across the street, in a window seat with clear sight of Lexie's apartment building.

Stephanie's place was only a few blocks away, and knowing it's where Stodden's men found the address of Lexie's hideout, he knew there would be eyes there too. Jackson parked around the block, out of sight from Stephanie's street.

"Stay in the car until I get back. I'm just going to make sure it's all clear." Lexie slid down in her seat and nodded.

Walking down the sidewalk, he noticed a suspicious car across the street from the townhouse. Two men were sitting inside. One was preoccupied with his phone while the other kept his eyes on the entrance to Stephanie's narrow townhouse situated in the middle of a line of identical-looking homes. Jackson pulled his hat down low, placed his headphones over his ears, and pressed play on his Walkman. The music sounded horrible, and it ate through batteries, but it brought him a strange piece of comfort knowing it was his father's. It was one of the few things he remembered about his father; he always played opera music to clear his head and focus. Jackson knew every song by heart but didn't know their names or the artists that sang them.

He shoved his hands in his pockets and walked down the sidewalk, approaching the vehicle in question. The two men barely glanced at him as he walked past. Jackson grabbed the rear door handle, pulling the door open. He slipped in the backseat.

"What the fuck?" The man in the passenger seat swung around.

Jackson pulled the headphones down around his neck. He could still hear the tinny sound filtering

151

out. "I have a message for John," Jackson said casually.

Jackson withdrew a knife concealed in his boot and jabbed it in the neck of the driver. The man sputtered as he grabbed for the hilt sticking out of his throat. The man slumped against the door with a moan, his hands grasping his neck without the strength to extract the knife. Jackson brought his elbow back and connected with the other man's face. "Fuck!" he screamed while scrambling for his weapon. Jackson wrapped a cord around the man's neck, pulling him back so he was pinned against his seat. The man grasped at the cord, but it was pulled taut. No sound escaped him as Jackson cut off his breath. It wasn't long before the man's struggles waned and eventually stopped. His body convulsed before it fell still.

Jackson sat back in his seat and placed his headphones back on his head, turning up the music as loud as he could stand. He grabbed a jacket that was lying on the backseat and wiped off his knife before slipping it back into his sheath, then spread the jacket over the man in the driver's seat to conceal the blood and reclined his seat. He pulled the hat down over the face of the other man and positioned him against the door. Jackson did not want to alert someone walking by. They would only assume the two men were asleep. He only needed to buy enough time to give them a head start.

Jackson walked back to the car and opened Lexie's door. "Let's go."

He led her around the back of Stephanie's town house. He signaled for her to stay back as he climbed the stairs, listening for any sounds inside the house. Jackson glanced inside the nearest window and confirmed the main floor looked clear.

Grabbing the door handle, he turned the knob. It wasn't locked. "Let's go." Lexie darted up the stairs into the house. He checked the lock from inside the door, revealing it was broken. He grabbed a chair from the small dining table and placed it under the handle. He didn't want anyone sneaking in here unbeknownst to him. His attention was called toward footsteps above as he looked around the main floor.

He pulled Lexie aside when the footsteps began descending the stairs. Jackson placed his hand on his gun. "Stephanie," Lexie breathed in relief when she saw her friend come into view.

"Holy crap, Lexie!" Stephanie came barrelling down the hall and threw herself into Lexie's arms. "I was so worried."

"You weren't answering your phone. I was scared."

"I can't find it anywhere. I've been tearing my house apart looking for it. Who's this?" Stephanie's gaze landed on Jackson.

"This is Jackson."

"Oh…Jackson from the cottage?"

"The very same," Jackson confirmed.

"I'm surprised to see you here. I thought you were waiting for…" Stephanie's words trailed off as she threw a glance Jackson's way, scared she may have said too much in Jackson's presence.

"I couldn't stay. An armed man showed up." Lexie took a deep breath.

"What?"

"Jackson stopped him," Lexie continued in a rush.

Stephanie looked at Jackson and back at Lexie.

"Jackson knows. It was no accident he ended up finding me. He's after the man who wants Mom."

"I can't even get my head around all of this." Stephanie looked at Jackson cautiously.

The doorbell rang, startling them. "Get back," Jackson ordered the girls. He pulled out his gun that was holstered under his jacket. Stephanie gasped when she saw the weapon and clung to Lexie's arm.

"We're gonna die, we're gonna die," Stephanie chanted in her panic.

Jackson walked into the living room. From what she could tell, Stephanie lived with her boyfriend or a male friend. A man's sweater was thrown over the back of the chair. A few game systems were situated in front of the television, and a football sitting on a well-worn La-Z-Boy didn't seem to fit with the soft feminine touches of the throw pillows and floral curtains. He walked toward the window, nudged the curtain aside with the barrel of his gun, and peered out at the front step.

"You expecting company?" Jackson asked. They both stared back at him with blank faces. "An idiot with flip-flops and bad sunglasses?"

"Evan," the girls both said in unison. He could see the relief wash over them.

Jackson walked over to the door and opened it just wide enough for his frame to be visible. "What?" he barked, not at all concerned with pleasantries. He didn't want him anywhere near

154

Lexie.

"Who the fuck are you?" Evan narrowed his eyes.

"Let him in, Jackson." Lexie grabbed the door handle and pulled the door from his hold. "Come in, Evan."

"You're here." Evan's face washed with relief. "Why didn't you tell me she was here, Stephanie?" Evan shot Stephanie an accusing look, making Stephanie look guilty.

"I just got here," Lexie defended her friend.

"Who's this guy?" Evan nodded his head toward Jackson, disbelief in his tone.

"He's a...friend," Lexie finished uncomfortably.

"Are you the boyfriend?" Jackson asked bluntly, after he did a quick scan outside and closed the door.

Evan answered yes simultaneously with Lexie's no. They both looked at each other; there was definitely history between these two, and it made anger simmer under Jackson's skin. Stephanie's gaze bounced back and forth between them with her mouth dropped open. He hated these emotions that suddenly felt as if they had a claim on him. Jackson led his life searching for facts. He didn't get involved with people for this very reason; they always complicated things.

"Where have you been? You just disappeared for days. The police even questioned me." Evan wrapped his arms around her shoulders and pulled her against his chest.

"I'm fine. I was just..."

Jackson noticed Lexie pulling on the hem of her

shirt, one of her nervous habits he picked up on.

Lexie's eyes sought out Jackson; he could tell she was unsure of how much information she could give him. She didn't return the embrace, and he liked knowing she had reservations toward Evan.

"She was with me." Jackson crossed his arms over his chest.

Evan spun around, with a narrowed gaze. "Who the hell are you?"

"He needs to leave," Jackson declared coldly, eyeing Evan.

"No, you need to leave." Evan threw Jackson's words back at him, pushing Lexie behind him.

"Stop it, Evan." Lexie refused his attempt to guard her.

"I don't like this guy. I don't want him near you," Evan bit off, his cold glower directed at Jackson.

"I don't need you protecting me, Evan. Don't you remember what happened to your brother? I don't need you. I don't want your help. I can take care of myself." Lexie pushed his hands away from her and squared her shoulders. "Jackson's right. You need to go." Jackson saw a brief glimpse of desperation in Lexie's voice. The look in her eyes spoke of her inner turmoil and grief. He knew the feeling well and recognized it instantly.

Evan shook his head. He looked wounded from her words. "I'm not leaving until you give me some answers."

Lexie looked into Evan's eyes, and her shoulders fell as her defiant stance melted away. "My mother's past caught up with her. Apparently she was involved with something dangerous. I'm just trying to lay low until I hear from Mom and we figure this out."

"You need to call the police," Evan demanded

Lexie looked over at Jackson. "He is the police."

Evan swung around and looked at Jackson in disbelief. "I'm staying," Evan declared. "I'm definitely not leaving you here with him." Evan stabbed his finger toward Jackson.

"You keep pointing that finger at me and I will break it," Jackson said impatiently.

"Oh yeah, I'd like to see you try." Evan swung around to meet Jackson face to face.

Jackson's tolerance rushed past its limit. He could no longer contain the rage that tightened its grip on him. He could think of nothing else than punching Evan in the face since he walked in the door, and he didn't hold back.

"Fuuuccckkk!" Evan screamed out as he stumbled backward, grabbing for his nose.

"Jackson!" Lexie gasped. Blood poured from Evan's nose, dripping down the front of his shirt. His eyes looked vicious as he glared back at Jackson. He started toward him, but Lexie stepped in front of him. "Stop this now." Lexie turned back toward Jackson. "Both of you."

"He's no more a fucking cop than I am!" Evan hollered.

The sound of a chair falling in the kitchen startled all of them, their attention snapped into focus. Jackson knew it was the chair he'd placed in front of the door. He placed his finger to his lips to silence everyone.

"Get upstairs now," Jackson whispered. Evan looked as if he was going to argue, but Lexie grabbed hold of his arm and pulled him toward the staircase.

Jackson withdrew his gun and moved slowly toward the kitchen. A man dressed in black, holding a gun, turned the corner toward the hall. He barely had enough time to register Jackson's presence before Jackson pulled his trigger. His aim was true as the bullet carved into the man's face, dropping him to the ground. It was one of the men from the café.

Jackson stepped over the man's body and walked toward the kitchen. He pressed himself against the wall, trying to hear any movement in the kitchen, but he was only met with silence. He pushed off and started forward. His gun was knocked from his hand before he had time to react, and it slid across the floor. Jackson grabbed hold of his attacker's arm, forcing his gun away. The man let off a shot, and the bullet lodged in the nearby wall as they struggled. Jackson spun the man around and slammed him into the kitchen island. The man lost his footing and stumbled. Jackson kicked the man's gun out of his hand before retrieving his knife. The man didn't notice the blade in Jackson's hand as he climbed back to his feet and ran toward him. Jackson sunk the blade into his side, twisting it deep, feeling the flesh give way. He could feel warm blood rush over his hand. The man gasped as he clung to Jackson's shoulders for support, growing weak, until finally he slid to the floor.

Jackson looked down at his blood-soaked shirt

and hands. The sight caused Jackson's chest to constrict and his hands to shake. He squeezed his eyes shut and tried to push back against the memories that began to flood his thoughts. He tried to focus solely on pulling long deep breaths into his body.

Jackson wiped his knife off on the back of the man's shirt and slid it back into his sheath. He walked over toward the door and picked up the chair to reposition it under the handle. He did quick surveillance to make sure there were only two men before he walked back into the living room and sat down. He reached carefully inside his pocket, careful not to smear too much blood, and retrieved the Walkman tucked inside. He placed the headphones over his ears and hit play. His head was suddenly swimming in the strong female voice that sang as if she were the finest of instruments. He closed his eyes and let the music drown out the dark thoughts that clawed at his mind.

CHAPTER TWELVE

Lexie

Lexie had her back to the bathroom door as the three of them huddled inside. The sound of the gunshots had them rattled. Minutes passed and the silence became almost deafening. They stared at each other trying to process the turn of events.

"Jesus Christ, Lexie. What are you involved in?" Evan whispered. He grabbed the hand towel from the ring to hold to his nose.

"Hey! That's my good towel," Stephanie complained, keeping her voice low.

Evan threw her a "are you serious" look before he dismissed her. Stephanie didn't put up any more of a fight as she sat down on the edge of the bathtub with a sigh.

Blood had saturated the front of Evan's shirt, but the bleeding had slowed considerably. He turned the water on low and washed the blood from his hands and examined his nose in the mirror.

"I wish I knew," Lexie whispered.

"How long do we wait?" Stephanie asked

nervously.

"I'm going to check." Lexie grabbed the handle of the door, but Evan's hand closed around hers.

"Stop," Evan demanded.

"Let me go, Evan." Lexie gave him a stern look.

Evan retracted his hand. "I'm coming with you," he said, breaking eye contact.

"Don't leave me here alone." Stephanie jumped to her feet as Lexie swung open the door. The silence in the house felt heavy as they walked down the hall and peered down into the foyer. Nothing seemed out of sorts until Lexie began descending the stairs and noticed a body lying in the hall.

Stephanie began to scream, but Evan clamped his hand over her mouth. "Shut up, Steph." Evan waited for her to nod before he removed his hand.

They moved toward the kitchen and noticed the other body lying in a pool of blood. "We have to call the police. This is insane."

"No," Lexie insisted. "No one is calling the police." She stared down at the body. Nausea swirled heavily in the pit of her stomach. She averted her gaze and took a deep breath.

"There are two dead men lying on the floor," Evan snapped, no longer trying to keep his voice down. "Why are you protecting this guy? Are you sleeping with him?"

"That's none of your business." Lexie shook her head in disbelief.

"Fuck, this is a mind trip." Evan walked over toward the kitchen table, pulled out a chair, and collapsed in it. "Do you have any pain meds, Stephanie?"

"Yeah." Stephanie's eyes kept sliding back to the dead man on her floor as she walked into her kitchen and grabbed a bottle from the windowsill. "What are we going to do with the bodies?"

"Where's Jackson?"

Stephanie pointed into the living room. Lexie noticed Jackson sitting in the recliner, the one that Stephanie despised wholeheartedly.

"Jackson?" she gasped, running over to him.

His eyes were closed, his brow furrowed, and his jaw clenched tight. His headphones were turned up so loud she could hear the music. She knelt down in front of him hesitantly, touching his arm. Blood coated his hands and soaked the front of his shirt. "Jackson." She nudged his arm. He didn't respond to her touch, and she ran her fingers along his arm. She could see his long slow breaths from the rise and fall of his chest, and it eased her panic.

She slowly lifted his shirt to reveal the blood that saturated his side was not his own. Physically he seemed unharmed.

"Lexie?" Stephanie called to her. Lexie turned around to see Stephanie and Evan approaching.

"Just give us a few minutes," Lexie requested.

Stephanie reached up to grab Evan's arm to stop him from walking any closer.

"This is fucked up." He pulled his arm free of Stephanie's hold, throwing a scowl at Lexie before he turned on his heel and stomped out of the room. Stephanie shrugged nervously before she followed him.

Lexie turned back toward Jackson. His eyes were now open and staring down at her hand on his arm.

"Jackson, are you all right?"

She could see the torment brewing behind his beautiful dark eyes. She knew her feelings for him were irrational, and she should be fighting them every step of the way. She knew if she was smart she would keep her defenses up around him, especially now. She should be building walls, not trying to feed this strange connection they had. The intense feelings that were claiming her heart were winning the war against logic. They whispered for her to move closer to the edge, to jump and free fall without knowing what would be waiting when she landed.

He was lost in his mind, tormented by his own demons. She knew the look; she saw it every time she looked in a mirror. All she could think about was bringing him back to her. Lexie climbed on the chair, straddling his lap. She pulled his headphones off. The music filtering through the earpieces was surprising. It sounded like what nature would sound like if it had a voice.

"Look at me, Jackson." Lexie placed her hands on either side of his face. "Come back."

Lexie looked into his eyes, swirling with so much unreleased emotion. He focused on her face, slowly coming back from wherever he retreated to. Lexie ran her thumb over his bottom lip. She loved the shape of his full lips. In this moment, she couldn't think of anything more beautiful than this strong man that was now vulnerable to her will. She could see him searching her face for answers. She wanted to give him all the answers he sought. She wanted to be his answer. Throwing caution to the wind, she decided to let her desires take the front seat. She was walking a new line, one with danger close on her heels, but she didn't want to think about what was lurking around the corner.

Lexie leaned forward and pressed her lips to his. She wasn't expecting the swell of excitement that heated her, making her heart race. It hit her fast and hard, shoving all the other emotions she was dealing with aside and taking center stage. She indulged in the sweet escape as she reveled in him. He kissed her like a starving man, and she encouraged him to devour her until reality seeped in and pulled them apart.

Lexie leaned back. She was breathless and staring into his now-clear eyes. His focus was back, and he was staring into her soul. "Where were you?" she whispered.

"Nowhere." His eyes closed, and he leaned back into the chair.

Lexie wanted to understand Jackson. She wanted to know what horrible truth caused him to shut down. She needed to establish trust between them, and to do that she needed to open up to him. Lexie took a deep breath. "Evan's brother and I were together for a long time." She looked up into his face. His eyes were open again, and he was listening. She could feel her lip tremble. "I had given him my heart, and he promised we would be together forever. A year ago we were at a concert. It was one of our favorite events of the year. On the way home, we were attacked. There were three of them." Lexie placed her hand against her neck. "Sometimes I can still feel the knife pressed against my throat." A sob escaped her, and she covered her mouth, taking a deep breath so she could continue. "Alex fought two of them." Lexie's shoulders began to shake as she let the emotions take over. "I replay it over and over all the time, wondering if I hadn't insisted on taking the scenic walk home, or if I could have just fought harder...he'd still be here."

Jackson looked down at his hands; he was struggling with something. She could see it brewing behind his eyes.

"My father died when I was four. I don't remember him much, but I knew that my mother loved him so much that part of her died with him. I was twelve years old when I found her..." Jackson wiped his face on his arm. "I found her in the bathroom. There was so much blood." He looked at his blood-covered hands.

Lexie didn't care about the blood on Jackson's shirt as she wrapped her arms around him and sought comfort for both their sakes. She wondered if the tragedies they both endured was the reason for her intense attraction toward him. Maybe her soul was drawn to his because like hers, his was torn and bloodied.

The sound of a phone ringing cut through the silence. Lexie recognized the ring immediately. She pushed herself to her feet, looking down at Jackson with wide eyes. Lexie frantically pulled it out of her pocket.

"Hello?" Lexie said in a rush. "Mom?"

"Lexie, you don't know how good it is to hear your voice. Are you safe?"

"Yes, I'm at Stephanie's. Where are you?" Lexie

stood up, running her hand through her hair and twisting the strands around her fingers until it bordered on painful.

"I tried to keep you safe. I didn't want him to know about you, but everything has changed." She could detect panic in her mother's words. "I went to the cottage, but you were gone and there were signs of a struggle."

"I'm fine. I managed to escape." Lexie locked eyes with Jackson.

"I thought he took you." Lexie could hear her mother's voice shake.

"Are you talking about John?"

Her mother grew quiet for a moment. "How do you know his name?"

"I found your diary."

"Oh Lexie, you shouldn't have found out that way. I am so sorry. I shouldn't have kept this all a secret, but I hoped it would always stay in the past."

"It's all right, Mom. I just needed answers. I just need to see you."

"It's not safe for you to stay there. Can you meet me at that little diner off the highway in Oxford? "

"Yes, of course. When?"

"Tonight at seven."

"I'll be there." Lexie didn't mention Jackson. She knew her mother wouldn't understand if she tried to explain over the phone. She would break the news to her in person. Hopefully her mother would see the value of having him on their side.

"I love you, Lexie."

"I love you too, Mom. See you soon."

Lexie hung up the phone and looked at Jackson,

who was awaiting the new information. "My mom wants me to meet her tonight."

"Lexie?" The both turned toward Evan. "I need to talk to you."

Lexie followed Evan as he led her upstairs to the spare bedroom. Her stomach felt heavy because she knew Evan was going to try and talk her out what she needed to do. He shut the door and leaned against it.

"Lexie…" he began, his tormented gaze pleading with her. "Don't do this. This whole situation is fucked to no end. You're going to get yourself killed. There are two dead men downstairs, lying in pools of blood, and you're putting your faith in a stranger whose intentions are God knows what. He's not stable. I don't believe he's a cop for one second. I saw the way he completely lost it down there." Evan reached for her, but Lexie took a step back.

"Evan, what we did that night was a mistake."

"Don't say that."

"Evan, listen." Lexie took a deep breath and forced herself to continue. "I love you—I do—but we were never meant to be more than what we were. I know you know it in your heart. I miss your brother every moment of every day, just like you. Us being together isn't going to make it easier. It won't make us miss him less. It won't solve any of our problems. It will only make things worse. It's not going to fill that hole we feel." Lexie felt emotionally drained as she spoke, but she needed to say this. She had let things go too far. She needed to be clear where the boundaries fell. "After we were together, I know you felt regret. I could see it in your eyes, and I could feel it in my heart. I also can't have you trying to protect me. If anything happened to you, I wouldn't be able to live with it. The only person I want you to worry about is yourself. I can take care of me."

"He'd want me to protect you."

"Look where it got him, Evan."

They both stood silent for a moment, staring at each other. She couldn't remember the last time Evan smiled. He had always been so easy going, care-free, but now he couldn't get through a day without getting high. Like her, he wasn't dealing well with their loss. It left them confused and in the dark when it came to moving on with the rest of their lives.

"I have to meet my mom tonight. I need you to stay here with Stephanie."

"Lex…"

"Do this for me, Evan. I put you both at risk coming back here. I have to face this. It's no longer a choice for me. More and more of those men are going to keep coming until my mother and I face this. Jackson knows what's coming for us. He might be our only chance to survive it. I trust him. Promise me, Evan. I need to know that you two are safe."

Evan looked so tormented. She knew he wanted to say more, but he held his tongue, and she was grateful. He gave the slightest nod. She threw her arms around him and squeezed him tight. His arms wrapped around her.

"Don't blame yourself for Alex's death, Lexie. I

know if given the choice he would have given his life for you a thousand times."

Lexie buried her face into Evan's shirt. "Remember that day when you, Alex, Stephanie, and I spent the night at Russet's Cove?"

"Yeah."

"I think about that a lot. How we spent hours by the campfire talking about our futures and where we would be in ten years. I remember laughing so hard my face hurt. Life was so perfect then. I wish we could go back to that night."

"Me too, Lexie, me too."

CHAPTER THIRTEEN

Jackson

Jackson stood out on the back porch of Stephanie's house. "I've got four bodies I need to make disappear." Jackson didn't bother with pleasantries when Max answered the phone.

"Fuck, Jack. Sliding over to the dark side, are you? Be careful where you step. Even you can get caught stepping in shit if you're not careful."

"Yeah, well, desperate times." Jackson ran his hand through his hair. He knew he was heading into territory that he might not able to return from. "Can you take care of the bodies?"

"Yeah, I got it, but you owe me big."

"Done." Jackson rattled off the necessary information before he ended the call. He barely slid his phone in his pocket when it rang. He held it up and looked at the name of the caller, Giles. "This is fucking great," Jackson mumbled before he accepted the call. He knew better than to ignore this call.

"Giles."

"When you asked for time off, you failed to divulge that you were running off doing God knows what. What are you up to, Jacks? I know you're not sitting poolside like you led me to believe."

"I have a meeting with Mary Connors. Don't take me off this, Giles. I'm close. I can feel it. I need these answers," Jackson argued. "I won't do anything stupid."

Giles was quiet for a moment before he continued.

"You found her?"

"Yeah."

"I think it's a little too late to not do anything stupid. Fuck, Jackson. What am I going to do with you?" Jackson could hear his exaggerated sigh on the other end of the line. "What makes you think she's going to give you the answers you're looking for?"

"I have her daughter."

"Her daughter?"

"Yeah, turns out Mary had lots of secrets. I suspect she's John's."

"Mary is part of a much bigger picture, Jackson. You can't lose your head. It won't bring him back, and it will leave us none the better."

"I know, Giles. I'm good. You know it."

"Jackson, I can't believe I'm saying this...I'm sending some backup. Don't make a move until they're with you. I want you to keep me posted about every goddamn move you make."

"You won't regret it."

"I already do. I want Mary brought in. Don't hurt

a hair on that woman's head. Do you hear me, Jackson? Bringing her in can finally be the break the case needs."

"Yeah. Keep the circle close, Giles. Only need-to-know basis."

"I will."

"I also need protection for a few of the daughter's friends. They were on the radar. I don't want to leave it to chance Stodden's men won't go after them once we leave."

"I'll make some calls and get some bodies on them."

Jackson gave Giles the rest of the details and planned a meeting location for the men Giles was sending. He slipped his phone into his pocket and sat down on the step.

"What am I missing, Dad?" Jackson spoke thoughtfully to himself. He had gone over his father's notes from his last case more times than he could possibly count. He knew the answers to his father's murder were tied with it. None of it added up; there were too many holes.

The door opened behind him, and he looked up into those blue eyes that made the rest of the world fade away. Every time he looked at her, it was like being hit with a bucket of cold water. The emotions she stirred in him were overwhelming. A part of him wanted it all to go away, but another was desperate to hold onto it, to her. He turned back around and took a deep breath. He needed to stay focused.

"Is everything all right?" Her voice broke through his dark thoughts.

"Yeah. We need to go."

"Evan is taking Stephanie to his place until…" Lexie nodded back toward the house. "Everything gets cleaned up."

"It won't be long. Someone is on the way," Jackson assured her.

"Will they be safe?" Lexie asked before biting her lips, her beautiful eyes wide with fear.

"Safer than with us," Jackson offered.

***

Jackson pulled into a gas station about thirty minutes from the diner where they were meeting Lexie's mother. They still had a few hours before Mary would be expecting them, and he intended to spend it with Lexie. She was quiet for most of the drive, twisting the hem of her shirt in her fingers. She seemed so far away—lost in thought.

He knew what should be on his mind, but instead his thoughts were of Lexie, the feeling of her soft lips against his. She had opened her heart to him, and he glimpsed the beauty within, the bright light that was haunted by sadness and guilt, and he wanted her.

These thoughts both thrilled him and terrified him. He had lived most of his life on his own, relying on no one but himself, but when it came to Lexie, he felt his resolve slipping away. His focus was suddenly pulled toward her, and he was scared she would knock his feet out from under him. He could already feel his world begin to tilt. Even when he closed his eyes he could still see her, still see those beautiful deep sea eyes that pleaded for answers. He was scared she would find the answers she was looking for. He knew it was only a matter of time now before she discovered the truth.

Jackson parked the car in front of a pump. The lot was nearly empty with only a few vehicles next to the small building. Jackson did a quick scan of the perimeter before he turned off his car, satisfied they were alone. He looked over at Lexie sitting beside him. She was watching him. So many questions looked like they were ready to burst from those beautiful lips, but she remained quiet, waiting for him to make the first move. He placed his arm on the back of her seat and flicked her hair, eliciting a small smile.

"Everything will change once we meet your mother."

"I know," Lexie said, releasing a deep breath.

"I'm not good with words, Lexie," Jackson said, his eyes set on hers. "I have so much I want to say to you." Jackson broke eye contact and looked out the window, trying desperately to reach inside himself. The feelings that swirled around deep inside him were scarier than any situation he had ever been in, and he had been in many situations that seemed impossible to walk away from alive. "I want to tell you how I feel about you, but I don't know how."

Lexie bit her bottom lip. "Show me then," Lexie whispered.

Jackson smiled, completely captivated by everything that she was. He pulled his door open and stepped out. He grabbed the nozzle for the pump and began fueling his car. He ran his fingers through his hair and wrestled with his better judgement. He knew he should not be making this move now. Every logical thought screamed at him to stop this before it went any further, but he couldn't help himself. He wanted to know what could have been.

Jackson pulled Lexie's door open and held his hand out for her. She slipped her hand into his…the contact made his blood heat.

He placed his hands on either side of her, leaning against the car. He could see how nervous she was as he gazed into her beautiful eyes. He wanted to memorize every detail of her so he could relive this moment again and again when it was nothing but a memory. Jackson pressed his body against hers, loving the feel of her body against him. Lexie felt too good to be true, and it made his head swim. Running his fingers along her jaw, he tilted her mouth up to meet his. She tasted so good, like strawberry lip gloss, and he wanted to devour her as he explored her mouth. She filled his mind with thoughts so wonderful he wanted to grab hold of every one so they would never disappear.

Lexie's hands grasped his shirt, pulling hard until it threatened to rip. Jackson leaned back, taking a much-needed breath. Her eyes were filled with both lust and fear. "Not gentle," she gasped. "Gentle is for…"

"Love," Jackson finished. He stepped back and grabbed the nozzle, placing it back on the pump. "Come with me." Jackson laced his fingers into hers and headed toward the building. He pushed the glass door open to the station and waved to the man behind the counter. "We'll be right back," Jackson called to him. The cashier nodded his head as he watched them head to the back of the store.

Jackson swung the washroom door open and pulled Lexie inside with him. She didn't question his intentions. She knew full well what was on his mind; he made it very clear that he was a man desperate to dive into all the pleasures she could offer him. She was a drug, and he was an addict. He threw the lock on the door and turned his savage eyes on Lexie.

She backed against the wall with a playful look upon her face. Jackson waited for reality to come crashing down on him. This was a piece of heaven that mistakenly fell into his hands, and before the error was realized, he planned to take advantage of it. He grabbed hold of her waist and pressed his lips against hers, sucking her bottom lip into his mouth, pulling his teeth along her soft flesh. He swallowed her moan before her kiss became just as frenzied.

Jackson lifted Lexie up and pinned her against the wall, supporting her weight. She wrapped her legs around his waist, positioning her body perfectly for him. He wanted to be inside her. He throbbed with need to the point of pain as he pushed against her. Her gasps of arousal excited him. The skin on her neck and stretching down toward her chest turned beautiful shades of pink, and he kissed every inch of it.

Jackson pulled her skirt up and wrapped his fingers around the delicate material of her underwear, pulling them aside. He could feel her excitement melt around his fingers. Instead of being overwhelmed with the need for release, he wanted to stay in this moment forever. He wanted to freeze time and have Lexie's legs wrapped around him until the end of time. He wanted to touch her, kiss her, look into those eyes that reached deep inside of him and made him want more. This was where he wanted to spend the rest of his life. He wanted her to want him to be gentle, but Heaven was never meant for men like him.

Lexie grabbed for his belt, unfastened it, and pushed his pants down. There was no denying how much he wanted her. He was a man on fire, and she was his relief. Lexie clung to his shoulders as he pushed inside her. He could feel her nails digging into his flesh as he pushed himself deep into her center. The combination of pleasure and pain made his head reel. He was driven by instinct, with deep thrusts as he pushed Lexie into the wall. Her moans of pleasure grew in intensity as she clung to him. He couldn't think past the hot pool of bliss he was enveloped in. Lexie had an ability to pull him in and make him lose touch with reality. An escape that was addictive. This would never be enough. He would never have enough of her.

She represented everything he thought he could never have. Now that she was in his grasp, he knew it was only a matter of time before she slipped through his fingers, and he knew it would be of his own doing.

Lexie ran her fingers through his hair, pulling him in to her kiss. Her hunger made him dizzy. He could feel her body tense in his hold. He forced himself to hold on until she found her pleasure before he found his own. Lexie's teeth sunk into his shoulder. She moaned against his skin, and it sent an explosion of pleasure to his groin. He held onto her melting body as he came, hot and hurried, inside her.

Her limp, sated body collapsed against him as he held her tight, his arms wrapped around her, clinging to the moment a little longer before setting her on her feet. He brushed her hair back off her shoulder, letting his fingers trail along the soft skin of her arm. He leaned in and pressed his lips softly against hers; he was overwhelmed with the desire to let her know that what he felt was more than sex and pleasuring needs. She meant something to him.

"Don't." Lexie pulled back, her eyes filled with tears, but they never fell. He gave her a slight nod in understanding. He crossed the boundaries she set. She didn't want gentle with him. He refastened his pants and let her situate herself. Neither one spoke, and as quick as it came, the moment they shared was over. Jackson had an overwhelming feeling of loss as he pulled the door open.

"Fuck...you're early." Jackson sighed when he noticed two men standing on the other side of the door. The men Giles had sent were both standing next to the aisle, their gaze dropped to Lexie behind him. There was no denying he crossed the line. He could see the "you're in deep shit" expression on Dane's face.

Jackson knew both Dane and Teddy well. As relieved as he was with the choice of men Giles sent him as backup, he knew they would both voice their opinions about what he got himself into. Dane was a straight shot, could probably hit a target with his eyes closed. Jackson met him the first day of the academy. They both had a similar past, growing up surviving the streets, wanting to rid the world of some of the darkness that lurks like a disease, the same evil that almost brought them to their knees when they were lost in their youth.

Teddy joined the force because his sister was raped and murdered when she was only twelve years old. He wanted answers for the injustice. He needed to follow a path that gave him a way to fight the evils that could destroy such a young beautiful girl before she had a chance at the life she deserved. Jackson understood his feeling of loss. He understood the feeling of being cheated of the joys of life.

"Grab something to eat, Lex. I need to talk with these guys." Jackson stepped back to let her pass. Lexie gave both men a quick look before she slipped down the aisle.

"I can't blame you. She's fucking A," Teddy said as his eyes followed Lexie.

"Fuck off, Teddy," Jackson said impatiently.

Teddy raised his hands in surrender.

"You should be glad Giles sent us. We actually care what happens to your ass," Dane said.

"I know. I need your ugly faces, but she," Jackson nodded his head toward Lexie, "is off the table. I don't want your opinion."

They both nodded in understanding. Both men were dressed in plain clothes. No one could tell they were loaded with weapons, carefully concealed. The three of them brought together by some force of nature and shared an unusual bond. "Does anyone else know you're here, besides Giles?"

"Rosh, he was with us when Giles briefed us," Dane said. "And a few others that Giles is keeping close. He said it was on the down low."

Jackson nodded. He knew his father's old partner would want to know any details on this case. He was with his father when he lost his life. He understood he would need closure as well.

"When Giles told us what you were up to, there was no stopping us. You should have told us," Teddy added. Jackson knew they were concerned for his clarity of mind. They knew his obsession with solving the case his father lost his life for, still open and far from having closure. No one wanted him to touch it. In fact, no one wanted to. Digging around John Stodden got you killed. His father, among others, was a testament to this.

"What's the plan?" Dane asked. He was always ready to get down to business.

CHAPTER FOURTEEN

Fifteen Years Ago...

Jackson threw his baseball up into the air high enough that it looked like a tiny speck in the vast sky. Sometimes it looked like it would disappear for a moment, swallowed by the endless blue stretching as far as the eye could see, but it would always fall back down into his readied glove. Jackson found it in an old box years ago when he was looking around in the garage. He knew it was his father's without even having to ask his mother.

He kept it, a possession he cherished. He brought the glove with him everywhere, even sliding it under his pillow at night. It gave him something real to hold onto when he barely had any memories of his father. He was so young when his father died. He only had fragments of memories. Small pieces that barely allowed him to picture the man his father was.

Jackson always stayed outside as long as he could. He didn't like being inside his house. It felt

181

cold, strange, and nothing like a home should feel like. His mother insisted on keeping the curtains closed and the lights dim. The walls were bare, not one picture to show that it was actually a home. She didn't like any reminders of before his father died, and she hadn't taken a picture since.

When night began to claim the sky, Jackson finally decided to go inside. He swung the door open and was surprised by the tantalizing smells that filled their normally stale house. It instantly made his mouth water and his stomach spin excitedly. "Mom?" Jackson called.

"In the kitchen," she called back. Her voice was lighter than normal, floating in the air around him. He slipped off his shoes, placing them neatly by the door. He was careful not to disturb this strange sense of peace his mother seemed to be emitting. The house had never smelled this good. This was how his friends' houses smelled like, not his.

He slowly walked into the kitchen and noticed his mother stirring a pot over the stove. Her hair was pulled up and curled. Red was painted on her lips, and she wore a dress with red flowers spattered over the material. She looked beautiful, and it brought a smile to his face.

"There you are. Sit. Supper is ready."

Jackson quickly slipped into his chair. The table was set with candles and dishes he didn't even realize they owned.

"It smells really good, Mom," Jackson said softly.

"It's your favorite. Spaghetti and meatballs, just like Sam's mother makes." She approached the table and collected the plates.

Every once in a while Jackson was invited to stay for dinner at his friend Sam's house. Sam's mother always made the most delicious food, and he always looked forward to it. He normally would eat cereal, granola bars, or whatever he could find in the cabinets because his mother never cooked. He didn't even realize she knew it was his favorite, and it made his heart swell.

"Thank you." Jackson could feel tears rise to the surface when his mother looked him in the eyes and smiled. He felt like it was the first time she really saw him. Her eyes were clear, without their normal dull cast. Her red lips turned up beautifully into a perfect smile. Jackson couldn't help but wonder if this was what his mother was like before his father died. It was the first time he met this version of her, and he wanted to hold onto her forever.

She sat down across from him with her own plate as Jackson dove into his food. It was delicious, better than any food had ever tasted before. Every time he looked up at his mother, her smile would broaden as she slowly picked at her food. Jackson wanted this moment to last forever. He wanted her to see him every time she looked at him. He wanted her to smile at him because it made that pain in his chest ease. He felt loved. He felt wanted.

"Do you like it, Jackson?" she asked.

"It's the best," Jackson said after swallowing a mouthful.

"Good." She set her fork down and stood up, smoothing out her dress. "Be a good boy, Jackson."

Jackson nodded his head and watched her

cautiously as she left the room. He stared at the doorway of the kitchen, waiting for her to return. Wanting desperately to see that beautiful floral dress and his mother's face light up when her eyes fell on him. He wanted to feel the warmth of her love to burn away the chill that crawled over his skin. He was terrified to get out of his seat and realize the moment was over. His hope that she could be like other mothers was slipping through his fingers.

Jackson sat in front of his plate, his food untouched since his mother stood to leave. He watched the minute hand on the clock make a complete rotation before he dropped his fork. His stomach knotted uncomfortably with the realization that she wasn't coming back.

Grabbing his plate, he set it next to the sink before he walked toward the stairs. He looked up at the unlit staircase. He knew something was wrong; he could feel it taunting him.

Jackson slowly climbed the stairs, grabbing hold of the railing to pull himself along. When he reached the top, he could see the bathroom light spilling from under the door across the hallway floor.

Taking a deep breath, he approached the door and knocked gently. "Mom?" Jackson looked down when a wet sensation pooled around his toes. He looked down to see a dark viscous liquid seeping out from under the door. Jackson's heart beat so hard it felt painful against his ribs as he turned the knob and pushed the door open.

His mother was slumped against the vanity, her

beautiful dress soaked in red that flowed from her wrists and puddled around her, covering the tiles. Jackson couldn't avoid stepping in her blood as he reached for her. "Mom?" He grabbed her shoulders to give her a gentle shake. She didn't respond. The red lipstick now looked so harsh against her pallid skin.

Jackson grabbed a towel and tried to wrap her wrists. He knew it was too late. His mind knew that her chest failed to rise and fall with breath. Her color did not speak of life, only death. The realization that she had been happy because she decided to leave him squeezed tightly around his heart. Her smile was not because she suddenly saw him after all these years. It was not because she had suddenly decided to live but because she'd decided to give up. The first time he thought he saw love in his mother's eyes was the joy of saying goodbye to him.

Anger stabbed him hard and fast as tears welled in his eyes. She was all he had, and she left him alone in a world that wanted him even less than she did. Jackson looked down at his hands, completely covered in his mother's blood. There was blood everywhere. He couldn't breathe. He tried to pull air into his lungs, but his chest constricted painfully. The pain pulled him inside out as he collapsed on the floor.

CHAPTER FIFTEEN

Lexie

Lexie peered over the top of the aisle, watching Jackson in a hushed conversation with the other two men. The three of them together was a sight that was hard to ignore; they looked scary beautiful. All three men towered over her in height, built of power and intensity that thrummed in the air around them. When Jackson said he was expecting a few men, she wasn't exactly prepared for what arrived. They were all attractive in their own right. Jackson drew her eye the most with his dark, enchanting features that spoke of danger and sex. When he looked at her, it was as if he could see all her secrets and she was naked before him. He was an obvious weakness for her, which explained her actions of late. The one Jackson referred to as Dane had close shaven hair and the bluest eyes she had ever seen. She knew they must be real because he did not look like a man that would take care with contacts. The other, Teddy, had blond hair. He threw an easy smile her way when he noticed she was watching them. She looked away and turned her attention to the rows of products in front of her. Heat crawled across her face.

Lexie noticed the cashier looked nervously at the three men huddled close in the back of his store. He obviously picked up on the energy these men exhibited and probably feared their intentions.

Lexie busied herself looking at the items lining the shelf, trying to hear what Jackson and the others were discussing, but they were too far away. She noticed a row of nail polishes sitting on a shelf with a handful of cosmetics the store carried. Her stomach stirred with an emotion when she saw the color she had been searching for. Revlon Knockout stared back at her from the white metal shelf. Lexie looked down at her toes. She hadn't even noticed the last of the color had disappeared. She didn't understand how she could not have realized. Guilt carved away painfully at her.

"Alex," Lexie whispered.

Lexie looked up past the nail polish to Jackson's handsome face. He was standing on the other side of the shelf watching her. Those deep dark eyes searched hers. His face was unshaven, and she could still feel the delicious burn on her face from his rough kiss. He was absolutely stunning. He couldn't have been more perfect if she'd created him herself. She wanted to walk up to him and throw herself in his arms. She wanted to know what it would feel like to be loved by a man like Jackson. So strong, brave, and able to take life on like it was made to bend to his will.

The very thoughts twisted the blade deep inside her. Her heart belonged to Alex. He gave his life to save her, and she was thinking of another. How could she even consider wanting to find comfort in the arms of another?

"We have to head out, Lexie," Jackson said softly.

Lexie looked up at him before dropping her gaze back toward the polish. She ran her finger over the label. Jackson grabbed the four bottles remaining on the shelf.

"What are you doing?" Lexie asked, surprised.

"Making your decision easier." Jackson walked over to the cashier and placed the polish on the counter, along with a couple bottles of water and bags of almonds. The cashier was probably no more than eighteen. His hands shook slightly as he watched the three men standing in front of him, intimidating in every way.

Lexie was scared to know who Jackson really was. She just wanted to hold onto what they had right now because it felt so real. It felt so raw and imperfectly perfect. It made her feel something other than sadness again. Lexie's emotions pulled her in so many directions she felt brittle and confused. The only thing that reminded her she was alive was looking into Jackson's dark brown eyes, feeling his skin against hers. Listening to that voice that plucked strings so deep within her that she felt the hum of life again. Jackson made the deep chill that settled in her bones thaw, but she knew it was time to start asking questions.

Lexie slipped into the front seat of Jackson's car.

She watched Dane and Teddy walk toward a different vehicle. "Are your friends coming with us?"

"Yes. They're here in case we need backup."

"In case John's men find us?" Lexie turned toward Jackson as he started his car.

He nodded before passing her the bag that held her nail polish.

"When are you planning on using us as bait?" Lexie asked, opening the bag to retrieve the bottles. She looked up and noticed Jackson's eyes on her. "I know that's your plan. It's the only thing that makes sense." Lexie picked up her purse from the floor by her feet. "Can you promise me something?"

"What?"

"To keep my mother safe." Lexie dropped the polish in her purse and zipped it closed.

"What about you?" Jackson ran his hands down the steering wheel.

"I can take care of myself."

"It seems as though your mother has done a good job of taking care of herself so far."

"I wouldn't be so sure. I think the only thing she has ever done was take care of me."

Lexie wrapped her fingers around Jackson's hand that he rested on the gearstick. He placed his hand against her cheek. She wanted to feel closer to him as she leaned in to his touch. "Do you think beautiful can grow from horrible beginnings?"

"I don't know."

"Me either." Lexie sighed.

***

Lexie looked out the window at the diner. Jackson had parked and turned off the car. He was quiet as his loaded gaze remained on her.

"What are you thinking about?" Lexie asked nervously, smoothing her hair.

"I'm making you nervous." Jackson let a small smile play on his sensual lips.

"You keep looking at me like you have something to say, and yes, you always make me nervous."

"Good."

Lexie noticed Dane and Teddy walk into the dinner, looking casual as they carried on with one another. Their eyes never even glanced toward Jackson and Lexie, still in their car. Lexie looked back at their car; two other men still waited inside, smoking with the windows down. "Are they with you too?"

"They are just keeping eyes on the outside. Just pretend they aren't here." Jackson leaned closer and grabbed Lexie's hand.

"What do you think will happen? Do you think John's men will show?" Lexie tried to pull her hand free, but Jackson held tight.

Jackson said thoughtfully. "This meeting was kept tight. There should be no way John should catch wind of it. I just want to make sure we're being careful."

"What happens now?"

"I want to talk to your mother."

Jackson's words gave Lexie a sinking feeling in her stomach. "About what?"

Jackson leaned back in his seat and pulled his

phone from his pocket. He glanced at the screen. "She's inside."

Lexie grabbed for the handle and opened the car door. Jackson followed close behind her as she walked toward the front door. She was excited to see her mother and couldn't wait another moment. She pushed the door open and looked around the interior of the dated diner. The bright red material lining the booths was worn and cracked from years of use, and the floors showed years of traffic, but it had a certain charm that Lexie could appreciate.

She skimmed the faces of the customers, passing Dane and Teddy sitting at the end of the bar that ran the length of the interior. They were foolish to think they blended into the crowd. They looked ready to step into a ring and do some serious damage. Their physiques were honed to perfection and did not fit the sea of soft bellies that filled the dinner, gorging on pie and sweets. Lexie found her mother, tucked in a booth along the wall. An expression of relief washed over her mother's face as she watched Lexie approach. She looked different from the last time Lexie saw her. Her hair was darker and cut just above her shoulders. Dark circles lined her eyes, and she looked exhausted. Her normal healthy glow was dimmed from the stress of the last few days.

"Mom." Lexie wrapped her arms around her mother, who stood when she neared. These last few days had been a roller coaster, and seeing her mother was a huge source of relief. "You cut your hair and the color…"

"Who's this?" Beth asked, pulling away, her eyes on Jackson.

In the excitement of finding her mother, she had forgotten that her mother would be thrown off by Jackson's presence. "Mom, this is Jackson."

Her mother watched him calculatedly. "Lexie—" she started, with heavy warning in her tone, before Lexie cut her off.

"He's the reason I made it this far, Mom. You left me completely unprepared for any of this. He's on our side."

Her mother sighed. "Sit down, both of you." Her mother slid back into the booth and made room for her daughter. Jackson sat down across from them. His dark eyes trained on Lexie's mother as he clenched his jaw. Lexie was surprised to see anger in his gaze. Her stomach dropped.

"Jackson stopped the men at the cottage. I don't know what would have happened if he wasn't there," Lexie whispered, waiting for Jackson to make a move. She could see his thoughts fuming for release.

Beth leaned back in her seat and took a deep breath. "You know who I am, don't you?"

"Yes," Jackson spoke through clenched teeth. "I know exactly who you are."

"Who are you and what do you want?" Beth asked, taking her daughter's hand in hers. Lexie squeezed back as she watched her mother and Jackson intently, trying to place the pieces together.

"My name is Jackson Finley. I believe you knew my father."

Her mother leaned back against the seat. "I should've known. You look like him." Her mother smiled sadly.

"What's this about?" Lexie looked between the two of them. Something was unfolding, and she didn't understand how the whole situation felt like it was picked up and turned full circle.

"Jackson, what's going on? What are you accusing my mother of? I don't understand." Lexie's voice became frantic.

Her mother squeezed her hand. "Lexie, calm down. You're drawing attention." Lexie looked into her mother's warm eyes. "I knew Jackson's father a long time ago. He was trying to help me escape a bad situation. Unfortunately, things didn't go as planned."

"You mean you shot him," Jackson accused.

"I didn't kill him." Beth looked across the table into Jackson's dark eyes. "I swear it. I had no reason to kill Officer Finley. He was helping me escape an impossible situation. I owed your father everything."

Jackson narrowed his gaze. "Why should I believe you?"

Her mother took a deep breath and rubbed her forehead. "I didn't kill your father, but I was the one who killed his partner."

"What? Mom?" Lexie asked in disbelief.

"Rosh isn't dead," Jackson said with a heavy scowl upon his face. Lexie had never seen his anger boil so hot under his skin. "He's alive and well and insists you are the one who killed my father."

"Officer Rosh isn't dead? But...of course he would point the finger at me. He's the one who killed your father."

"You're a liar," Jackson seethed.

"He betrayed us all. I can prove it," Beth insisted.

"How?" Jackson gripped the edge of the table so hard his knuckles turned white.

"You let me and my daughter go, and I'll make sure you have all the evidence you need."

"I can't let you go." Jackson shook his head.

"Jackson…you promised me," Lexie spoke up.

Jackson rubbed his hands down his face and turned toward her. "I didn't promise anything."

"Yes, you did." Lexie smacked her hands on the table. Many of the faces in the diner turned toward them with Lexie's outburst, their interest piqued. "I trusted you," Lexie said with a quieter tone, but the emotion was still heavy in her words.

"Jack," Dane called out as he stood up suddenly from his seat. There was only one reason Dane would acknowledge him. Jackson swung his attention toward the door to see a black car pulled up in front of the building.

"Did you tell Officer Rosh you were meeting me?" Lexie's mother asked in a panic.

"What's happening?" Lexie asked.

Jackson pushed himself out of the booth and pulled out his gun. Panic exploded inside Lexie. This was not how she imagined her reunion with her mother. She still had no idea what was happening. A couple of screams erupted in the room as people noticed their weapons. Two more cars pulled up directly in front of the diner.

"What's happening?" Lexie asked with wide eyes as they watched men exit the vehicles through the front windows and enter the diner.

Lexie's mother grabbed hold of her arm. "Oh God," she whispered as her grip became almost painful.

The waitress froze when the armed men started to pour in the entrance. They were here to cause trouble, and anyone who laid eyes on them knew the dangers that would soon follow.

The waitress's fear spilled from her as she visibly shook. She dropped her pot of coffee, and it shattered over the floor. The dark liquid splashed across the black and white tiles running along the floor until it pooled against the shoe of the nearest man who entered. The waitress retreated behind the counter, tears streaming down her face. The men walked in and took various positions around the diner. All the customers looked terrified as they cowered in their seats, too terrified to move. Dane and Teddy both had their guns aimed toward the men.

A man walked in, dressed in a suit and tie. Everything about him spoke of money and power. From his suit to his well-manicured appearance, he was a man that was accustomed to giving orders. Lexie could feel the cold shift in energy as his polished shoes crunched the glass upon the floor. His gaze fell on her, and she shifted uncomfortably in her seat. Her mother's nails would surely leave a mark as she refused to lessen her hold.

"Don't even think about pulling the trigger." The man looked at Jackson with a challenging expression.

"Fuck you, Stodden," Jackson replied with malice. He seemed unfazed by all the weapons now aimed at him.

Lexie gasped when she realized this was the man she had read about in her mother's journal, the man that very well might be her father—John Stodden. Waves of nausea hit her as she placed her hand against her throat.

"Tell your men to stand down," John commanded. "I'm sure you don't want any of these lovely people to be killed." John held out his hands, indicating all the people in the diner. A few whimpers could be heard around them as well as a small child that began to cry. "I know who you are, Jackson Finley. As much as I despised your father, at least he knew what side of the line he stood on. I'll advise you to stand down or you'll meet the same fate as your father."

Lexie watched Jackson clench his jaw. She knew he was struggling to remain in control of his emotions. "I'm surprised to see you here. From what I hear, it's not your style." Jackson refused to lower his gun as he looked at John over the barrel.

"I agree that these are not usual circumstances." John placed his hands in his pockets casually.

Jackson didn't back down, despite the fact that he knew he was outmanned and outgunned. Lexie didn't understand how he could seem so confident in the face of danger. She, on the other hand, wanted to crawl under the table. His bravery astonished her.

"It's been a long time, Mary. Or should I call you Beth?" John's attention slid over toward her mother.

"What are you doing, John?" Lexie's mother's

demanded. Her voice was strong considering the fact she could feel her mother tremble.

"Taking back what's mine." John raised his brow. Though he remained perfectly composed, Lexie knew he must be angry with her mother with their history. It scared her how cold and unfeeling he seemed. He almost appeared to be amused by the situation.

"Nothing here belongs to you," her mother said, narrowing her eyes in contempt.

John dismissed her mother's words, letting them roll off his impenetrable cold, dark shell.

"I know the circumstances are not ideal, but it is nice to meet you, Lexie," John stated with a certain charm that was surely a key to his success and power. The way he looked at Lexie, she could understand how people could be drawn to him, but she knew the truth behind those deceiving eyes. He was the embodiment of a trickster.

"How do you know my name?" Lexie asked.

"I know a lot of things." John extended his hand toward her. She looked down at it and made no move to accept. Her instincts screamed to retreat.

"Don't fucking touch her," Jackson demanded, raising his gun. All of Stodden's men shuffled forward with their guns trained on him.

"You're outnumbered." John raised his brows. "You and I know how this works. You're going to lower your gun and let us walk out of here."

"I can take you down before anyone of these shitheads gets a round off," Jackson said coldly.

"And if a stray bullet happens to hit a poor bystander...are you enough of a cop to care about the innocent, Jackson? What happens if Lexie gets hurt because of you?"

Jackson's gaze flashed toward Lexie. She could tell he was struggling with the truth of John's words. There was so much torment in his dark eyes.

"I believe you just revealed your weakness." John smiled confidently.

"And you being here reveals yours," Jackson countered.

"That's where you're wrong. I have no weakness."

"You're full of shit."

John began to look impatient as he glanced at his watch. "Stand down and I promise Lexie won't get hurt."

"She's not yours, John. Leave her out of this," Lexie's mother demanded. The calm, collected woman Lexie had known her entire life was stripped away to reveal something altogether different.

There was a flash of anger so deep and volatile in John's expression it dropped the temperature of the room before he composed himself as he smoothed his tie. "If Lexie and Mary come with me, Lexie's friends will be spared." John nodded toward one of his men. Lexie's eyes followed to see someone pull Stephanie and Evan out of the back of one of the vehicles visible through the diner window. They both looked disoriented. Their arms were tied and their mouths covered. Lexie gasped in terror as she watched her friends manhandled by John's men.

"No!" Lexie cried when Stephanie's eyes locked

with hers through the window. "Don't hurt them."

"Fuck," she heard Jackson mutter under his breath.

Lexie couldn't take her eyes off Stephanie and Evan. The man who pulled them out of the vehicle had a gun trained on them. Stephanie was in tears, and Evan barely contained his anger. Lexie was terrified he would do something to get himself killed. Evan was never one to think through a situation, always diving in head first.

"I'll go." Lexie swung her attention back toward John. "I'll go with you if you promise not to hurt them."

CHAPTER SIXTEEN

Twenty-Three Years Ago...

Mary Connors

Mary ran her fingers through her hair, straightening her silk nightgown. Looking at her reflection in the mirror, she took a deep breath. Her hands paused on her stomach, rubbing gently as she sought strength. She needed to be strong for her baby. She had known for weeks now that she was pregnant, but she had not spoken a word about it to anyone. Her stomach was still flat and did not tell of the secret she held tight, but soon this would change. Knowing this, she needed to make her move.

The plan was made, and she was about to set it into motion. She walked toward the large mahogany bar that was lined with John's favorite spirits. All were worth more than she would ever consider paying for a bottle of liquor. She ran her fingers over the labels and selected an opened bottle of whiskey. Pouring a generous amount in a glass, she tipped it to her lips. She let the harsh liquid swish around her mouth before spitting it into the sink. She pulled a small baggie out of her garter belt. It was filled with crushed sleeping pills she had been saving. She poured it into the drink and used her finger to stir it. When she could see no remnants of the powder, she wiped her finger along her neck and down the front of her nightgown.

Mary leaned against the bar and stared into the amber liquid. She had been dancing with the devil for far too long. "Please let this work," she whispered. She picked up the glass and ignored the fear that twisted her insides.

Mary knocked on the large wooden doors that led into John's office. He had been home for hours now, working away in his office, while she tried to gather the nerve. He would normally have had several drinks by now and would be starting to unwind from his stressful day, or so she hoped.

For the last few weeks, she had been playing her part perfectly. When she discovered she was pregnant, she knew she could not fall apart. She forced herself out of bed, forced a smile upon her face, and forced the image of love and adoration toward John. She swallowed all of her hatred, knowing this moment would come.

"Come in," John called distractedly. Mary took a deep, shaky breath. Her heart raced so fast she felt nauseous. She turned the knob and let it swing open. Mary ran her hand along the doorframe and conjured a playful smile on her lips. "Mary." John looked up from his work, the scowl falling from his face as he leaned back in his chair.

"I've been waiting for you." Mary stepped forward, making herself stumble slightly. "Oops…" She giggled at herself.

She watched a smile form on his lips as he watched her walk toward him. She was wearing his latest gift to her—a red silk nightgown that barely covered the curve of her bottom, matched with a black garter set. His eyes traveled up her body as she approached. An appreciative sound rumbled from his chest.

Mary deepened her smile. It was moments like this that made her remember why she fell into his trap. Monsters shouldn't be so beautiful. "I'm a lonely girl," Mary drew out, biting her lip as she leaned against his desk.

"We can't have that." His smooth voice washed over her, as he assessed her appreciatively.

"Do you want to know what I have been thinking about?" Mary ran her fingers along the edge of John's desk as she walked around to stand in front of him.

He glanced at her legs before looking up, his desire painted all over his perfectly evil face. "What is going on in that pretty little head of yours?"

Mary leaned down and pulled his bottom lip into her mouth before giving him a gentle bite. She sat on his lap while looking mischievous. Mary tipped her glass up to her lips and pretended to take a drink before handing the glass to him.

He took it without question, his normally suspicious mind drunk on lust and the illusion she painted for him. He tipped the glass to his own lips and took a long draw as he watched her unbutton his shirt. Mary moved slowly, fumbling the buttons as she maintained the illusion that she was drunk. She wanted to make sure she stalled long enough for him to drink enough of the whiskey to be effective. Mary kissed his chest, running her hands down his hard lines until she slid down on her knees. John drained the rest of the glass as Mary pulled his belt from his pants.

She knew how much he loved it when she took him in her mouth. She stroked him as she slid her warm mouth over him. John growled in satisfaction as he wound his hand through her hair, pushing into the back of her throat. Mary tried not to gag as he took pleasure in her. She squeezed her eyes shut and tried to make herself sound as if she was enjoying every moment, no matter how much she wanted to cry and run from him.

He suddenly pulled her hair, forcing her to stand. A whimper escaped her from his rough hold. He spun her around and yanked her nightgown up. Pushing her against his desk, papers scattered to the floor as she braced herself. She had to stifle her gasp as he pushed her chest down against the surface of his desk. The only thing she could think of was that she didn't give him enough—her plan was not going to work.

When he suddenly released her, Mary looked over her shoulder and noticed John rubbing his hands down his face. "What the fuck!" He shook his head before his eyes met hers. He stumbled, placing his hand on his desk. Realization dawned on his face.

"What did you do?" His eyes filled with so much rage that a chill raked over her, stealing her breath. Mary stumbled backward out of his reach when he grabbed for her. He missed and collapsed, taking most of the contents of his desk with him as he fell to the floor.

Mary looked down at his unconscious body. Fear froze her in place. She tried to calm her breathing as she covered her mouth to stop the sob that tried to escape. She needed to move; she only had so much time to act before he would wake up. She knew that she would not survive his wrath this time. She had pushed too far.

Mary quickly ran over to the wall where she knew he kept his safe. He had opened it a few times in her presence, and she hoped that what she thought was the combination would actually work. She swung the painting open to reveal the number pad. Mary stared at the numbers, trying to remember the sequence. She knew the first three numbers. It was only the last that she was unsure about. She had become really good at pretending that she was not paying attention when she was in his office. With her first few attempts, she was only rewarded with a flashing red light. Mary shuffled her feet and tried to calm herself down. She tried one more time, swallowing the panic that was rising in her throat. The safe clicked and then flashed green. *"Thank God!"*

Mary swung it open. Her eyes fell on stacks of cash. She ran over to the closet and grabbed a black duffle bag. Grabbing as much cash as she could, she stuffed it into the bag. She noticed a box of computer disks tucked it the side of the safe and a few folders. She grabbed them all, not sure what would be relevant or not.

Mary went back to John's desk, cautiously stepping over his still body. She could hear his long slow breaths, giving her some comfort that he was still unconscious. She wasn't sure how long she had. She tried opening his desk drawers, but some were locked. She ran her hand on the underside of the desk, searching for a key, only to turn up empty.

Leaning, she patted John's pockets. When she felt something that might be what she was looking for, she reached in and pulled it out. A small silver key sat in the palm of her hand. If she wasn't so terrified, she would have screamed out in triumph. She pushed the key into the lock and pulled the drawer open. A few more files sat in the desk along with a handgun. She picked up the folders and tucked them into the bag before picking up the gun. It felt heavy and cold in her hands. She wondered how many people John had killed with this very gun as she gripped it and pointed it at his still form. It would be so easy to pull the trigger and rid the world of John Stodden forever.

Mary's hands shook as she kept the gun aimed on John. Tears blurred her vision. They ran like a river as all the emotions she kept hidden for so long rose to the surface. Her sob broke the silence in the room. She wanted to pull the trigger, but she couldn't. She couldn't let her baby grow up without any family. She would be all her child would have and she wouldn't risk being locked away. She let her arms drop as she looked down at the man who took so much of her life away.

She wanted to trust Officer Finley. She needed to believe that he would keep her safe like he promised. She just needed to get this information to him, and he would protect her. She tucked the gun in the bag and ran from the room.

Mary dropped the bag on the floor in her closet and pulled on a pair of jeans, a sweater, and practical shoes. Mary wiped her face and took deep calming breaths. She didn't want to look anything but poised when she left.

She had to walk past the office door on the way to the garage. It was still quiet within, giving her reassurance he was still out as she quickened her pace. She threw the bag into the passenger seat of her car and started it. She pulled out of the garage, hoping it would be the last time she ever saw John again. Excitement started to fight with the fear in her chest. As she watched the condo disappear in her rear-view mirror, it didn't seem so impossible to escape John's hold.

Mary drove to the meeting place she had arranged with Officer Finley. It felt like the ten-minute drive took hours as she constantly watched for a tail. When she pulled up in front of the coffee shop, Officer Finley was waiting for her. She parked her car, grabbed her bag, and walked to his car. As she approached, he stepped out and opened the rear door for her. She slipped in without a word.

Mary knew that Finley would have his partner with him. She hadn't met him, but he sat in the passenger's seat and gave her a quick nod when their eyes met. He looked down at the duffle bag she had thrown over her shoulder. She pulled it tight against her side, unprepared to trust anyone but Finley.

His partner looked to be about the same age; they both looked to be early thirties, though she wasn't certain. Finley turned on the ignition and pulled out of the parking lot. They drove for a few minutes before the silence was broken.

"Are you all right?" Finley glanced back at her before his eyes returned to the road.

"I don't know." Mary sighed. She kept her eyes on the passing scenery as they drove.

"This is Matt Rosh, my partner. We're going to take you somewhere safe, and then we can talk."

They both seemed to respect her need for quiet for the rest of the drive. She had just made an enemy out of a very dangerous man, and she knew it would not be easy to betray him without serious consequences. She hoped she had made the best decision.

***

Mary looked around at the rundown interior of the motel room. The floral wallpaper was stained and peeling in sections. Her hands were wrapped around a cup of tea. It was almost too hot to hold, but her insides felt chilled and her body needed the heat. Finley and Rosh were both looking over the paperwork as she looked on, curious what information they entailed.

Mary rolled the name Rosh around in her mind. She knew she recognized him from somewhere but couldn't recall where. Something about him did not sit well with her. He seemed to be uneasy and constantly throwing glances her way.

"I want to keep the money." Both men looked up at her when she spoke. "When you find me a place like you promised," Mary directed her words toward Finley, "I want to keep the money to start my new life."

"I'm sure we can work something out." Finley didn't seem surprised by her request.

Mary took a deep breath and sipped her tea as she slipped back into her comfortable silence.

"John's reach extends much further than we realized. Look at these transactions. He's got contacts all over the country." Finley flipped through the nearest file as he absentmindedly scratched his chin. "Most of these accounts are from overseas." He was oblivious to his partner's anxious behaviour as he consumed the information.

"I'm gonna call this in. I will be right back," Rosh excused himself, slipping out of the room.

Realization hit her where she had seen Rosh before. She had seen him at the club. He was one of the men she had seen in the private rooms. Her stomach dropped.

"I've seen your partner before." Mary's fear spoiled her words.

Finley looked up at Mary questioningly. "What do you mean?"

"He was at the club…he was at the club the night I found the girl with the rose tattoo. When she was beaten and barely conscious. He knew about her. He was there." Mary stood up from the chair, her eyes on the door, fearful of his return.

"Rosh?" Finley face dropped in confusion. "Are you sure?"

Mary nodded her head, her eyes widening in fear. "He was there," she whispered. "Do you believe me?"

Finley shuffled through a few of the files. A scowl formed upon Finley's brow as he read the contents of the file in his hand. "It's hard not to when his name is listed in John's contacts." Finley dropped it on the bed. "*Goddamnit, Rosh!*" Finley racked his hand over his face.

They both looked at each other as footsteps neared. Finley's hand moved toward his gun as the door swung open, but he wasn't quick enough. Rosh's gun was already drawn and aimed when he entered.

"Don't move, Finley," Rosh ordered as he kicked the door closed behind him.

"What the fuck, Rosh? We've known each other for years," Finley said in disbelief. "We're practically family."

"Yeah well, things change."

"Why'd you do it?" Finley pleaded, seemingly desperate to find insight into his partner's betrayal.

"It doesn't fucking matter why I did," Rosh snapped, his demeanour becoming unraveled.

"How'd he get you to turn on your badge?" Rosh didn't answer as he stared down the barrel of his gun at Finley. "You're gambling again, aren't you? If you needed money, you could have asked me."

"Fuck you, Finley. You and your perfect family can go fuck yourselves. I'm not your little project to

209

fix." Rosh waved the gun at the files laid out on the bed. "I'm not letting you take this in. My name is tied to those files, and I'm not fucking going to prison."

"I'm sure we can figure something out."

"It's too late. You think I'm the only one in our department that John's sunk his fucking teeth into? If I don't make this disappear, someone else will." Rosh's grip tightened on the gun.

Finley's whole body tensed. "Don't do this."

Mary backed against the wall. She knew something horrible was about to take place. Finley had confiscated her gun when they arrived at the motel, and she had no way to protect herself.

"Goodbye, Finley," Rosh said in a cold, stagnant voice.

Finley made a move for his gun, but he didn't have a chance against Rosh, whose weapon was already trained on him.

The sound of the gun rang out in the room. Mary didn't realize she was screaming until the sound faded from her lips.

Finley dropped to his knees; his gun dropped from his hand before he collapsed on the floor. Mary saw the bright red color seep into the carpet as she stood frozen in fear. She looked up and noticed Rosh moving toward her.

Mary spurred her feet into motion. She jumped across the bed in an attempt to evade him, but he was too quick. He grabbed her leg and pulled her backward. Mary managed to land a kick to his chest and slip from his grasp, tumbling to the floor next to Finley's body.

Her hand landed in the scarlet puddle that now saturated the carpet. Mary gasped as Rosh grabbed her by the hair. She tried to fight him, grabbing for anything to hold onto to give her leverage against his pull. Her hand touched something hard; when her fingers wrapped around it, she realized it was Finley's gun. Holding tight, she wrenched her body around and pointed it at Rosh and pulled the trigger.

His eyes widened in shock. He rolled off the bed and collapsed on the floor with a strangled breath. Mary didn't waste any time. She grabbed for all the files on the bed. She threw them into the bag with the money. She knew she needed to take them for leverage. She needed to keep her head if she was going to survive this.

Grabbing the box of disks off the desk, she tossed them in and zipped up the bag. She could hear Rosh moaning as he remained slumped on the floor. She grabbed the car keys and slipped out the door.

Mary now knew she could not count on anyone but herself to save her baby.

CHAPTER SEVENTEEN

Jackson

"Did you honestly think your little security detail would stop me?" John boasted as he looked past the barrel of Jackson's gun. This man truly thought he was invincible. Jackson's finger itched to pull the trigger and end the sick bastard. "It only took a moment to apprehend Lexie's little friends. Your men never even saw us coming."

"What about my mother?" Lexie asked John, tears welling in her eyes, as she kept glancing through the window at her friends.

"She's not fucking going with you," Jackson said to John, reaffirming his grip on his gun. All the men around him moved in. Jackson couldn't care less about the men pointing their guns at his head. The only thing he could see was John in his sights, on the side of the gun he wanted him on.

John ignored Jackson, turning toward Lexie. "Your mother and I have unfinished business, Lexie."

"You can't hurt her," Lexie demanded.

A shout outside drew everyone's attention. Evan had tackled the man who had them hostage to his gun, shoving him into the side of the car. Stephanie was knocked to the ground, and Evan struggled against his bindings as he threw his body into the armed man. A shot went off during the struggle.

Lexie screamed out; her mother shoved her to the ground and withdrew a gun she had tucked away. Beth barely had the gun raised when one of John's men knocked it from her grasp. The force of the hit threw her backwards into her seat. Lexie's scream echoed through the entire building before a flurry of action followed suit.

Jackson aimed at John, but one of his men threw himself in the way and his bullet lodged into the other man's chest. Jackson was tackled by a man beside him, but he managed to get a grip on his gun, twisting it from his grasp as his fist contact with the man's face. Lexie and Mary were pulled out of sight by a few of John's men.

"Get the girls, Dane!" Jackson screamed out as he struggled. Shots started firing throughout the room, followed by a sea of screams by the bystanders. He couldn't even see Dane and Teddy through the chaos that erupted. A sharp, raw sting tore across Jackson's shoulder that burned like fire. He knew the feeling well. It was not his first time being shot. He could still manipulate his arm, which gave him a good indication it was only a flesh wound.

Jackson grabbed hold of his attacker's head and brought it down on the edge of the table with as much force as he could manage. Blood sprayed over the front of his shirt as the man slipped from his grasp and fell to the ground. He wasted no time grabbing for the gun of another, twisting the man's arm so his gun was aimed at his own chest. Jackson pulled the trigger, releasing two rounds into the man. Blood sprayed from his mouth before he fell.

Jackson ducked for cover as a bullet rushed past him. "Lexie!" Jackson called out. He lost sight of her. Teddy approached him from the side as Jackson knocked over a table for some cover. Teddy had a gash on his forehead; blood ran down his face and dripped off his chin. "I lost Dane. He was trying to get the girls." Jackson leaned up and unloaded his gun at the remaining men still firing. He noticed Lexie struggling against one of John's men trying to pull her toward the exit.

"Fuck!" Jackson screamed out in frustration. "Find Mary," Jackson ordered Teddy. Most of John's men were already pulling out. He ducked back behind the table to avoid gunfire.

"Lexie!" Jackson screamed.

"Jackson," Lexie called back desperately. Jackson threw his empty gun on the ground and grabbed another from his holster before he stood up with his gun aimed. He jumped over the table and toward the man that still ushering Lexie toward the door. He aimed, his focus snapping clear and true before he pulled the trigger. The man was thrown back by the force of the blow.

He need to get to Lexie; he couldn't let John have her.

A sudden blast caught Jackson off guard, his

eyes blurred, and he stumbled to the ground. Lexie was so close. He could still feel her near him. He frantically grabbed for her, but he was too disoriented. His feet refused to cooperate. His ears rang, drowning out the cries from the people in the diner.

"Lexie," Jackson tried to scream, but he couldn't hear his own voice. He pulled himself to his feet. His surroundings snapped back into focus just in time to see Lexie and her mother being forced into the back of one of the cars. Jackson grabbed a gun off the ground and ran outside. He aimed for the tires of the vehicle as it pulled away, but the other car drove toward him. He barely managed to jump out of the way just before it collided with him. He unloaded a few rounds into the windows before it tore out of the parking lot.

Jackson took off toward his car. Swinging the door open, he slipped in behind the wheel. The passenger side door opened, and Evan slipped into the car.

"Get the fuck out!" Jackson spat angrily. He had no time to waste.

"I'm coming." Evan pulled the door shut awkwardly because his hands were still tied behind his back.

Jackson shook his head and stepped heavily on the gas, and the car jolted to life as he sped after the cars. He saw Teddy come running out of the diner, but he was already in pursuit.

"You let them take her. You were supposed to protect her. She trusted you," Evan hollered angrily.

Jackson pulled his blade from his boot and held

it out for Evan. "I'll get her back."

"I swear to God, if something happens to her, I will kill you," Evan seethed.

"If something happens to her, you won't have to." Jackson turned toward Evan, locking eyes. Evan twisted in his seat to grab the blade Jackson offered. He immediately began working on the bindings, only taking a moment to cut himself free.

Jackson tore down the street, paying no mind to controlling his speed as he drove with determination. When one of the black cars came into view with his handiwork that had destroyed the back window, it was an easy target. Jackson floored the pedal, swerving around the last two civilian cars between him and his target. Car horns blared in response to his invasive driving as he forced his way toward the black car.

Jackson crossed the lines of the road and forced the driver toward the shoulder. "Shit!" Evan muttered as he braced himself on the dash. The sound of his car scraping against the other made his head throb, but he needed to stop the vehicle. His shoulder burned painfully as he held on tight to the steering wheel. He needed to find out where they were taking Lexie.

The car finally hooked onto the shoulder and lost control, spinning off the stretch of road and down into the ditch. Jackson slammed on his brakes, coming to a stop and kicking up a cloud of dust around the two cars. Jackson grabbed his gun and swung his door open. He barely missed a bullet that caught the roof of his car. Jackson aimed his gun and shot the gunman in the head. The side of his cheek sprayed against his door window before he dropped to his knees and then landed face first into the dirt.

Jackson approached the car slowly with his gun readied. The dust slowly began to settle, and he noticed there was no one else in the vehicle. Jackson stepped over the man's body, looking for a phone or anything inside the car that would be helpful. There was nothing. He flipped the man's body over, looking for identification or anything to give him direction, nothing.

"Fuck!" Jackson screamed out in frustration. He unloaded a few more rounds into the dead man's body.

"Where the fuck is she?" Evan screamed. He rounded the car, looking down at the dead man at Jackson's feet.

"Not here," Jackson bit off in irritation.

"Where then?" Evan raised his hands.

"I don't fucking know. If you quiet the fuck down, I might be able to think."

"Fuck you, Jackson. This is all your fucking fault!" Evan shoved Jackson backward into the open door.

Jackson clenched his jaw, trying to curb his anger, but it flared hot. He couldn't contain the emotions that suddenly suffocated him with the realization that Evan was right. It was his fault that Lexie was taken. He knew what evils John was capable of. He had studied the man's files for years, wanting to solve his father's last case. Swinging his fist toward Evan, he connected with Evan's jaw, causing him to stumble backward. He was not going to let Evan put his hands on him. Evan regained his footing before bringing his fingers up to his lip to see blood. He spat on the ground before he threw himself at Jackson. Evan's fist connected with Jackson's stomach before he could twist out of his path.

"Stop, Evan!" Jackson screamed. "Get the fuck off me. I need to get back. I need to figure out how to get Lexie back. I don't have time for this shit." Jackson shoved Evan backward. Evan wiped his mouth with the back of his hand, taking a deep calming breath before he nodded in surrender.

Jackson jumped back into his car, raking his hands down his face before he hit the steering wheel with his fist so hard that pain shot up his arm toward his shoulder. He noticed the blood that saturated his shirt and dripped down the back of his arm. "Shit. This is fucking great!" He had forgotten about his injury.

Evan slipped into the passenger seat, and Jackson threw the car into gear. The car was a decoy to allow the others to get away. He fell right into their trap, and it infuriated him beyond measure.

"Why do you have to keep hitting me in the face?" Evan asked angrily as he looked in the mirror. "Fuck." Evan used his sleeve to stop the blood that seeped from his lip.

"'Cause you keep pissing me off."

Jackson drove at full speed back toward the diner. He needed to figure out a plan, and having Evan next to him did nothing to clear his head. He couldn't stand him.

Jackson swung his car back into the diner parking lot. He could hear sirens in the distance. A few rattled customers lingered in the doorway and were startled by his approach. He jumped out, ignoring the extensive damage to the body of his car. The entire driver's side was marred beyond repair. Many of the customers were hovering outside the building now, awaiting the authorities' arrival. Most looked to only have minor injuries.

He walked past an older man, trying to calm his shaking hands long enough to light his cigarette. He looked ready to pass out as he leaned against the wall. Jackson recognized him from before the attack. He had sat a couple tables over, his attention on his newspaper as he sipped coffee and ate a slice of apple pie. The man's eyes widened when they looked at Jackson. He knew that Jackson was involved in the dramatic turn of events that brought the violence from the pages of his safe paper to the world around him, where the threat was real and inescapable.

Jackson walked past him and into the open door of the diner. A sullen mood was painted on all the faces of the people lingering inside. People were slowly getting to their feet, still skittish that the threat would return. He only noticed a few fatalities.

Jackson spotted Teddy, motioning him over. "Where's Dane?" Jackson asked as he approached. Other than the blood seeping from his head wound, Teddy looked to be in good condition.

"Fuuuccckkk," he heard Dane moan. He looked down and saw his friend slumped against one of the booths. Blood saturated his shirt from a wound on his side.

"He'll live." Teddy shook his head. "He's just being a fucking baby." Teddy tried to sound light, but Jackson could tell he was feeling the weight on his shoulders.

"Give me…my gun. I'm gonna shoot…this fucker." Dane's words clenched his teeth through the pain.

"What the fuck happened?" Jackson ran his hands over his face.

"I don't fucking know. This was supposed to be a closed meeting."

"Pete and Josh?" Jackson asked, looking for their backup who had their eyes outside.

Teddy shook his head. His eyes said it all without having to speak a word.

Jackson turned on his heel and walked back outside. Teddy followed on his heels. Two police cruisers pulled into the lot as he walked toward Pete's car. Jackson didn't know Pete and Josh well, but they were both dependable officers. He knew Josh's wife was expecting a baby in a few months, and the thought made the news hard to bear.

Jackson grabbed the door handle of the car and swung it open. Both Pete and Josh were slumped over in their seats, gunshots to the head. Jackson squeezed his eyes shut and slammed the door closed. "Fuck!" he yelled.

Two more cruisers pulled in, and the officers exited their vehicles with their guns drawn. "Put your hands up," an officer called to them. Both Teddy and Jackson looked at each other before raising their hands.

"They automatically think it's us because you look like a shady motherfucker." Teddy smiled wickedly.

"And you look like a fuckwad," Jackson retorted without humor. He was still reeling with anger about having lost Lexie to John.

"I've been called worse." Teddy shrugged. He was the type who seemed to let everything roll off his shoulder and turned to humor in all situations.

Two officers approached with their guns trained on them. "My badge is in my pocket," Jackson said impatiently as the officers neared.

"Turn around and put your hands on your head," the officer ordered.

Jackson turned around with an irritated sigh. He grabbed Jackson by the back of the shoulder. "Don't move."

"Right pocket," Jackson offered. The officer pulled Jackson's out and opened it up. "Can I put my hands down now?"

"Can you please tell me why you are outside your jurisdiction? And what the hell is going on here?"

Jackson dropped his hands and took his wallet from the officer.

"I'll fill him in. Why don't you go check on Dane?" Teddy nodded as he flashed his badge to the officer.

Jackson headed back toward the entrance. The only people remaining inside were the victims that were too injured to walk. Jackson heard the sirens of the ambulance pull into the parking lot. A few more people had managed to exit the building, and police officers were assessing the damage. Jackson flashed his badge when their eyes fell on him in question. "Dane, how you holding up?" Jackson said, kneeling in front of his friend.

"It hurts like a fucking bitch," Dane moaned. His hand pressed to his side was covered in blood.

"The paramedics are here now. It shouldn't be long before we get you patched up."

"You know what this means, right?" Dane turned his icy blue eyes on Jackson.

"Yeah, it means the fucking traitor is someone we know." Jackson looked down at his hand. Blood dripped from his fingers and splattered on the floor.

"Looks like you need to get checked out too."

"Just a scratch," Jackson dismissed.

Jackson turned when someone approached. Evan came to stand next to him, blood still smeared across his lip. Bruising had already formed under his eyes from the first time Jackson punched him in the nose.

"I'm gonna find Lexie and her mother," Jackson said with complete certainty.

"And Stephanie. They took her too," Evan said, deflated.

"Shit." Jackson shook his head. He had completely forgotten about Lexie's friend in the commotion.

A couple of paramedics approached them. They assessed Dane's wound before placing him on a gurney to transfer to the hospital.

The female paramedic took a quick look at Jackson's shoulder. "You'll need stitches," she said as she grabbed some gauze out of her kit.

"I got it." He took the gauze from her hand and pressed it on his shoulder.

"What about you?" She turned toward Evan.

"I'm good." He raised his hands. "Just a few cuts and bruises."

She nodded before moving on to the next patient. Jackson walked over toward their table. He kicked a broken dish and some debris aside, noticing Lexie's purse. A sickening feeling swirled in his stomach with the thought that he had no idea where John had taken her. All the consuming thoughts that normally haunted him were pushed aside. He needed to make sure Lexie was safe. He needed to find her and bring her home.

CHAPTER EIGHTEEN

Jackson

"Almost done. You're gonna have a nice scar," the doctor said, pulling the last stitch through the skin on Jackson's arm. The bullet had torn a deep gash in his shoulder.

"Yeah, story of my life." Jackson took a deep breath. He couldn't concentrate with all the scenarios running through his head about how the course of events was going to unfold. The cute redheaded nurse stood behind the doctor, her eyes lingering on his shirtless chest. Jackson didn't miss the way she bit her lip and the subtle tells when a woman had sex on her mind. She ran her fingers along the neckline of her uniform. Her breath quickened and her pupils dilated just a fraction. This woman was walking sex, and the doctor seemed oblivious to her wildfire needs. Part of Jackson wished he could step back into his old shoes before Lexie came into his life and turned everything upside down. He could take the nurse

224

and walk away without ever thinking about her again. He loved living day to day, his singular goal of revenge in mind and his sexual wants scratched by whoever was convenient when he felt the need. Now his insides were twisted with new emotions—fear and desperation. Everything in him was pulling him toward the desire to hunt down the man who took Lexie. Revenge for his father's death was now filing in line behind Lexie. The way she looked at him had him spun close to insanity. He wanted to be in her world. It was an impossibility that his heart refused to give up on.

"Well, you're lucky it wasn't any worse," the doctor said. He was an older gentleman with graying hair, and reading glasses perched on the end of his nose. He dropped the instruments he used to apply the sutures on a metal tray, along with the bloodied gauze. "That should do it. Keep it clean and dry…" the doctor began before Jackson cut him off.

"Yeah, yeah, I know the drill. I'm in a bit of a rush, Doc."

The doctor raised his brow at him before handing off the used medical supplies to the nurse. The nurse's eyes continued to drink him in as she collected the tray.

The idea of bending the nurse over the examination table had its appeal. It even caused his dick to flicker to life, pulling at his thoughts, but it was not the redhead he was envisioning. It was Lexie with her petal soft skin and captivating beauty that mesmerized him like a bug drawn to a light. He had no choice but to be pulled to her on every level, even knowing what the outcome would be. A happy ending was never in the cards for him—something he had long since accepted. Though now he realized he might no longer have the blissful, unattached pleasures of sex because Lexie had infected him with something that had taken hold—like a drug, pulling him toward something he never wanted but now feared he could not live without. A man like him should not know the meaning of gentle, but now it was all he wanted. He wanted a gentle life with Lexie.

Teddy leaned against the doorframe of the examination room, crossing his arms. He had a small bandage on his forehead but was otherwise uninjured. He seemed to pick up on the sexually beaming nurse, and an amused smile crossed his face.

"How's Dane?" Jackson asked, grabbing his shirt off the examination table.

"He's still in surgery."

"Hear from Giles?" Jackson pulled his shirt over his head.

"Yeah, he wants us to come in immediately, as in yesterday."

Jackson rubbed his forehead roughly. "Fuck. Let's go." Brushing past Teddy, he walked out into the hall.

"I wish my nurse was a hot little number like that."

"Yeah well, be my guest." Jackson waved back toward the room he just exited.

"Fuck man. What's got into you? Does your girl have a magic pussy or something?" Teddy asked.

Jackson spun around and shoved Teddy into the wall, pinning his arm against his throat. "I told you she's fucking off limits. Don't talk about her like that!" Jackson bit off before he realized he shouldn't have lost his temper. He was wound too tight. There were too many uncertainties when it came to Lexie. Too much risk involved now. He released Teddy, raked his hands through his hair, and kept walking.

"Sorry, man. I didn't mean it," Teddy said as he caught up to him, his hand against his throat.

"Let's forget it."

"We'll find her, Jack," Teddy said seriously. Jackson looked up into the eyes. Teddy was always so carefree, wearing a smile wherever he turned, but now that façade was stripped away. The real Teddy behind the front was standing beside him, the Teddy that understood Jackson in a way that others couldn't.

"Let's go."

***

The precinct was more familiar to Jackson than his own apartment. He found more comfort sitting at his desk with his files in front of him than he did surrounded by the blank walls of his home. He had moved into his apartment five years ago and still had yet to unpack most of his things. Boxes were still stacked along the wall, the only furniture in the space was a small table with a few bottles of whiskey as a centerpiece, and his king-sized bed was the lone piece of real furniture in his bedroom.

His clothes were stacked on top of boxes. He had no desire or know-how to make a place feel like a home—a luxury he never had. He barely spent any time within the walls. It was a place to sleep and nothing else. Since he had taken his oath he had existed as nothing but his job.

The only things pinned to his apartment wall were all the evidence he collected on John since he found his father's file. Jackson spent the entire night staring at it, hoping he would see something he missed. Anything that would give him some insight as to where John would take the girls but he only came up empty. He needed to find out where to start, and unfortunately the one person who would have insight into the head of John Stodden was a person he hoped to have never crossed paths with again.

"Giles is waiting for you in his office," Mera said as they pushed through the front glass doors to the precinct.

"Thanks, love." Teddy smiled wickedly at the middle-aged woman. Mera had been with the precinct before Jackson earned his badge. "Do you have a kiss for me?" Teddy leaned over her desk, wiggling his eyebrows.

She rolled her eyes at Teddy's flirtatious behavior. "Honey, you couldn't handle my kisses." She was a loyal employee, as dedicated as they came. She thought of the officers as her children. She was as sweet as candy to those she loved. She was always showing off the latest pictures of her grandchildren and making sure everyone was taken care of, but should anyone step on her toes or cross someone she cared about she turned vicious as a snake.

"Hold onto your hats, boys. Giles is ready to blow today," Mera called after them.

Teddy spun back around, unable to leave Mera's statement alone. "I got something for you to bl—"

"Teddy! You keep your dirty mind to yourself. I'm too old for such talk." Mera shook her head with a chuckle. "Run along."

They walked past rows of desks that lined the way to Giles' office until someone stepped into their path—a woman with shoulder-length chestnut hair and deep chocolate eyes. She wore a tight-fitting shirt and a blouse. Jackson couldn't help but be impressed by her long lean legs that led to a pair of heels. It was definitely questionable whether they were proper for the office. She gave Jackson a once over before she honed in on Teddy. "Teddy," her voice bordered on whiny. "You didn't call me."

"Sorry, sweetheart. I was off saving the world." He gave her a wink. "I'll call you when things die down."

She watched after them with a pout. "Okay, but you better call me."

"Gives me something to look forward to." Teddy turned around and placed his hand against his chest, flashing her a smile that was always a deal closer.

"Tell me, Teddy, have you fucked every single female in this office?" Jackson shook his head.

Teddy turned his lips down thoughtfully. "Almost. I can't get past the fact that Trish in evidence can grow a better mustache than me."

Giles called Jackson and Teddy into his office as

229

soon as he noticed them approach. "Shut the door," Giles said as soon as they entered the large office. Large bookcases flanked the wall on either side of his mahogany desk. A large window was directly behind his desk, with the blinds drawn tight. Giles was approaching sixty, his hair having long since turned white. Jackson had a hard time picturing him any other way. He had always looked the same to Jackson for as long as he could remember. He kept it trimmed short with clean lines. He was a man that held power and presence. He was the perfect embodiment of what a chief of police should be.

"So the little rendezvous was a complete clusterfuck." Giles leaned back in his chair and assessed the two with a sigh. "Why is it that nothing goes according to plan when the three of you are involved?"

"Someone tipped off John. He was expecting us," Jackson informed him. Giles looked at him thoughtfully.

"Are you sure you weren't followed?" Giles asked.

"Positive. I made sure of it," Jackson confirmed with confidence.

Giles ran his hands through his hair, tapping his fingers on his desk. "No more playing by your rules, Jackson. I've got two good men dead."

"They never saw it coming. John's men took them out before they could even warn us." Teddy rubbed the back of his neck. The truth hung heavy in the air of the loss they endured. No one could deny errors were made.

"Someone leaked the info, Giles. It has to be

someone close." Jackson placed his hands on Giles' desk. He looked into the eyes of the man who had been the closest thing he had to a father. Giles was the person who pulled him off the street and gave him something to work for.

"I know. The problem is that until this went down, everyone in the circle was a man that I would have laid my life down for on their word." Giles shook his head in disbelief.

"Do you have an idea who?" Jackson asked.

"Let me deal with that. You need to be debriefed. I just got off the phone with Haffey before you arrived. Let's just say her feathers are a little ruffled," Giles informed them.

"You mean she's on the war path?" Jackson corrected.

The phone rang, and Giles sighed before he grabbed the receiver. "Giles." Giles looked toward the door as he listened to the person on the other end of the line. "Thanks." He hung up the phone and raked his hands down his face. "We'll finish this conversation later, but until then, anything about this case goes directly from you to me. Understood?"

"Yes sir."

Jackson swung the door open and walked out into the hum of voices floating around the room. The volume of the room dropped as eyes followed their exit from Giles' office. Desks were situated throughout the large room, people constantly moving around the space. It looked like chaos, but it was a well-oiled machine that made up the some of the working parts of the precinct that enforced the laws of the city.

Jackson's gaze found Josh's wife talking to one of the officers. She clutched the desk, tears streaming down her face. Her belly was swollen with a child that would never know its father. Sadness twisted like a knife deep in Jackson's stomach. He knew what it was like to grow up without a father, and his heart went out to her child.

"I'm handing this file over to Haffey, Jackson. John is her case."

"I'm not walking away from this, Giles. It's my fault they were taken. I'll get them back." Jackson meant business. There was no way he was going to walk away now. Giles knew better than anyone the reasons Jackson entered law enforcement. The case that was unfolding before him was what he'd been working toward and the very thing Giles was trying to keep him away from unsuccessfully, and now that Lexie was involved, Jackson was out for blood on a completely new level. "I'm going to Belhaven."

"I'll keep him out of trouble, Giles," Teddy interjected.

"Yeah, I figured as much. I told Haffey to expect you two," Giles said with a sigh.

"That must have made her shit bricks," Teddy said with a thoughtful smile.

"You don't know the half of it." Giles shook his head.

"Thanks Giles," Jackson added. Detective Haffey was a determined woman out for Jackson's head and deservingly so. He knew she would not be happy to see him.

Giles looked thoughtfully at Jackson before nodding his head. Jackson knew he had more to say about the whole situation that Jackson put himself in, but he had a pregnant widow to deal with.

"Go see Anders for debriefing before you leave." Jackson watched Giles approach Josh's wife. The news had been delivered, and now her grieving had begun in full force. He knew Giles would feel heavy guilt for Josh's death. They all did, and seeing the life that Josh was torn from made it worse. Jackson had met Josh's wife at the last Christmas function thrown at the precinct. She was an elementary school teacher and had been Josh's high school sweetheart. He couldn't remember her name, but he never forgot a face.

She grabbed hold of Giles and collapsed under the weight of her grief, and Giles wrapped his arm around her for support. Jackson knew now more than ever that his purpose in life was to bring an end to John Stodden, but now he also had to make sure that Lexie came out of this unharmed. Though if Mary Connors really did kill his father, then hurting Lexie would be unavoidable. He would not be able to let his father's murderer walk away even if it meant Lexie's hatred.

CHAPTER NINETEEN

Ten Years Ago...

Jackson

"Keep the fucking light still, Nate!" Jackson snapped in a harsh whisper as he shuffled through papers in the desk drawers of the darkened office.

"If we get caught, he's gonna kill us," Nate said skittishly as he tried to still his shaking hand by using both hands to grip the flashlight. "Like seriously fucking kill us. Slowly and painfully, I might add," he whispered.

Jackson stopped to glare at Nate when he knocked a stack of papers to the floor. "If you don't get your shit together, I'm gonna kill you myself, you *fuck*."

"I've seen what Seth does with people that steal his shit." Nate's voice broke. He continually looked behind him to the door and out the window, watching the street. "And we are in his *fucking house* with his goons in the *next fucking room*."

234

"Shut the fuck up or they'll hear you. We can get out a lot faster if you keep the light down so I can see what I'm doing," Jackson bit out in frustration.

Nate shone the light up to see Jackson's face, which currently displayed his annoyance. "Give it to me, for shit's sake, and go wait outside."

"Yeah, yeah, here." Nate passed the flashlight quickly as if it were suddenly scorching to touch. "I'll keep watch outside." He couldn't get out of the room fast enough. Jackson could only shake his head as he heard Nate knock something over in his hasty retreat from the house.

"What the fuck was that?" Jackson heard one of the guys in the next room holler. Jackson flicked off the flashlight and ducked under the desk when he heard footsteps from the next room.

"Turn the fucking TV down!" one of the men shouted as he moved down the hallway outside the office. Jackson waited and listened, hoping that Nate made it outside. He knew they were in deep shit if Seth found out they were in his house; he did not want to be responsible for bringing that shitstorm.

Jackson sighed in relief when he heard the footsteps return to the room across the hall and the television return to its deafening volume. Jackson placed the flashlight in his teeth and searched through the remaining drawers until he found the bottom one to be locked. He quickly picked the lock and pulled it open to reveal bags of blow. Black was right: Seth had been skimming his product. He found a file in the drawer with Seth's contacts. Taking the papers out, he folded them up and shoved them in his pocket. Closing the drawer, he looked up when he noticed headlights turning in the driveway. Jackson quickly turned off his flashlight and grabbed the scattered papers that Nate knocked to the floor and placed them neatly back on the edge of the desk. He didn't want to raise any flags when Seth returned home. He knew that eventually Seth would realize the papers were missing, but he would be long gone at that point, and Seth would have no one to point a finger at.

Jackson moved quickly down the hallway as he heard footsteps upon the front step. The smell of rotten food reached out toward him as he slipped past the kitchen. Even in the dark he could see old takeout boxes stacked upon the counters. The sound of keys in the lock met him as he stepped out of the line of sight from the front entrance. Jackson listened to the voices of the people entering the house. Seth's voice was the first to register with Jackson, and the other was a willing female, eager to show Seth her talents. Satisfied he had retrieved all relevant information needed, Jackson slipped out the window and pulled it closed behind him. The window pane was immediately set aglow as they entered the bedroom he'd exited from. His feet were silent as he made his way through the backyard and over the fence, where a very anxious Nate awaited him.

"Holy fuck, that was close," Nate spat out as Jackson's feet landed on the other side of the fence.

"We're good." Jackson smiled, satisfied, waving the papers.

Nate was a good guy. He was the closest thing to

a friend that Jackson had if he would even really call him that. Nate liked to pretend he was fearless, but in the face of actual danger, he ran with his tail between his legs or sacrificed his dignity to save his hide. Jackson didn't know if he could actually count on Nate, but then again he never let himself count on anyone. He depended on himself and no one else.

The two of them walked down the street, discreetly and quietly, avoiding any attention that would alert anyone they were in the area. The evening air was heavy with humidity, offering no relief from the heat even with the sun far from sight. Jackson looked up at the sky; it reflected the city lights and made it impossible to see the stars. It wasn't long before the stretch of houses began to change to storefronts and bars as they moved from the residential streets into the inner workings of the city.

"I need a fucking drink. It's hot as shit out tonight," Nate said before he veered into a corner store. They walked into the brightly lit interior. The only person that inhabited the store was the clerk behind the desk, who eyed them suspiciously over his paper. His thick eyebrows scowled at them as he took in their presence. Nate walked toward the back and grabbed a soda from the fridge in the back. "You want one, Jacks?"

"Water," Jackson hollered without looking up. He was eyeing the magazine rack with half-dressed women stretched out on the hood of a car, both very pleasing to the eye. Nate returned from the back; holding his up to shield his face, he placed the bottles on the counter.

"These and all the cash in the register," Nate said firmly to the cashier. Nate laid the barrel of his piece on the edge of the counter. The cashier's face drained of color as he stood up from the stool. His paper fell to the ground, forgotten in his panic.

"*Fuck,* Nate." Jackson rolled his eyes. "Thanks for the heads up." Jackson deadpanned as he pulled his hood up to conceal his face.

The man opened the register with trembling fingers. His glasses slid down the length of his nose as sweat beaded on his face. Jackson watched Nate and couldn't help but wonder where this confidence was when he was practically pissing his pants in Seth's house.

Jackson grabbed some licorice from the candy shelf as he watched the man fumble the money before practically throwing it at Nate. He held the door open as Nate dove toward the exit. They moved with quick steps to get away from the area.

"You are a fucking piece of work, you *shithead*." Jackson shoved Nate's shoulder as they jogged down the street, keeping to the shadows. "What happened to keeping a low profile tonight?"

"Sorry, man. I got bills to pay, you know."

"Yeah, whatever. I hope you're ready to run." Jackson noticed the police car approach, and its lights began flashing on cue.

"Shit," Nate spat, turning on his heel to run. "That was fast."

"This way," Jackson called as he ran down an alleyway. "Do you ever think things through?" Jackson scaled the fence and flipped himself over.

The sirens were loud, and the officer was yelling for them to freeze. Once they were out of the officer's line of sight, they split up in separate directions. Jackson knew the drill…when the heat rained down, it was important to split up and find a place to hide out or lay low until the coast was clear. Jackson couldn't recall the amount of times he found himself in this very situation; lately he was always watching his back. It felt natural for him to run from what was coming for him. He heard an officer in pursuit stumble as he tried to follow Jackson over a fence.

Jackson pulled off his hoodie and threw it in a dumpster as he passed by before turning the corner to a street peppered with people enjoying the nightlife the busy street offered with its pizza shops and corner stores that sold cigarettes to anyone willing to pay regardless of age, causing it to be a regular hangout for the underage smokers. A group of girls drew his attention. He recognized one immediately. They all turned and smiled ridiculously at his approach. He couldn't hear their whispers, but the look in their eyes told it all, and he would use their adoration for his benefit.

"Hey, Jackson." Bethany bit her lip seductively as he held her gaze and walked up to her. The other girls giggled and stepped back in welcome as he walked into their circle.

"Ladies. I just wanted to tell Bethany something." He took Bethany's hand, lacing his fingers through hers. He pulled her into a kiss without explanation. He had barely spoken to her before, but he had seen her watching him. Bethany melted into his chest, her hands grabbing the material of his shirt. She moaned against his mouth before he pulled away.

Bethany's face was almost as red as the shirt she was wearing. Her long brown hair was dishevelled from his fingers and her lips were swollen. She had a satisfied, awed expression on her face that made his lip turn up in a smirk and made his groin tighten in response.

The officer rounded the corner, breathless from the chase as he scanned the street. "Evening, Officer Mack," Jackson said when the officer looked at him. Jackson knew the officer; in fact he knew most of the officers at the precinct. He pulled Bethany to his side and wrapped his other arm around a petite blonde with a severely low neckline that Jackson took advantage of as he towered over her.

"Jackson, you little shit. How is it whenever there's trouble, you're lurking in the shadows?" The officer spit on the sidewalk, clearly out of breath as he held his side.

"Now, now, Mack, is that any way to speak in front of these beautiful young ladies? I'm disappointed." Jackson shook his head in mock disapproval.

"Run along, girls," Mack ordered as he approached Jackson. The girls quickly scattered.

"I'm taking you in this time," Mack warned.

Jackson couldn't help but smile at Mack when he tried to make his stout figure look intimidating. Jackson still towered over the overweight man. The officer grabbed his radio and called for his partner to bring the car around.

"I didn't do anything. I was just hanging out with my girls. You saw me."

"You have been getting away with this shit for way too long," the officer scolded.

Jackson just rolled his eyes in response. "Sorry to disappoint you, Mack. I will try really, really hard to be good next time," Jackson said sarcastically. The patrol car pulled up to the curb, and Jackson noticed the street was suddenly bare.

"Come on," he sighed as he grabbed Jackson's shoulder and directed him toward the car. "Get in, and no trouble or I will cuff you, I swear to God, Jackson."

"Yes sir." Jackson saluted.

"That's the smartest thing I ever heard you say," Mack said as he closed the door after Jackson climbed into the back seat.

"Jackson," the driving officer acknowledged.

"Wells," Jackson responded in kind as he leaned back against the seat for the silent drive to the station.

When they pulled up to the front of the precinct, Jackson's stomach knotted tight. It had been years, but every time he was brought in he got that same sadness as memories haunted him. Mack opened the door and noticed Jackson's hesitation as he looked up at the building. "You wouldn't have to keep coming back here if you would get your shit together…at least not in the back of a police car, not like this." Mack let out a defeated sigh. "Come on."

"Good times," Jackson bit off as he climbed out of the car.

All eyes fell on him when they pushed through

the front doors. All of the blue suits looked at him with the same looks of pity that caused anger to heat his blood. He clenched his jaw tight and kept himself in check as he followed Mack and Wells. They led him back toward Giles' office, a place he had frequented many times over the last few years.

"Thanks, Officers," Giles said as they walked in. Jackson sauntered over to a chair. Dropping down, he swung his feet up onto the top of the desk.

"You want us to stay?" Wells asked as they lingered in the doorway.

"Not necessary." Giles gave them a tight smile and nod as they closed the door behind them. Giles pushed Jackson's feet off the desk.

"Your eighteenth birthday is four months away," Giles said, running his hands through his hair.

"I'm so honoured you remembered," Jackson said shallowly.

Giles gave him a cold look before he shook his head. "Once you turn eighteen, I'm not gonna be able to save your ass anymore. You'll start suffering the consequences of your actions, Jackson. I can't keep you out of jail if you keep trying to put yourself there."

"I never asked for your help," Jackson muttered.

Giles ran his hand down over his face, clearly tired. His sun-darkened skin did not hide the lines that were beginning to form around his eyes. "You have to clean yourself up. Everyone understands how hard it was for you, but now it's time to grow up and be the man your father could have been proud of."

"I can't be that." Jackson picked at the arm of the

chair he sat in. He was uncomfortable with the topic of his father. His chest felt too tight and the room too small to contain him.

"Why not? Why are you throwing your life away?" Giles pleaded with him in a stern voice.

"What life?" Jackson looked up and met Giles's eyes. He knew Giles could see his anger. The one emotion Jackson could still access, it was wound so tight around him; it fueled him and drove him to carry on. "Tell me, Giles." Jackson grabbed the name plate off his dark wooden desk. "Why do you care what happens to me? I sure don't give a fuck." He tossed it back up on the desk. Giles watched it tumble over a stack of papers and come to rest haphazardly on his desk.

"Because you were dealt a shitty hand and I owe your father at *least* that. I can't stand seeing you going down a road that you were never supposed to be on in the first place."

"Well, you can clear your conscience, Giles. This is me letting you off the hook." Jackson waved his hands.

"It doesn't work that way, Jackson. I care what happens to you. I can't just stop."

Jackson put his hand over his heart. "I'm touched, really," Jackson said sarcastically.

Giles reached for his phone. "I'm calling Mark and Jenna." Jackson frantically moved to put his hand over Giles' on the receiver.

"Don't." Jackson cringed when his word sounded like a plea. "I'm not going back there."

Giles tried to read Jackson's expression, searching for something, when he noticed Jackson's arm. His shirt was pulled up, revealing a deep purple bruise that marred his skin. "How did that happen?" Giles asked as Jackson pulled his sleeve down. "Let me see."

Jackson shook his head. He didn't want to have this conversation with Giles.

"Take your shirt off, Jackson."

"Sorry, Giles, I don't swing that way."

"Shirt off now!" Giles ordered, anger slipping into his usual calm demeanour.

Jackson stood up with a defiant look on his face. Giles was tall, well over six feet, but Jackson met him eye level. Reaching over his shoulder, he pulled his shirt over his head, revealing a map of colors encompassing his entire torso. He didn't say a word. He didn't need to.

"Jesus," Giles gasped. "Why didn't you say anything?" Jackson watched Giles's eyes gloss over as he raked both hands down his face.

Jackson looked down at his chest; the bruises had been there so long he didn't remember what it looked like without them. It didn't hurt anymore; it had been a long time since he could feel the sting of the impact of Mark's belt or fist. The beating was ultimately not the reason why he would never return. It was what Jenna did when she crawled in his bed to offer comfort.

Jackson watched Giles wipe his eyes and lean against his desk, his head down. Jackson just stared in disbelief, wondering why Giles would shed tears for someone as worthless as him.

"You're coming home with me, Jackson. We are going to turn your life around."

CHAPTER TWENTY

Lexie

Lexie huddled next to her mother in the back of the vehicle. One of the men had tied her hands and placed a cloth over her head. She had no idea where they were taking them. They had driven for what felt like hours. She clung to her mother, pressed close beside her. The vision of Jackson before the deafening flash exploded haunted her. She had been trying to get to him before the world was suddenly picked up and dropped in front of her, and she didn't know which way to turn. Someone had grabbed her and pulled her out of the diner before she could process what was happening. Something about Jackson found a hold deep inside her, and very real fears tightened her chest painfully. She wanted to know he was safe. She wanted to know who he really was and how he knew her mother.

The need to ask her mother about Jackson's accusation clawed at her. She knew her mother was terrified by the almost painful hold she had on her hand. The words in her diary spoke of much hatred and fear of the man that now held them captive. She worried for her mother, knowing what John was capable of. She hoped desperately that Stephanie and Evan escaped unharmed. She needed to hold onto the hope that they all would survive this. It was the only thing keeping her sane.

Lexie felt herself drifting to sleep as the car pressed on; the only sound she could hear was her own breath, accentuated by the cloth over her face. She tried to force her eyes to stay open, but her body was exhausted, and as time passed she found it harder and harder to stay alert.

Lexie's eyes snapped open when the car engine cut off. Adrenaline surged through her blood as the door opened and cool air rushed in. The temperature felt like the early hours of the morning before the sun rose. They must have driven all night. Lexie felt a hand clap on her arm and pull her toward the open door. "Get out," a man barked close to her ear.

"Lexie!" her mother called out, trying to keep a hold on her, but Lexie was pulled out of the car. Her fingers slipped from her mother's, and she was left grabbing at nothing. "Where are you taking me?" Lexie tried to gain traction by planting her feet firm and pulling against the man's hold.

She spun around when she heard her mother struggle. "Mom!" Lexie screamed. The man pinned her arms against her chest and wrapped his arm around Lexie's waist, pulling her feet from the ground. "Mom!" Lexie screamed again, but she could feel herself being carried away from her mother's fading voice. Lexie tried kicking her feet, but the man did not even react to her efforts.

"Okay, okay, you can let me down. I'll walk." Lexie didn't want to be manhandled anymore, and she had a hard time trying to pay attention to her surroundings while he carried her. "I won't do anything stupid. You're hurting me."

"If you try to run I'll catch you, and I promise I'll make you regret it." His voice was hard and unfeeling.

"I'm sure you will." Lexie tried to adjust her shirt the best she could with her hands tied. "Where's my mother?" she demanded.

"Walk." He pushed her forward, ignoring her.

Lexie growled in frustration. "Can I take this cloth off my face so I can see where I'm going?"

"No. Keep walking." He nudged Lexie between the shoulder blades with what felt like his gun.

"Is John here?"

"Walk," he demanded again. His patience seemed to be wearing thin. The sound of elevator doors grabbed her attention.

"Where are you taking me?" Lexie refused to move her feet. She turned around and grabbed for the cloth over her eyes. "Mom!" Lexie screamed.

The man pinned her against the wall and repositioned her blindfold. "Trust me when I say you do not want to cause any more trouble for your mother. She's in enough already." He leaned in so she could feel his hot words against her neck.

Lexie nodded her head. "Okay," she whispered when she could get her voice to cooperate.

He grabbed Lexie by the shoulder and pushed her inside the elevator. She tried to remain brave, but she couldn't stop the thought that she might not return from wherever she was going. She had no idea why John brought them here, though she was certain it was not for a happy reunion.

When they exited the elevator, they took a few turns before he told her to stop. She heard him open a door before leading her inside. "You'll wait in here," he said.

"For what?" Lexie asked; she could feel her voice shake slightly from fear. When Lexie heard the door click closed and then the turning of a lock, she wasted no time grabbing for the cloth from her head. Fresh air washed over her, and she took a deep breath. Brushing the hair out of her face, she immediately went to work trying to untie the knot binding her hands. Using her teeth, she managed to loosen it enough to pull her hands free.

Lexie looked around the room. It looked like an upscale hotel room with a large king-sized bed sitting in the center of the room. Abstract paintings of flowers brought color into the otherwise monochromatic color scheme of varying shades of grey. A large television sat on an entertainment unit, and a small mini bar was situated in the corner of the room. It was a nicer hotel room than she had ever been in, but it did not take much to overshadow the outdated motels she had been in. She immediately searched the room. There was no phone, and the windows that overlooked untouched forest land were sealed shut. She tried the door, but it was locked from the outside.

"Damn it!" Lexie ran her hands through her hair before sitting on the edge of the bed. She wrapped her arms around herself and took a deep breath. She needed to stay strong if she was going to get through this. She closed her eyes and thought of Jackson, trying to figure out where he really fit in this huge puzzle that became her life. Even knowing he kept secrets from her about her mother did not change the fact that she missed him and yearned for the comfort of his embrace. The thought that something happened to him carved at her chest, causing a slow ache to gnaw at her insides. For so long she was lost and felt like her whole life was slipping through her fingers as pain consumed every aspect, but then Jackson showed up. He felt solid and real. He made her remember she was still alive. When she held onto him and looked into those dark, bottomless eyes, she felt like the world finally came back into focus. He numbed her pain, and she needed him right now.

Lexie kicked her flip-flops off and curled up on the bed. She looked down at her bare toenails, and a sharp pain twisted in her chest, making it hard to breathe. She wondered if this was her punishment for betraying Alex. That night she let Evan come to her bed was the beginning of this unraveling. Alex had been a huge light in her life—he deserved better than her. He gave his life for her, and then she let herself fall apart. She wasn't worthy of the love he gave her.

Alex deserved better than this broken girl, who couldn't stop her betraying heart from having feelings for another. The problem was that she could not turn back time and convince him that she was not worth his life.

CHAPTER TWENTY-ONE

John

John opened the car door and stepped out into the hotel underground parking. He ran his hands over the sleeves of his suit jacket, making sure it was spotless. He straightened his tie and noticed a red spot on the light grey fabric—blood. He ran his finger over the stain before he snapped his head up and narrowed his gaze on the nearest man. He was a new recruit, and John couldn't remember his name nor did he care. The man did nothing to earn his attention; he was just a number. "Get me a new tie," John demanded as he loosened and pulled it from the collar of his shirt.

"Yes sir," the man answered eagerly before he turned on his heel and left.

Jason Flint, who had been riding in the same car as John, rounded the vehicle. He was a man who had earned a place next to John's side long ago, his loyalty paid in blood.

Flint held his phone against his ear as he listened. "Good," he said before disconnecting the call. "Jacobs and Rayner are holding Mary in the conference room, awaiting your orders. They just took Lexie to the room you requested." Flint slid his phone into his pocket.

John had known Flint for years, since their school days. Trust was something John didn't offer lightly because he had made too many enemies in this lifetime. Many had worked years to fall into John's good graces, but he always made sure to keep people at arm's length. He knew this life well enough to know that everyone had a price and ultimately everyone stood for themselves. Loyalty was a dying breed with the exception of Flint. He and Flint were the closest thing to family either one of them had. Some had even mistaken them as actual brothers before because of their similar appearances. He was the only man John trusted enough to show his back to.

"Good."

"Masten is here to see you. He arrived twenty minutes ago." Flint raised his brows, knowing John would not have the patience to deal with him right now. Masten had been a thorn in John's side for a long time, a man who blurred every line ever drawn. He was dangerous and unpredictable, but luckily the man had tastes that allowed John to exert power over him. They had established a working relationship many years ago that benefited them both, and he knew the terms of their arrangement did not leave much room for Masten to have a change of heart.

Lexie's friend was pulled out of one of the other vehicles. Rogers, one of John's security crew, was struggling to keep her under control. She was kicking and fighting him like a trapped animal. Even blindfolded with her arms tied behind her back, she managed to kick herself free of Roger's hold. John was tired and didn't have the tolerance for her disruption. She was obviously not scared enough and needed a reminder that he was the one in control.

John walked over toward her and grabbed the material from her head. He wrenched her head back by her hair, causing her to gasp out in pain. "You certainly have a death wish, sweetheart." John pulled his gun from his holster tucked neatly under his jacket and placed it under her chin, pressing it into her soft flesh, knowing that it would leave a bruise. It would be a reminder that he had power over her.

"Please..." she whimpered as tears began to run down her reddened cheeks.

"If you value your life and the lives of your friends, you will shut the fuck up." John watched the fear of his words bloom in her wide eyes. Her fight deserted her with the threat of death. Fear was like a drug to John; he could taste it in the air, and it made him hungry for more.

"Take this one to Masten. She seems to fit his profile." John released her, and she stumbled backward. Rogers grabbed her by the arm and headed off toward the elevator with the subdued girl.

***

John walked into the conference room to see Mary seated in a chair, her arms tied and a gag placed in her mouth. Her beautiful blue eyes flared with rage when she saw him enter. Her words were muffled by the fabric tied tightly in her mouth. After all these years, she still looked every bit the prize she was in her youth. Now her features carried a maturity to them that did not distract from her beauty. He hated knowing he had missed so much time that should have been his. The thought of another man touching her, having her, made his blood boil. She was his, and she would not have the opportunity to escape him again…he would make sure of it.

Jacobs and Rayner were in the room, awaiting his arrival as they made sure she remained under surveillance. They both knew John would not tolerate any mistakes in handling her. Rayner was intimidating with his wide shoulders, large build, and tattoos that stretched up his neck and along his jawline. A cigarette hung from his mouth as he stood dutifully awaiting John's orders. The man instilled fear in everyone. He was a wolf among dogs. Jacobs was not as large, but with a violent past there was no line he wouldn't cross, a trait that came in handy many times in John's dealings. His eyes revealed a man who had taken a dip in the sea of hell and was not afraid to show his wrath.

"Mary," John said, trailing his fingers along her cheek. "Did you think I'd forget about you?" His touch was almost loving as he caressed her skin, trailing his fingers down her neck and along the neckline of her shirt. "That you could just run away and forget about me?"

"Fuck you." Mary's words were muffled through the fabric. She pulled back from his invasive touch, leaning back as far as she could in the chair.

John grabbed her face and squeezed tightly, eliciting a whimper. Leaning in, he made sure she was looking him in the eye. "Is she mine or *his*?" His voice was harsh and demanding.

Mary narrowed her eyes but refused to make a sound. She tried to pull free of his hold, but his grip was too strong.

"It's easy enough to find the truth." John released her. She squeezed her eyes shut before she tried to speak.

"Untie her gag." John motioned toward Rayner. The large man stepped forward and loosened the fabric.

"Please, John, don't hurt her," Mary whispered as she pulled against the ties on her arms. "She doesn't know this life. She's innocent of all this. Please let her go."

John let a sly smile curl his lips before he looked down at his hand. He ran his fingers over the rings that lined his fingers. He slowly turned them, lining the emblems up on the inside of his open palm. He looked up to see Mary watching him with a desperate plea in her eyes. John reeled his hand back and slapped his open palm across Mary's face. Her scream excited him. He had always revelled in the sound of her cries. It had been too long, and his groin responded in hot fury. Blood dripped from her lip, running down her chin and dripping on the exposed skin on her chest before sliding down toward her cleavage. His drank in the sight, like the sweet taste of liquor that warmed his stomach. He would never let her leave him again. She was his, and he would make her pay for turning on him.

"I want what you took from me," John said in a voice so cold it caused goosebumps to flash across Mary's skin. He could see in her eyes she would be willing to do anything to protect her daughter.

"I don't have it. I burned it all. I wanted to forget about my past."

John shook his head. "You are too smart for that, Mary."

Rayner cleared his throat when someone entered the room. John turned to see the man he had sent for a tie standing in the doorway with a new tie in his hand. John waved him in the room, holding his hand out to receive it. The young man had light hair that was in need of a cut. He couldn't have been more than thirty years old, with the look of hope in his eye that only youth held.

John looked at the tie. The fabric was rough against his skin, and a department store tag hung from the end of the tie. "Come here." John motioned him closer. "What is your name?"

"Marshall, sir," he said nervously.

John took the tie and wrapped it around Marshall's neck. John could feel him tremble beneath his touch. "Tell me, Marshall, do you think I look like a man that wears a department store tie for thirty dollars?"

"No...no sir. I am sorry, sir. It was the quickest

option."

John proceeded to tie it around Marshall's neck, straightening it to perfection before he grabbed the lengths of the material and pulled, wrapping it around his hands to gain leverage. Marshall gasped as the pressure on his neck made it impossible to breathe. "I don't care what you thought." John continued to tighten the tie around his neck. The young man grabbed hold of John's hands in an attempt to fight for breath. He tried to plead for his life as it was squeezed from him. Mary's screams rang out behind him as she pleaded for him to stop. She was always so soft, always pleading for him to be a better man. What she didn't know was that better men took what they wanted and demanded power. He was the better man. He climbed to the top of his world and would make all those under his feet know who he was. He was unstoppable, the very best of men.

John did not release his hold until all life was drained from Marshall's eyes and pools of nothingness stared back at him. When he let go, Marshall's body slumped to the floor and Mary's screams died away.

"Is she mine, Mary?" John demanded, reeling from the high of taking a life. He tipped her chin up and looked into her tear-soaked eyes. He searched those blue eyes that stole a piece of his dark heart so many years ago. He wanted to own her then, the very first time he saw her in that night club line up. Throwing that beautiful hair back and laughing like she had no cares in the world. It was then that she fell into his hands. He would never let her escape him again. "You don't know, do you?"

Tears fell from her eyes, down her cheeks, and mixed with her blood. "You can't have her," Mary sobbed. "She will never be yours, you sick bastard."

A sinful smile spread across John's face as he leaned in close to her. Her scent filled his senses once more. It had been too long. "You've never been more wrong."

Mary sobbed and tried to pull away from him.

"I'll give you some time to think, Mary. Maybe you will remember where you put what you took from me. Until then, I think I'll go get acquainted with dear, sweet Lexie. She reminds me so much of you." John trailed his finger along Mary's jaw and across her chin. When he pulled his finger away, it was coated with the blood from her lip. John brought it to his lips and sucked the coppery liquid from his finger.

"Stay away from her!" Mary struggled against the ropes; the chair scraped against the floor as she pulled desperately at the ties. John walked away, a cold chuckle leaving his lips.

He walked out into the hallway. The owner of the hotel owed John steeply, and when he could not deliver the funds, John found a way to make the situation benefit him. The grand hotel, bordering the edge of Sugar Hill, was only a short drive to Belhaven. It was a perfect location to stay under the radar, especially with some current rumblings of the new detective sniffing around his town. Belhaven had some changes in their police force, and the female detective was out for his blood. Until he found her weakness he had to lay low, especially now after the incident at the diner in Oxford. It would only be a matter of time before she got word of his involvement, if she hadn't already. John currently had men on damage control to keep any witnesses from talking. Most would be easy to persuade to keep their mouths shut. Fear was good motivation, but as for Jackson Finley and the other officers involved, he would have to take more extreme measures. The very thought made a smile curve his lips. John hated Finley's father, and he would take great pride in having his son meet the same fate.

Three levels of the hotel were blocked off for renovations for an extended period of time. It was the perfect place for John to conduct private business matters without drawing attention. John headed toward his room. Sliding the key into the door, he swung it open and walked straight toward his bar. He picked up his whiskey and poured a generous glass.

"There you are, love."

John looked over toward his bed to see Rebecca lounging on the bed. She was rousing for the day as she blinked sleepily at him. She slid her scantily clad body off the bed. Her blue eyes always had reminded him of Mary, but hers lacked the depth. After just coming from Mary he realized how different they actually were. The similarities were not close enough to appease him anymore. The thin strap of her dress slipped off her shoulder, exposing the swell of her breast as she sauntered toward him. "I missed you last night," she cooed before she ran her hands over his chest.

John drained his glass as he looked at her calculatedly. The differences between her and Mary almost disgusted him now. They stood out in stark contrast. Rebecca was oblivious to his thoughts as she leaned in for a kiss. John turned away from her approach; reaching for the bottle of whiskey, he refilled his glass.

"What's wrong, baby?" She let her hands fall to her sides.

John tipped the glass up to his lips and drained it again. "Don't fucking talk."

A scowl creased the skin between her eyes, and a pout turned her lips. John grabbed the strap of her dress and ripped the material.

A gasp of surprise escaped her. "I loved that dress," Rebecca whined. A frown pulled her lips as she looked down at what was left of the dress.

"I'll buy you another one." John set his glass down.

A seductive smile turned her lips. Rebecca was as shallow as they came, and money always brought a smile to her Botox-filled lips. She dropped to her knees. Looking at him with heavy lids, she unzipped John's pants. Her experienced hands pleasured him before she slid him into her mouth. She was well skilled in how to pleasure a man, but right now John wanted the control. He grabbed the back of her hair and pushed himself further until he could feel the resistance of the back of her throat, and she gagged around him. He loved the sound as she struggled to work with his demanding thrusts.

He grabbed hold of Rebecca's hair and wrenched her off the floor and threw her against the bed. His hand grabbed her by the neck and pushed her down into the mattress. He shoved himself into Rebecca's hot center, while thinking of his Mary strapped to the chair, helpless and in his control again after all these years. "Scream for me," John demanded as he brought his hand hard against Rebecca's backside. Unlike Mary, Rebecca found pleasure in his rough hands. He came fast and furious while she writhed beneath him.

CHAPTER
TWENTY-TWO

Jackson

Jackson pulled to a stop in front of his apartment building. He'd had a tail on him since he left the precinct. It didn't worry him—instead it irritated him beyond measure because he knew exactly who it was. He flexed his fists, praying for patience that he knew would never come. Jumping out of his car, he slammed the door and stalked toward the Civic, parked a few spots down the street. He grabbed the handle and swung the door open of the rusted grey car.

Evan sat behind the wheel. He threw his hands up in surrender. "Don't fucking hit me! I just need to talk to you."

"You are the last person I fucking want to see, let alone talk to right now." Jackson grabbed Evan by his shirt and wrenched him to his feet. He slammed him against the side of the car. "Don't. Follow. Me.

261

Go back to Freyview and wait for me to call you like I told you." Jackson released him and Evan stumbled, grabbing the side of the car for support.

He started for his building. He only had twenty minutes until he needed to pick up Teddy and no time to entertain Evan's stubbornness. He wasn't surprised when he heard Evan's footsteps following him. "You know I carry a gun, right?" Jackson called back over his shoulder.

"Yes."

"I will shoot you," Jackson threatened.

"I'm not leaving. I told you I need to talk to you." The tone of Evan's voice spoke of desperation. Jackson closed his eyes and took a deep breath before he spun around to face him.

"What?" he barked impatiently.

"I can't just sit here and twiddle my thumbs waiting. I need to find them. I need to find Lexie." Evan ran his hands through his hair. He looked terrified.

"How sweet. I don't care about your little fucking love story," Jackson bit off.

"Listen, I know she doesn't feel the same. I can live with that—but she's all that I have left of my brother."

"You have mistaken me with someone who gives a shit."

"I can shoot," Evan blurted. "I can help. I'm a good shot. I want to take that fucker down." He pulled out a gun that was tucked in the back of his pants.

Jackson rolled his eyes. "I'm a cop. You can't go waving guns around."

"I know you have a badge, but you don't convince me for one minute that you wouldn't cross the line if the opportunity presented itself."

"I don't have time for this shit. Take your toy gun and go home, Evan." Jackson spun around and pulled out the key to the front entrance of his apartment building. Evan insisted on following him inside, but Jackson proceeded to ignore him.

"Do you know where he took them?" Evan asked. He was close on Jackson's heels as he jogged up the stairs of his building.

"Not yet, but I will. Go home, Evan."

"I can't."

"Listen, Evan. You are a fucking junky," Jackson accused. "You would only get in the way."

"I don't want to be anywhere near you either, but you are the best chance I have of finding her. I need to make sure she's safe. I know you have feelings for her too. I can tell by the way you look at her."

"You're wrong. I don't do *feelings*." Jackson pushed his apartment door open and spun around. "Don't follow me." Jackson slammed his door in Evan's face.

Jackson headed straight toward his bedroom and grabbed a duffle bag. He threw all his necessities in before zipping the bag and swinging it over his shoulder. Grabbing his gun, he turned and aimed toward the doorway to his room when he heard movement.

"Whoa!" Evan put his hands up.

Jackson narrowed his eyes as he looked over the barrel of his gun.

"I know how to pick locks. I told you, I can be

helpful," Evan defended himself. "I'm going with you. I have to."

Jackson narrowed his eyes at Evan. He could see something in Evan's determined gaze that reminded him of himself. He tucked his gun back into his holster and walked toward Evan. He wound up and punched him in the face, causing Evan to slam back into the wall.

"Fuck, that hurt. God dammit. Stop hitting my fucking face!"

"I can't help it. It fucking annoys me. You get in my way at all, I will shoot you in the face next time. I will not save your stupid ass if you get yourself in trouble." Jackson walked past him and toward his door.

"Does this mean I can help you find her?" Evan asked, shuffling his feet behind Jackson. "Where are we going?"

"Bellhaven." Jackson spun around and looked back at Evan, who had his hand against his jaw. "You just need to promise me one thing."

"Yeah, what's that?"

"When I get Lexie out of there, you need to take her as far from me as you can."

"Done." The relief on Evan's face gave Jackson the urge to hit him again, but he clenched his fist and instead headed for the door.

***

"Who the fuck is this?" Teddy asked as he slipped into the front seat of Jackson's car. He turned to look at Evan sitting in the backseat. "Oh shit. You are fucking bringing Lexie's friend? You're shitting me, right?" Teddy looked at Jackson for clarification.

"Nope. He has a death wish, and who I am to deny his hopes and dreams?" Jackson turned his lips in a frown but was completely unfazed by the idea of putting Evan in harm's way.

"I take it Giles doesn't know we're playing babysitter." Teddy shook his head.

"If anyone asks, he's your baby brother who just earned himself a brand new shiny badge and we're breaking him in."

"Are you fucking serious, Jackson? Why?" Teddy shook his head.

"Because he knows I'll come regardless," Evan piped up from the backseat.

"We could just arrest him," Teddy offered with raised brows. "Lock him up."

"I never thought of that." Jackson rubbed his chin thoughtfully.

"Fuck no. Jackson already said I was in. I'll take care of myself." Evan leaned back in his seat. Jackson could feel Evan's eyes burning a hole in his back. As much as he wanted to kick his ass out of the car and speed off, he could see the determination to track down Lexie reflected in Evan's eyes. Being reckless was not new to Jackson. He didn't know why he should start playing by the rules now. If Evan wanted to get himself killed, he wouldn't stand in his way. The only thing Jackson cared about was crumbling the very foundation beneath John Stodden's feet and making sure that Lexie wasn't in the way when it all came crashing down. An ache formed in his chest when he thought of Lexie. Time was of the essence, and he had to find her now.

"And you thought Haffey was going to have your balls. Just wait until Giles finds out we brought a civilian with us on our field trip. Fuck, I love hanging out with you, Jacks. You always make for a good time." Teddy chuckled. "And why the fuck does he have to be my baby brother? Why can't he be yours?"

"Because you both have the same stupid look on your face."

Teddy shrugged, turning his lips into a frown. "Buckle up, baby bro. We don't want you to die before the guns come out."

"Shit." Evan grabbed his seat belt as Jackson tore out of the parking spot. Jackson's only thought was those sweet beautiful blue eyes that desperately pleaded for him before John's men took her. He would tear down the whole world to get her back. There was nothing that would stand in his way. A part of him needed to believe that she would hate him after discovering the truth about his intentions with her mother.

Solving his father's murder was above him; it was something he could not walk away from, even knowing that it meant that he would never again indulge in the sweet, beautiful pleasures her body offered him. Desires that flowed straight to his heart that roused only for her. He wanted to stare into those eyes that saw something he didn't know existed. He wanted to hold her, touch her, and smell her sweet scent until the end of days, but he was not a man who deserved that part of her. Lexie needed a man that knew how to love, that knew how to put a smile on those beautiful lips. He didn't know how to love. The only thing he knew was hatred, and eventually it would crush what he loved about her. She could never be his, and it made his anger that always swirled deep in his stomach flare hot and fiery.

CHAPTER TWENTY-THREE

Evan

Evan was restless in the backseat of the car, shifting constantly to ease the discomfort that grew in intensity as the hours passed by. He looked down at his hands—trembling. He grasped them together and swallowed the nausea beginning to claw at his insides. It had been too long since he had a hit.

"Are you feeling all right, man?" Teddy spun around in his seat to assess him.

"Yeah, I'm good." Evan wiped his forehead with the back of his hand. "I could use something for this headache."

Evan looked up and noticed Jackson's narrowed his eyes on him in the rear-view mirror. Evan knew he was going downhill fast if he didn't get a hit to ease the shakes that were becoming hard to hide. He could feel cold sweats begin to break out over his skin.

"What's your poison?" Jackson asked with an irritated tone.

"No, man, it's not that."

"What is your *goddam* poison, Evan? We can't do this if you are going through fucking withdrawal."

Evan sighed and leaned his head back on the seat. "Smack."

"Jesus," Teddy breathed out in a rush. "My little brother is not only a cop impersonator, he's also a junky. Fuck me. What's Mom gonna say?" Teddy shook his head.

"I know a place," Jackson said, throwing the car into a U-turn without any warning, jarring him.

"I'm gonna be sick," Evan mumbled with his hand on his mouth. Jackson slammed on the brakes. He was barely stopped when Evan flung the door open and stumbled out. The contents of his stomach spilled over the ground, but it did little to alleviate his discomfort. He took a deep soothing breath before walking back to the car. Evan didn't say a word as Jackson continued to drive with purpose. He needed this hit if he was going to be of any use to anyone. Jackson was right.

Jackson pulled up to a mechanic shop about twenty minutes later. A dozen rusted-out vehicles of various makes lined up along the property. One of the three overhead doors was open, showcasing three rough-looking men working on a white pickup. They all wore full sleeves of tattoos and looked anything but the typical mechanic. Evan would have bet his life savings that all three of these men spent time behind bars.

"Stay here." Jackson opened his door and approached the men. It only took a moment for recognition to show on their faces. Jackson knew these guys. The man closest to Jackson, sporting a full beard and shaved head, gave him a pat on the back.

"Who are these guys?" Evan asked Teddy, leaning against the center console.

"I have no fucking clue." Teddy began tapping his fingers on his knee. "Our Jackson likes his secrets."

Jackson disappeared in the building with the man that welcomed him, while the others remained watching Teddy and Evan closely.

"Whoever they are, they're scary as shit."

"Yep, that pretty much sums them up."

Jackson returned ten minutes later, walking straight toward the car. There were no waves or friendly send offs from the three grim faces watching Jackson leave.

"Here." Jackson threw a small black case into the backseat as he slipped inside and threw the car into reverse.

"Friends of yours?" Teddy asked. His eyes still lingered on the men as they drove away from the garage.

"My past," Jackson said curtly.

Evan's attention was solely on the small black case in his hands. He unzipped it and grabbed the small vial and one of the needles inside, ripping the packaging off. He set to work; he could feel the discomfort ease with the anticipation of what was to come. His body craved the drug like air to his lungs.

He pushed the needle through his skin, pressing the fluid into his bloodstream. The effect was immediate, and the suffocating feeling of being submersed in water washed away, and he was left feeling light and powerful. It was the reason he fell for the drug. He needed the distortion of reality to deal with the emotions of his life. The pain that strangled him every moment of every day seemed more bearable while under its effect, and for those fleeting moments he felt free. Though it was different now, he couldn't let himself drift away in the bliss. He needed his focus. He only allowed himself enough to be functional.

Evan looked up to see Teddy watching him. "One of my prouder moments." Evan sighed as he leaned back into the seat. He didn't even look in Jackson's direction. He just let the silence fill the car as he watched the scenery change.

Jackson's phone rang, breaking the silence. Evan listened as Jackson spoke to the caller. "Yeah, we couldn't stick around. We have to stay on the case. We're on the way to Belhaven...fuck you too...you do that...we'll check in with you later." Jason dropped his phone in the console. "Dane said we could all go fuck ourselves for leaving him in the hospital."

Teddy laughed and shook his head. "He shouldn't have gotten himself shot if he didn't want to miss the fun."

When they entered the border of Belhaven, Evan couldn't help but be intrigued. He had never been to the large city that drew people from all over for its nightlife and entertainment.

"So this is Belhaven, huh?" Evan leaned forward between the seats. Jackson had been quiet most of the drive, seemingly lost in thought.

"The one and only," Teddy replied with a smirk. "I got my first blow job in the washroom of…" He leaned closer to the window. "That night club." Teddy pointed at a rundown building with a few people lingering out front, cigarettes hanging out of their mouths and dark circles under their eyes. They looked as if they had just emerged from an endless night of drinking. Teddy turned back toward Evan, a satisfied smile on his face. "It was fucking awesome."

"Did you grow up here?" Evan asked curiously.

"Yeah, until my sister was taken. Then my parents picked up and ran." Teddy leaned back in his seat. His usual light-hearted mood was suddenly washed with mud. He splayed his hand out on the window and just stared at the passing city streets. It was strange to see Teddy in a solemn mood, radiating so much pain. Jackson reached over and gave Teddy's shoulder a squeeze.

"Sorry, man." Evan knew better than to dig into Teddy's past. It was the last place he wanted to be by the look of his face. He leaned back in his seat and watched the people walk up and down the street. He was used to his small town of Freyview; here everyone looked as if they came from different corners of the earth as they passed each other on the street. The sidewalks looked full of lonely people. He tried not to let his thoughts dwell on Lexie and where she was. The thought of her in danger made his heart race with fear. He needed to protect her.

He needed to make sure she was safe. He had already made too many mistakes, and he needed to start making things right. He owed his brother better than this.

Evan glanced up at a large brick building as Jackson pulled into a parking lot. The Belhaven Police Department definitely put the small town sheriff's department of Freyview to shame. The building and lot looked as if it consumed an entire city block.

Evan followed Jackson and Teddy into the building. They walked up to the main desk and asked the full-figured woman behind the counter where they would find Detective Haffey. The woman pushed her glasses up her nose, giving them a calculated onceover. "Who should I tell her is here?"

"Detective Finley," Jackson said impatiently. He seemed a bit uneasy, and Evan could tell he was not looking forward to this meeting.

"Just a moment." The woman sat back down and grabbed her phone.

Teddy leaned against the counter and picked up the woman's pen and began flipping it around in his hand. She snatched it away from him, shooting him a scolding look before she began to speak with someone on the line. Teddy turned around with a sigh, leaning against the counter like a bored child.

"She's in a meeting right now. She'll probably be about twenty minutes. If you'd like, you can wait for her in the blue chairs to your right." The woman waved her hand before she set back to her work.

"I'm gonna make a call," Jackson informed

273

Teddy and Evan, pulling his phone out of his pocket and walking off.

"Let's take a walk, little brother." Teddy slapped Evan on the back of the shoulder.

Teddy led them down the hall. "So tell me why Jackson is really letting you tag along?" Teddy asked with raised his brows.

Evan shook his head. "I don't know."

"It's the girl." Teddy seemed satisfied with his conclusion. "I never usually question Jackson. He can see the bigger picture better than any of us, but something is different, and I know it has something to do with Lexie. Do me a favor and don't get us killed because of your sorry ass." Teddy spun around and placed his hand on Evan's shoulder. "I'm serious. Don't do something stupid."

Evan shook his head. "I won't."

"Good talk." Teddy gave him a tap on the side of the face. "Wait here and keep watch. Let me know if anyone comes this way."

"What?" Evan asked in confusion as Teddy walked into an open office.

"Tell me how much you missed me," Teddy said to the attractive woman behind the desk. Evan barely got a glimpse of her before Teddy swung the door shut. He turned around and leaned against the wall with a sigh. Evan was feeling anxious and didn't want to hang around waiting for whatever Teddy was up to. He watched the minutes tick by and people walk up and down the hallway.

The woman they had spoken to at the front desk motioned for his attention from down the hall. He gave her a wave before he opened the door to tell

Teddy they needed to head back. He was not expecting the scene that met him. Teddy had the brunette bent over the desk with her shirt unbuttoned, her breasts exposed, and bouncing with each thrust as Teddy entered her from behind. She moaned and looked up to meet Evan's shocked expression. A gasp escaped her as Evan swung the door closed. "Holy shit." Evan erupted into laughter as he leaned against the door.

Teddy opened the door a few minutes later, slipping out before closing the door again. "Sorry, man. Give me a heads up next time. The woman at the desk wants us."

"She's fucking hot, isn't she?" Teddy pointed his thumb back toward the closed door. "I love a woman with no morals."

"Yeah, man." Evan shook his head. "From what I saw, she looked pretty exceptional."

"Let's find Jacks."

CHAPTER TWENTY-FOUR

Jackson

Jackson pushed the door open to the conference room and was immediately stung by the glare of Detective Haffey. She was bordered by pictures the familiar faces of John Stodden and his associates pinned to the white board. Papers and files were spread out over the massive table—content Jackson was dying to get his hands on.

"Finley," Haffey bit off harshly. There was no way anyone in the room could miss the poison in her tone.

"Always a pleasure," Jackson offered tightly. He was on thin ice as far as Haffey was concerned, and regrettably she called the shots on this case.

"Jackson has a fan club, I see," Evan whispered under his breath, and Jackson threw him an unamused glare.

"He made an office call but didn't follow up."

Teddy winked to Evan with a sly smile on his face.

"Shut the fuck up," Jackson spat quietly. He didn't have the patience for jokes. He was wound so tight he could feel the pressure on his chest. He needed to tackle this properly or Haffey would send him packing.

"Teddy," Haffey greeted. "Have you replaced Dane?" She raised her brow when she noticed Evan.

Teddy wrapped his arm around Evan's shoulders. "Dane got himself shot up. He's recouping. Meet my baby brother, new to the force and on his first assignment with the professionals."

"What happened to his face?"

"He's just clumsy," Teddy explained.

"Lovely. Do me a favor and keep him out of trouble," Haffey dismissed before turning her attention back toward Jackson. "Care to enlighten me why you decided to piss all over my case?"

All hope that she would set her anger aside fizzled out, and he was left looking into her fiery gaze. Haffey was a beautiful Latina woman; her dark hair hung loose around her shoulders, and her dark eyes held much wisdom as they glared angrily at him. Jackson had the liberty of discovering the extent of her anger six months ago when he, Teddy, and Dane were in Belhaven for undercover work. Their street smarts made them a draw for the undercover cases, and they were never ones to turn down a chance to kick up some dirt.

Jackson tipped his beer up to his lips and took a long draw. They were out celebrating with a few Belhaven officers for their successful case. Teddy and Dane were waging a game of pool. The bills were lined up on the side of the table, the pot for the winner to claim. One of them was leaving tonight with empty pockets.

Jackson chuckled and shook his head. Neither one of them could refuse a good bet even if it meant losing his rent money. Jackson drained his beer and set it on the bar, nodding to the bartender for another.

"Jacks, you play the winner," Dane called to him.

"Fuck you, guys. I'm drinking my money," Jackson said, grabbing the new beer the bartender slid toward him. A few other officers they had gotten to know over the last few weeks were mingling with them. A young office clerk from the Belhaven precinct was hanging off Teddy's arm, begging for his attention and eating up anything he threw her way. She was a pretty little thing if you liked the desperate type. Teddy loved the attention, and apparently even desperate fit into his type.

Jackson leaned back against the bar and stretched his legs out in front of him. Detective Haffey sat down on the empty stool next to him. She was hard to miss in a room. She had a fierce beauty with her dark, penetrating eyes. Jackson tried to determine what her perfume reminded him of, but he couldn't quite place it.

"To cleaning up the shit on the streets." Haffey held up her beer, and Jackson tapped his against hers.

"Cheers."

"You're not the betting type?" Haffey nodded

toward the pool table where Dane and Teddy were currently arguing about one of them cheating.

"Nope."

"Afraid to lose?" Haffey teased. It was strange seeing her without the uniform and strict demeanour she exhibited while in rank. She wore tight fitted dress pants that displayed exquisite curves that drew a man's attention like a magnet. Her white blouse flowed around her but dipped sinfully in the front, revealing she was blessed with all the curves that could cause a man to lose his way.

Jackson didn't even try to hide the fact he enjoyed the view. He had too many drinks warming his blood to ensure boundaries were kept intact.

"I don't want to take their money and have them sleep on my sofa because they didn't know when to quit."

"So you prefer to brood at the bar?" Haffey pulled at the label of her beer. She was always professional, but Jackson was good at reading people. He knew she was attracted to him; he also knew she was not the type to jump into bed without strings. She had warning labels all over her, but they blurred with each drink.

"I certainly do. It's working for me so far." Jackson looked into her eyes and watched her squirm. His libido had taken full control of his actions. The only thing he could think about was stripping the clothes from her body and losing his mind to the pleasures of a woman. "Can I buy you another drink?"

"If I have any more, I may not be able to find my

279

way home." Haffey bit her lip.

"I'll make sure you get home." Jackson waved the bartender over.

***

Haffey barely had her apartment door unlocked when Jackson grabbed her and carried her inside. She squealed in delight before wrapping her arms around his neck. Her lips pulled at the skin of his neck, nibbling his ear and jawline. Jackson laid her down on the sofa.

Grabbing the material of her blouse, he ripped the fabric open. Her moans fueled his blood as he pulled the cups of her bra down and pulled her beaded nipple into his mouth, grazing his teeth along the sensitive flesh. Grabbing the waist of her pants, he pulled them down the length of her legs. He was a man driven by instinct, a need that had to be satisfied.

Haffey ran her fingers under his shirt, exploring his flesh, making his blood rush in hot fury to his groin. Jackson pulled his shirt over his head and tossed it aside. She was already working on his belt. Jackson was barely free of his pants before she was guiding him toward her slick entrance. He reveled in her eagerness. Her hands were frenzied as she pulled at his flesh. He plunged deep inside her, massaging her swollen clitoris as he continued to thrust. Her full breasts bounced with their movements as he continued pushing and pulling at her hot center. Her legs tightened around his waist as she unraveled, screaming out in pleasure.

Jackson grabbed her hands, pinning them over her head. He let himself follow her, emptying his need inside of her, leaving him with only a few seconds of peace until his thoughts started chipping away at the fog.

Haffey pulled him against her, claiming his lips, but he could not bring himself to feel it. He was sated, and as much as he tried to scrape up some warmth toward her, his heart was too broken to try and pass off anything as real. He wasn't sure how he was supposed to feel, but the only thing he could think of was leaving. He needed to escape before she realized how cold he could actually be. He wanted to spare her that.

She ran her fingers along his shoulders. "That was wonderful."

Jackson leaned against her shoulder as she ran her fingers through his hair. "Are you hungry? I'm just gonna go get cleaned up and I can order us some food."

"Sure," Jackson said, pulling away.

"There's a great Chinese place down the street."

She grabbed her shirt and stood up. Stretching up on her toes, she placed a kiss on his cheek before shuffling off toward the washroom. Jackson pulled his pants up, grabbed his shirt, and headed toward the door. He couldn't stay. He had nothing worth giving her. It was better for him to walk away now before he caused any more damage. He was fine with her hatred. It was the one thing he knew well; anything else scared him.

"I had no intention of running into your guy."

"That's bullshit. I know how much you want to get your hands on this case."

"I was working a lead. The run in with John wasn't planned; we have a leak in Westford. Someone tipped him off about the meeting."

"Who?"

Jackson shook his head and frowned.

"Fucking great. You're telling me that John has one of your men under his skirt." Haffey rubbed her forehead.

"What does John want with—" Haffey grabbed a file off the table. "Beth and Lexie Wilder, and Stephanie Muse?"

"Beth is actually Mary Connors."

Haffey's attention snapped up to Jackson. "John's Mary? The one accused of killing your father?"

"The very one." Jackson clenched his jaw.

"How the hell did you find her?" Haffey shook her head in disbelief. Mary Connors was written off long ago as most likely tracked down by John's men and killed. She disappeared without a trace.

"I found her daughter, and apparently I wasn't the only one."

"How old is the daughter?"

"Old enough to make John think she's his."

"Did he give you anything? Do you have any idea what he's planning?"

Jackson shook his head. "I have no idea where they took them. That's why I'm here."

Jackson was grateful Evan was smart enough to keep his mouth shut and stay under the radar. Having Evan with them would be more than a slap on the wrist if they got caught.

"We haven't been able to find anyone willing to talk. John's got everyone in his mix either too scared or their wallets too padded," said Shane Sieks. Haffey's partner leaned back in his chair. He ran his hand over his bearded face before taking a sip of his large cup of coffee. "God, I would kill for a smoke right now." He shook his head. Haffey grabbed a package of nicotine gum off the table and threw it at him. "My jaw is fucking sore from chewing so much fucking gum."

"Stop being a baby." Haffey dismissed him.

"Stodden's slip up at the diner must be enough to get a warrant to move in." Jackson tapped his fingers on the table. "We have witnesses that place him there and can testify that he abducted the women."

"That move was out of character for him. Every move he makes is normally calculated, but then he drops in a diner in Oxford, hours from his location, and shoots the place up and abducts the women with countless witnesses. It doesn't make sense." Haffey picks up a pen and clicks it a few times.

"I think we finally found his weakness," Sieks concludes.

A knock on the door swings their attention. "Excuse me, Detective Haffey?" A young officer walked in with a stack of files.

"What do you have for me, Stevens?" Haffey addressed him.

"Nothing. No one is talking." Stevens dropped the files on the table, shaking his head.

"What do you mean no one is talking?" A deep

scowl creased Haffey's brow.

"Everyone on the list is either unreachable or denies knowing of John Stodden's involvement." Steven's raised his hands in surrender.

"Fuck…he's tidying up loose ends." Haffey hit the table in frustration. She looked up at Jackson. "You may have targets on your backs."

"Nothing new." Jackson dismissed the threat. "Do we have possible locations for Stodden?"

"We have a few. John's been lying low lately, well…until now, anyway. He might have brought them here." Haffey pointed at an aerial view map, spread out on the table. "We've had activity in the last few hours. Officers have seen a few of his men in the area recently." Haffey placed her manicured finger by a bright red circle. "If I had to place my money on it, I would say he's here."

"I believe three abducted women is a good reason to move in." Jackson leaned against the table. "Think you can get the paperwork together?"

"That's a big fucking area, Jacks." Teddy leaned in and viewed the map.

"How many bodies can we get?" Jackson asked Haffey.

She turned toward one of the other officers in the room. "Go gather some numbers for us, Quinton."

"When?" Jackson asked.

"We can move in tonight." She looked up at him from under her long, dark lashes. "I need to talk to you alone, Jackson."

"Well, I'm going to throw my head against a brick wall since I can't have a smoke." Sieks stood up from his chair. He gave Teddy a pat on the back as he passed. "Always fun seeing you guys." Sieks laughed and shook his head before he left the room.

Jackson turned toward Teddy. "Do me a favor and give Dane the heads up that Stodden is cleaning up his mess."

"Yeah, man." Teddy spun around toward Evan. "Come on." He gave Evan a smack on the face with the back of his hand as he walked toward the door.

"Fuck, can't you guys leave my face alone? It's still fucking sore," Evan complained as he followed Teddy.

Jackson looked back at Haffey, who had her brows raised. "Ignore them." Jackson swung the door shut.

"Just so you know, since you walked in the door, I have been envisioning shoving my knee into your balls."

"Fair enough, I deserve that." Jackson gave a quick tilt of his head.

Haffey sighed exaggeratedly. "The only reason I haven't sent your ass back to Giles is because truth be told, I could use you on this case, and I can honestly also say that the idea of you being in harm's way has its appeal."

Jackson crossed his arms and couldn't help but smile at the bite that this beautiful raven-haired woman had.

"I want to make one thing perfectly clear, Jackson." Haffey walked around the table and placed her finger against his chest.

"What's that?"

"This is my case, and I call the shots. You do what I say or you're out. Do you hear me?"

"Loud and clear."

"Oh and one more thing." Haffey's lips twisted into an evil smirk. Jackson didn't try to dodge her fist as it came for his face. A flash of pain radiated through his jaw, leaving his lip stinging. He ran his finger along his lip and found it coated in blood. He couldn't help but be impressed by how hard she hit.

Haffey shook her hand, a painful look etched on her face. "Fuck you, Jackson."

"Don't worry, Haffey. I'm already fucked." They stared at each other for a moment. He could see the wheels turning in her mind. She was trying to figure him out; little did she know there was no point.

CHAPTER TWENTY-FIVE

Dane

Dane opened his eye and stared up at the white ceiling of the hospital room. It was unfortunately becoming a familiar sight. The dark spot in the corner of the ceiling tile always drew his attention. It looked like an old leak had left darkened water rings fanning out across the one tile while the others remained untouched. He shifted his weight, causing pain to shoot up his side. The bullet ripped through muscle, and it ached up his entire side and radiated down his leg. As much as it hurt to move, he was restless and couldn't stand being left to his own thoughts. Dane was never good at being alone. It scared him to be left only with his thoughts. It would always stir up old memories that haunted him when his mind was at rest.

He managed to roll over on his side in an attempt to sit when his phone began to ring. Dane moaned in pain as he reached for it on the table beside his bed. Teddy's face lit up the screen from the time he drank so much he passed out. Dane had taken the opportunity to get a good shot of him. It was a picture that always made Dane laugh. "Have you called to apologize for leaving me alone in the boring ass hospital?" Dane said through clenched teeth as he pushed himself to a sitting position, careful not to pull out his IV.

"Stodden's been doing some house cleaning. He already got to the witnesses. Keep your eyes open. I'm gonna get Giles to send you a babysitter."

"Tell Giles not to send Mansfield. He annoys the shit out of me," Dane complained as he slid off and brought himself up to a standing position. As much as it hurt to move, it felt good to stand. He walked over toward the door and looked out in the hall. It was quiet, only a few nurses talking at the end of the hall. "Why the fuck haven't you and Jackson sent me any flowers or anything? All the shit I do for you guys."

"You fucking took all my money last time we played. Buy your own fucking flowers." Teddy laughed.

"Don't get killed." Dane rolled his eyes.

"You either," Teddy said before he ended the call.

Dane tossed his phone on the bed and raked his hands down his face. He needed to get out of the hospital room. He turned around when his door opened. A man entered, and he immediately knew he was in trouble. "Shit," Dane said in a rush when the man took out his gun. Dane made his move. His side burned with raw pain as he darted forward and grabbed hold of the man's arm in an attempt to disarm him. The man shoved Dane back against the wall, the impact jarred him, and he almost lost his grip on the man's gun. Dane struggled to keep the gun aimed away from him as he tried to gain the upper hand. The pain in his stomach took his breath away.

The door opened again, and his nurse walked into the room. She screamed when she noticed what was happening. The man attacking Dane reared back and knocked her down in an attempt to silence her. Dane took the opportunity to head-butt his attacker. He grabbed the IV that was ripped out of his arm and wrapped the tube around the man's neck and pulled. The man thrashed in his arms, hitting him in the stomach. Dane held on despite the fact the pain pulled at him like he was being gutted. His eyes watered as he pulled with all the strength he could manage.

The nurse scrambled to her feet and swung the door open. He could hear her screaming, but he couldn't make out her words. The man in his arms began to lose his fight, and Dane held with his waning strength until they both slid to the floor. When the man was no longer moving, Dane felt for a pulse. He let out a relieved breath as he tried to shove the dead man's body off of him. Dane realized he had ripped himself open, and his blood gushed down his hospital gown.

"Fucking great," Dane barely managed as he clenched his teeth through the pain.

The room of his door swung open, and two

armed security guards came in the room with their guns drawn.

"Now you show up," Dane said sarcastically.

CHAPTER TWENTY-SIX

Lexie

Lexie listened to the heavy silence as it closed in around her, a vast contrast to the chaos in her head. Though the room looked like a luxurious hotel room, it felt like the prison it was. The energy of this place was dark and twisted, and Lexie feared she was not the only person this room had ever held. She curled tightly in a ball, holding onto her legs, hoping to make herself small enough to disappear from this place.

She opened her eyes and scrambled off the bed when she heard the lock turn. She frantically pushed her hair out of her face and wiped away her tears. She held her breath as she waited for someone to enter. The sight of John Stodden as he walked into the room was like a punch in the stomach. A cold smile was on his hardened face when he looked at her. A chill crawled across Lexie's skin at the sight of the man that held her captive, the man who had brought so much pain to her mother, and the very man that could be her father. The thought made her sick. She wanted nothing to do with him, but she was his prisoner.

"How are you feeling, Lexie?" His voice was smooth, deep, and commanding.

"How am I?" Lexie asked in disbelief. "Where is my mother? What did you do with her?" Lexie positioned herself on the other side of the bed, putting as much distance between them as she could. She wasn't sure what his intentions were, but she planned on making whatever he intended as difficult as she could.

John watched her calculatedly, like he was trying to figure out how to play his cards. "I assure you your mother is fine."

"I want to see her," Lexie demanded,

"In time." John tilted his head. "When depends on you."

"How?" Lexie narrowed her eyes suspiciously. She was trying to stay on top of his moves. This man knew how to twist the world to his benefit, and she was terrified she would play right into his hand.

"I want your cooperation. You want to see your mother. I am sure we can work something out."

"Where are my friends?" Lexie held her breath in anticipation. Painful thoughts of the worst possible scenarios had been playing through her head since she was left alone in this room—taunting her.

"Your friends…does that include Jackson Finley?" John raised his brow.

Lexie nodded slowly, not wanting to give more information than necessary.

"How well do you know Jackson, Lexie?"

"Well enough." Lexie squared her jaw. She could feel John testing her edges, trying to find a way in. His eyes were terrifying because she knew she was looking into the gaze of a real life monster.

"Did you know that your mother murdered his father?" John sat on the other side of the bed. Watching her like a hunter watched its prey. Lexie didn't answer; she had no idea how to respond. She had been trying to make sense of the fact that her mother was in some way involved in Jackson's father's death.

"I have good sources that tell me Jackson had plans to exact revenge on your mother and you." John used potent words. She wasn't even sure if she could deny them. Jackson had kept so much from her, she wondered if she could trust him at all. It could have all been a lie, even his feelings toward her. She felt used and angry. "You could say that my little interference saved your lives." John looked pleased with himself. "He's a man who wears a badge, but he has always walked on the edge of crime because he could never fully leave his past behind him."

Lexie shook her head. "You're wrong." But her defense was weak at best. She wasn't convincing anyone that she truly believed her words.

"Am I?" John was unsettlingly calm. He was a man who believed he had control of all things, but she knew she would never let him control her.

"Jackson wouldn't…" Lexie shook her head. She

couldn't help that seed of doubt that took root in her stomach. She knew Jackson had lied, but she needed to believe he wouldn't have hurt them. She tried not to let John's words get inside her head and twist her thoughts.

"You have feelings for this man," John stated offhandedly. "Let me give you some advice, Lexie. Men that pretend to be something they aren't are the true evils that walk among us. I, on the other hand, will never try to deceive you. I may not be the most upstanding citizen, but I am true to my nature."

"I know exactly who you are. *You're* the one who can't be trusted," Lexie spat angrily.

"I'm sorry you feel that way. I'm sure in time you will feel differently. Jackson's father brainwashed your mother years ago. She made the mistake of taking his word over mine. Don't make the same mistakes as your mother. Jackson is too much like his father. Men like that don't have the ability to love. They only destroy. He wants revenge for his father's death, nothing more."

Lexie thought of all the words that her mother wrote. She knew John's true colors. She may not be able to trust Jackson, but she knew for certain she would never believe a word this man tried to sweeten her with. She would never soften to him.

John stood up from the bed and smoothed out his suit.

"What about Stephanie and Evan?" Stephanie asked nervously.

"My use for them ceased when I had you." His words dropped the temperature of the room.

"Are they…" Panic slipped into her voice, and

she wrapped her arms around her stomach.

"They are alive," John said reassuringly. A subtle smile curled his lips as if her fear amused him. He walked back toward the door and opened it, waving someone in the room.

Lexie watched a man walk in with a case in hand. He looked to be in his late forties. His hairline was diminished and feathered into the remaining thickness that still wrapped around the base of his head. He set his case on the table and opened it up to reveal medical supplies.

She shuffled backwards until the backs of her legs collided with the cool wood of the nightstand, causing the lamp to topple to the floor. She retreated as far as she could until she had nowhere to go and her back was pressed against the wall—trapped.

"Relax. He's only here to take a blood sample. I need to confirm if you're my daughter." John smiled, but it did not meet his eyes.

Lexie didn't want to know if she was part of this monster posing as a man. She feared this truth more than the four walls holding her captive. If he really was her father, she would never be able to escape his evil because she would be a part of it. She shook her head. "No," Lexie gasped. "I don't want to know."

"If you want to see your mother again, Lexie, you would do best to listen," John said impatiently.

Lexie's gaze met John's; he held in his hands the power to destroy her. A tiny drop of her blood could destroy what little hope she had for her future.

"What happens if I'm not your daughter?"

John walked around the bed. Lexie had nowhere

to retreat. Her back was still against the wall. His dark eyes swallowed her whole, but she couldn't read his expression. She had no idea what dark thoughts were swirling behind his stony features. "Dear Lexie, you remind me so much of your mother." Lexie pulled away when he touched her hair. A smile played at the corners of his mouth. "We will find a place for you, though the circumstances may be different."

"I don't want to stay here."

John laughed, deep and rich. "You don't have a choice."

"What did my mother take from you? Can't she just give it back and you leave us alone?" Lexie couldn't stop the tears that flooded her eyes.

"What she took is between your mother and me. Your mother was never free to leave in the first place. I will not allow it to happen again." John waved the waiting man forward. "This is Doctor Collins. He will take your blood sample for the test."

"What if I am your daughter?" Lexie asked, wishing the wall she was up against would disappear so she could run far away.

"Then we shall get acquainted. Make up for lost time, so to speak."

"Will I ever be able to leave? Will my mother be able to leave?" Lexie asked.

"Regardless of what this test reveals, you are mine. You and your mother belong to me."

Doctor Collins stepped forward. He seemed completely unfazed by the fact that John was keeping her and her mother against their will.

John grabbed Lexie's hand and held tight, despite the fact that Lexie tried to pull free. His hold was too strong. The doctor ignored her protest as he pricked her finger and took the sample. He proceeded to package and label it before he tucked it away in his bag. Lexie could only watch in devastation.

"I should have the results for you within the week," Doctor Collins said, pushing his glasses up the bridge of his nose as he grabbed his case.

"Be sure you do," John responded, his eyes not leaving Lexie's hand that he still held in his own.

Doctor Collins turned stiffly on his heel and walked out of the room without a backward glance.

"Shower and change. There are clothes in the closet for you. You will join your mother and me for dinner," John said as he ran his fingers along the inside of Lexie's wrist.

Lexie perked up with the mention of her mother, but a swell of discomfort filled her chest with John's touch. He leaned down and placed a kiss on her hand before releasing her. "I will see you shortly, Lexie."

Lexie held her breath as John left the room. Taking a deep breath, she let her body slump against the wall. Her heart still raced with fear as she slid down and collapsed on the floor. She didn't need her mother's diary to know this man was capable of great evil.

She wasn't sure how to play this game, but she was determined to figure it out. She would not be owned by anyone. She needed to talk to her mother, and this dinner with John may be the only chance she had. For now she would cooperate until she could find a way out. She was determined to find a way to get them both free of John Stodden for good.

Lexie pushed off the wall, wiping her face. She opened the closet doors to reveal it was stocked with many dresses. She ran her fingers over the various fabrics. They all looked exquisite and expensive. She selected a bright red dress with intricate lace detail and looked at the tag. She was surprised to see the dress was in her size. Kneeling down, she looked at the shoes lined up on the floor, of various styles and colors, in her size as well. The fact that he knew what size she wore made her stomach feel like lead. She walked over to the dresser and opened a drawer. It was filled with underwear and bras. Lexie picked up a bra and looked at the label. She dropped it quickly and shoved the drawer shut.

Flicking on the light, Lexie walked into the large washroom. She ran her fingers over the lip of a large white tub. A tiled shower ran the length of the back wall that looked to be as large as her entire bathroom in her apartment. She looked at her reflection in the large mirror over the vanity. She looked as exhausted as she felt. She walked closer and leaned against the vanity. Her eyes were bloodshot and her hair tangled. This was the look of a girl that life just beat the crap out of her, but she was determined to go another round—as many as it took.

Her attention was drawn to the products sitting on the counter—perfumes, makeup, creams. It was as if someone went into her apartment and brought all of her things here, but these were all brand new and a much broader selection than what she normally indulged in. Lexie picked up a tube of her favorite brand of lipstick. She looked at the label to see the shade was "Happy." It was her favorite color, and she wore it more than any other shade. "Happiness is only a color." Lexie sighed as she dropped it back on the counter and watched it roll off the edge and drop to the floor.

Lexie tried not to think about what it meant having someone go to the trouble of stocking the room with everything she needed. John's plan to bring her here was something that was premeditated. Someone had to have been through her entire apartment to know what to buy. The more she looked, the more unlikely it seemed she would be allowed to leave—ever.

She found herself drawn toward the large shower. She wanted more than anything to stand under the hot water and let it wash away the gross feeling that had a tight hold on her.

Lexie scanned the entire room; the uneasy feeling that was clamped around her stomach would not let up. In the upper corner of the room a small black device called her attention. She climbed up on the edge of the tub to get a better look. Anger burned through all her other emotions as she reached for a small black camera. She wrapped her fingers around it and pulled. It was small enough to fit in the palm of her hand and easily missed if she hadn't looked for it. She ripped the cord from the back of the expensive-looking device and threw it in the toilet and flushed. She watched it spin around the bowl until it disappeared.

Lexie searched every inch of the washroom before feeling confident it was the only camera. She walked out into the main area and quickly selected some clothes and threw them on the desk chair. She dragged the heavy piece of furniture across the floor and into the bathroom. Once in the washroom, she lodged the back of it under the door handle and made sure it was secure before she walked up to the shower and turned on the water. She knew it wouldn't keep anyone out that was determined enough to enter, but it would buy her time.

CHAPTER TWENTY-SEVEN

Jackson

"Your buddy all right?" Sieks gave Jackson's foot a nudge. Jackson looked up at Evan, sitting by his side. Evan's complexion looked as grey as a stormy sky. He was grasping the handle of his gun with white knuckles, while bouncing his knee nervously. He looked on the verge of having a panic attack. Sweat broke out over his forehead, and his eyes were unfocused.

"He's fine." Jackson rammed his elbow into Evan's side, causing him to grunt. Evan's eyes snapped to his. Jackson made sure the meaning behind his glare read loud and clear.

"He's just getting in the zone," Teddy assured. He was sitting on the other side of Evan. He grabbed Evan's shoulder and gave him a shake.

"I don't know, man. He looks like he's gonna pass out." Sieks looked skeptical. "Has he been on a

301

raid before?"

"Yes. He's just messing with you." Teddy chuckled before leaning in and whispering something in Evan's ear. A small smile forced its way onto Evan's face, and his leg stopped bouncing. Evan ran his hand down his face and leaned forward.

"I'm good."

Jackson leaned back against the side of truck, the hum of the tires on the road radiating into his bones. His thoughts never left Lexie. While Evan was practically crawling out of his skin beside him, Jackson was consumed with rage, a feeling that gave him pin-point clarity and a feeling of purpose. Throwing himself into danger was the mold best fit for him. He was not cut for a life of normalcy. He was most comfortable with a weapon in his hand and a target in his sights. Until Lexie he didn't want for anything. He didn't fear falling victim to shadows or crossing lines. He had lived day to day without much thought to his future.

Lexie made him question everything. She made him want something that was not his to take. That's why when he put her life back together he would walk away. He would take all the feelings she created in him and tuck them away deep inside where the darkness that lived in him could swallow them up.

"Here, Jacks." Teddy reached into his backpack and pulled out an iPod with small, sleek earbuds.

"What's this?" Jackson asked, taking the device.

"I can't keep fixing that relic. I know it means a lot to you, but maybe you can retire it so it doesn't fall apart. I uploaded all the songs on this. It's the exact same playlist."

Jackson wrapped his fingers around it.

"I fixed the other one, but if you keep playing it there will be nothing left to repair. The tape on that cassette is worn to shit."

"Thanks, man."

"Sure."

Haffey's voice flared to life on Sieks' radio, informing them that they were five minutes out. The men shifted restlessly, their guns in hand. Jackson adjusted his vest. He wasn't used to wearing so much gear and felt restricted. He didn't feel comfortable in a uniform; he much preferred slipping in under the radar, but he had to play by Haffey's rules. He knew she would be waiting for him to slip up so she could have an excuse to take him off her case. The only reason Jackson was here was because Giles had sway with their precinct, but it would not stick if Jackson made trouble. The Belhaven precinct was where his father had worked. Giles too until he moved to the neighbouring town of Westford ten years ago in an attempt to separate Jackson from his dark past.

The van pulled off the main road, and they all braced themselves as it continued on uneven terrain. All conversations died as they prepared themselves for what lay ahead. When the van came to a stop, the back doors swung open and all twelve men filed out, guns ready. They were on the perimeter of the large property. The lights could be seen twisting through the trees in the distance. They needed the element of surprise if they were to be successful.

John was quick on the draw, and any notice would give him too much time to react. Jackson grabbed Evan by the back of the shirt. "Stay behind me and don't get yourself killed. Got it?"

Evan nodded, his eyes sliding between Teddy and Jackson, who were both looking at him for confirmation he wouldn't screw things up.

"You're good, man," Teddy confirmed, giving his shoulder a reassuring shake.

"Let's go. Stay tight," Jackson started. The others were already moving toward their positions. Staying close to the treeline, Jackson headed toward the rear of the large property. The building was lit up with surveillance around the entire perimeter.

Haffey's voice buzzed in Jackson's earpiece. "Stay in position until my signal."

"This place is lit the fuck up," Evan said, ducking down behind brush for cover.

"You're staying right here and will be our eyes on the outside." Jackson pulled out binoculars and began scanning for bodies on the outside of the building.

"I thought I was coming in?"

"You are staying right here so I don't have to drag your dead body out." Jackson shook his head. "Fox Trot. Ready to dance. Over," Jackson said into his radio.

"Roger, waiting for the music. Over," Sieks' voice responded promptly before cutting out.

"Set the mood, Teddy," Jackson said with a nod.

Teddy dropped his backpack on the ground and pulled out a laptop. Lying flat on the ground, he booted it up and began typing away. Jackson kept his eyes on the building, watching for any signs of movement. A back door opened, and a man walked out carrying two large garbage bags.

"We got one taking out the trash." Jackson kept the man in his sight. He watched the man throw the two bags into a large dumpster before returning inside. "Clear," Jackson said as soon as the door closed.

"What's Teddy doing?" Evan whispered.

"What he does best." Jackson grinned. "Any minute now, Teddy."

"Got it." As soon as Teddy said the words, the exterior lights all shut off, leaving the building in complete darkness.

"This is our song. Over," Haffey said through the radio.

"We're up, Ted," Jackson said, sliding the earbud to the iPod in his right ear, tucking the device in his chest pocket. The comforting sound of his music flowed through his body. He had never heard it so clear. The constant buzz in the background was gone, and he was left with sharp clarity. Jackson closed his eyes and took a deep breath.

"You're listening to music now?" Evan asked in disbelief.

"Fuck off," Jackson responded as he picked up his gun.

"How can you hear with one ear plugged into tunes?"

"I can hear," Jackson said.

"That music fuels the unstoppable beast. It is a thing of beauty. Don't touch my stuff while we're gone or I will kill you." Teddy gave Evan a slap on the back before he followed Jackson. They moved through the thin barrier of brush onto the open pavement surrounding the building.

Guns in hand, they moved silently toward the building. Jackson took sight of Sieks and his men moving in on the west side of the building. Jackson and Teddy made it to the rear entrance just as the back door opened again. They pressed their bodies behind the opening door.

"I can't see shit," the man cursed. Jackson reached around the door and grabbed the man by the neck. He shoved the door closed and sank his blade into his throat. He was taken by surprise and didn't even attempt to struggle. Teddy grabbed the dead man by the shoulder and hauled him back against the building and out of sight.

Jackson grabbed the handle and slowly opened it. They had studied the blueprints of the building and knew the general layout, but they were blind to what they were about to face upon entering. Jackson and Teddy were joined by three other men as they walked into the narrow hallway. Guns raised, they headed in the dark interior except the emergency lights that cast an eerie glow along the ceiling.

The powerful voice centered him as the music pumped through his blood. The men inside these walls would be well armed. They knew John's crew well enough to know they all packed heavily. It was a necessity for their line of work. Jackson led his group down the hall and veered to the left. Three men were gathered in the center of the hall. Jackson motioned for his men to stand back. He approached alone. One man held a flashlight and shone it toward Jackson as he approached.

"Hello, boys," Jackson greeted slyly.

"Who the fuck are you?" one of them questioned. Jackson withdrew his blade and watched their postures stiffen. There was no need to alert everyone in the building just yet with gunfire. He dove into the group with his blades extended. The men scrambled for their guns, but Jackson was too quick. His blade cut across the throat of the first and impaled the chest of the next. The last managed to retrieve his gun. Jackson tried to knock it out of his hand before he could pull the trigger, but the shot rang off, embedding in the wall next to Jackson. Jackson threw his knee into the man's stomach. Pulling out his own gun, he placed it under the man's chin and pulled the trigger. Blood sprayed over the wall behind him. Jackson scanned the hallway. They would only have minutes before more men starting pouring in.

"Shit, man," Teddy whispered beside him.

"Let's keep moving." Jackson waved them forward as they stepped over the bodies and continued down the hall. When they turned the corner, six armed men approached. Gunfire erupted immediately. Jackson dove across the open hall and into an alcove on the opposite side. He leaned around and began firing at the men. Bullets tore through the air, tearing through walls and bodies, spraying debris. Jackson didn't stop firing until all the bodies were dropped. Motioning his men toward the common room, they indicated the target area from the blue prints.

They moved down the hallways clearing all rooms before moving onward. Some of the rooms were set up as temporary offices, while others were empty. The hall opened up into a large open warehouse space. Large pallets of boxes were piled high, filling most of the area. It made perfect cover for the men taking aim at them.

Jackson ducked when a bullet came dangerously close to his head, shredding the wall beside him. He could feel particles spray against the back of his neck. He moved for cover behind the nearest stack of boxes. Readying his gun, he shot a man who stepped into his line of sight. A new flurry of shots erupted. The men were cornered and lashing back in a last attempt at self-preservation; it was only a matter of time before John's men would have to admit defeat. Jackson shot at anyone who dared show himself.

Jackson dropped to the ground to reload his gun.

"We have a man down," Teddy said. He was on Jackson's left, giving him cover. Jackson looked over to see one of their guys slumped against the wall. He didn't know him well, but he remembered his name from Haffey's team. He had a wound that looked like it pierced through his shoulder.

"Mark?" Jackson called to him.

He lifted his arm in a wave, indicating he was all right. Jackson snapped his clip in his gun and stood up. After taking down a few more targets, the gunfire died off. With a readied gun, he moved in closer, weaving through the boxes. Silence began to rain down heavy in the large space, allowing him to hear the hushed frantic whispers of the remaining men. He stepped out into a small clearing, his gun trained on the men. He knew as soon as he looked into their eyes that these men were too scared to fight back. They surrendered, throwing down their weapons. Teddy walked up beside him. "Looks like the party is over, boys."

CHAPTER TWENTY-EIGHT

Lexie

Lexie pulled a simple black dress over her head and smoothed the material over her curves. It practically sang against her skin. No wonder her mother fell victim to the charms of this life before it reared its ugly head. Lexie was not naïve to the truth. She would not let anything but hatred color her vision of John.

She searched the entire room, but the only clothes she could find were dresses. She chose the most practical of the selection after deciding not to put her soiled clothes back on. The cut of the material fit her as if it was specifically made for her. She opted out of the shoe selection and wore her flats. There was no way she was wearing heels. She needed to be prepared for anything.

Once Lexie was ready, she sat down on the bed. She had no idea what time it was because there was no clock. She grabbed the remote control off the entertainment unit and tried turning on the television, but it was channel after channel of static. Turning it off, she threw the remote against the wall as hard as she could, shattering the back and sending the batteries scattering across the floor. She lay back on the soft mattress, staring up at the ceiling. Exhaustion was pulling at her consciousness. Her body felt heavy and sluggish, and she could feel the desire to close her eyes growing strong, but she continued to fight it.

She wanted to be able to look into the face of danger like Jackson, not fearing it but embracing it. She couldn't afford to be scared anymore. Being scared would only get her and others killed. She knew that better than anyone. Lexie was done being a victim, and the thought gave her some peace of mind. Whatever John had planned, she would be ready for it. She would not go down without a fight.

She focused on her anger with John for imprisoning her mother and her, for believing they were his to control. The words in her mother's diary haunted her. She knew now without a doubt that every word her mother wrote she had paid for in blood. This man was the embodiment of evil, and she was terrified of what would become of them if they could not escape. The only thing Lexie knew for certain was that she would not write about her fear…instead, she would turn her pen into a weapon and fight her way out of this place.

She was also angry with Jackson. She couldn't deny his deception. The truth was staring her in the face. She felt like the sliver of light he had shown her was torn away and she was left exposed and vulnerable. She tried to rationalize his behavior, tried to think of something to give her hope that she had seen truth in his eyes when he touched her, kissed her, and expressed his desire for her, but John's words clung to every memory—taunting her.

The part of her that had fallen under Jackson's spell hid in shame. She deserved the humiliation after recklessly allowing a piece of herself to desire another. If she was honest with herself, she knew it was more than physical with Jackson. She allowed him stir the broken remains of her heart, and now she deserved the fallout.

She hadn't realized she had fallen asleep until a sound pulled her awake. Lexie pushed off the bed as the door swung open and backed up as far as she could. A man that she didn't recognize stalked into the room. "Who are you?"

CHAPTER TWENTY-NINE

Jackson

"Where the fuck are they?" Jackson hollered, grabbing one of the men by the neck of his shirt and throwing him into a stack of boxes. A couple of them knocked free of the pile and fell to the ground, their contents spilling onto the floor.

"I don't know...I don't know anything about these girls you're talking about...I just work here." The man raised his hands, visibly terrified of what Jackson planned on doing.

"Holy fuck." Teddy grabbed for something that had tumbled out of one of the boxes. "They're fucking sex toys." Teddy held up a box for a bright pink dildo. Teddy opened the box to take a closer look at the merchandise.

"Where's John?" Jackson demanded, tightening his hold until the man began gasping for breath.

"W-Who?"

"John Stodden. Where is he?"

"Dildos filled with fucking crack," Teddy said excitedly. "Talk about double your pleasure." Jackson cursed under his breath and swung around to glare at Teddy. "Sorry, man." Teddy threw up his hands in apology, still holding the dildo.

Jackson threw down the man next to the others huddled on the floor. "Someone better tell me where to fucking find John Stodden," Jackson hollered, raising his gun and aiming it at the group. They all cowered in the face of danger.

"We were hired to pack boxes. Nobody tells us nothin'. We don't know no John," one of the other men said, his eyes darting around the room as the rest of the men with Jackson's group joined them. Mark leaned against a pallet of boxes, the entire front of his shirt saturated in blood.

"Who hired you?" Jackson waved his gun demandingly in their faces.

One of them pointed a shaky finger toward one of the dead men on the floor. "He did. He pays us cash per shift. I told you we don't know nothin'." Jackson raked his hand over his face.

"Check him, Ted." Jackson nodded toward the body. Teddy knelt down and flipped the body over. The man was definitely dead, with a bullet hole to the forehead. Teddy reached into his pocket and pulled out the man's wallet.

"Says he's Pete Winters. Sound familiar?"

"No. He must be new blood." Jackson rubbed his temple with his free hand. "Someone has to fucking know something. Tell me." Jackson could feel his rage tightening his chest. "Or I'll shoot every one of you."

"Lower your weapon, Finley," Haffey ordered. Jackson turned to see her and a group of officers file in lead by Haffey. "John's not here. We already cleared the building." Jackson tightened his grip. He wasn't ready to admit defeat. "Lower your goddam weapon, Finley, or I will shoot you myself."

Jackson dropped the gun to his side. Clenching his jaw, he stepped back. A few of Haffey's men moved in and cuffed the men he had in custody, none of them putting up a fight.

"I'm sending a team in here. We will find something to link John to this place. For now, go cool down." Haffey glared at him. Jackson could see he was testing her patience.

Finley looked down when her foot kicked a box next to her feet. "What's this?" She picked it up, and realization dawned on her face.

"Crack-filled pleasure sticks. What's your color preference, blue or pink?" Teddy laughed despite the tension in the room. He never ceased to take a serious situation and find humor in it.

Haffey rolled her eyes and shoved the box into Sieks' hands. "Get evidence in here to process this shit."

"And you." Haffey pointed at Teddy. "Get Finley out of here before he gets himself into trouble."

"Sure thing, Detective Haffey." Teddy saluted.

Jackson shoved his gun into his holster and walked away. He needed to get some fresh air before he tore something apart. Their best lead turned up a dead end. He knew that the chances of finding John's name on any of the paperwork in the building were slim to none.

"Jackson," Teddy called behind him. Jackson was on a mission, and he stalked from the building. Swinging the exit door open, it smashed against the outside wall. "Jackson, wait up. Where are you going?"

Jackson spun around when they were outside and away from Haffey's team. "Change of plans, Teddy. I'm finding John my way."

"I'm in." They both turned to see Evan approach with Teddy's bag in his hand.

"Give me that," Teddy demanded. "I told you not to touch my stuff."

Jackson looked at Teddy. He was going to need him for this plan to work. Teddy assessed his bag, making sure everything was accounted for before he swung it over his shoulder. He looked at Jackson with a deep sigh. "You know I'm in, man, until the end."

Jackson nodded. "Good."

CHAPTER THIRTY

Stephanie

The air smelled stale. It reminded Stephanie of the locker room of her gym, but putrid. She felt herself rousing. Her mouth felt like it was filled with cotton. She tried to open her eyes, but they felt so heavy. Her disoriented mind was trying to pull facts from the dark cloud that filled her head.

Stephanie lifted her head when the memory of being taken by men with guns penetrated the fog. A sob escaped her as an ache began throbbing in her jaw. The feeling in her body began to return. She remembered being taken into a room where she was locked inside.

She scrambled around the room looking for something to cut the ties that bound her arms. It wasn't long before the door swung open and two men walked in. One of the men wore an expensive suit. His appearance was well manicured and his demeanour refined. It didn't match the cold, evil glare that flared in his eyes when his gaze fell on

317

her. He terrified her.

The other man looked like one of the men that had taken her. Tattoos covered the right side of his neck, and his head was shaven. Though he looked dangerous, it didn't compare to the darkness that filled the shadow of the other man.

"What do you think?" the tattooed man asked the other as they both watched her.

"Yes," he replied.

"Good. I'll let John know." The tattooed man approached her then, pulling something from his pocket. Stephanie had backed against the wall, pleading for him to let her go. That was when she saw the needle. He grabbed hold of her, and she struggled against him until she felt a sting in her arm. Her fight wavered as her body began to fail her. The last thing she remembered seeing was the cold, sinister smile of the man in the suit.

Stephanie was now on the hard, cold floor in a dimly lit room. She turned her head to see the source of the light. Across the room, a lone lamp sat on a table in the corner of the room. She could see it through black metal bars that stood in front of her.

It took all the strength she could gather to push her body off the floor. She grabbed for one of the bars to pull herself up to her unsteady feet. Her body began to throb as her blood rushed through her body as she began to move. Her stomach rolled with nausea.

She grasped the bars with both hands, looking around the room. Tears streamed down her face at the haunting sight. A small run of cabinets sat in the corner with boxes stacked on the counter, and in the center of the room sat a large bed with chains hanging off the headboard.

"Help," Stephanie managed to whisper. Her tongue felt too big in her mouth, and her throat was so dry it made her words feel sharp. "Help." She tried to shake the bars that would not give under her hold. "Help me!" she shrieked, pulling at the bars.

She had woken up in what she could only describe as hell with darkness lingering in every corner. The promise that she would suffer in the dank, murky place had fear clawing at her. She pulled on the bars until her hands ached and her skin felt raw. There was no escape. She had no idea what was happening or why she was here.

Stephanie jumped back when the door across the room swung open. It was the man she remembered with the suit; his red tie was the only thing that stood out as shadows obscured his face. "You're awake," he said in a tone that lifted the hairs off the back of her neck. "I've been waiting."

Stephanie backed away from him until the cold wall pressed against her back. There was no escape.

ACKNOWLEDGEMENTS

A huge thank you to:

My family, who are always my biggest fans.

Limitless Publishing, for giving me the opportunity to share this series with the world.

Toni Rakestraw, my fabulous editor, who has to fix all of my annoying writing habits.

Author J.L. Drake, for being wonderful.

Dawn Canfield, Hot Pressed Books, for her great advice.

Readers, these were only words upon the pages until you brought them to life.

ABOUT THE AUTHOR

Aimee McNeil was born and raised in Nova Scotia, Canada, where she continues to live today with her husband and three children. She is a stay-at-home mother that loves every colorful moment with her family.

Aimee spends most of her free time indulging in her love of writing. You can also find her lost in the pages of a good book, or making a mess with her paints. Aimee loves to explore anything that promotes creativity. It is one of the many reason she enjoys writing.

Facebook:
https://www.facebook.com/aimeemcneilswriting

Twitter:
https://twitter.com/aimeeswriting

Website:
http://www.aimeemcneil.com/